T0164769

Wish Me Dead

Wish Me Dead

Diane Nielsen

Order this book online at www.trafford.com
or email orders@trafford.com

Most Trafford titles are also available at major online book retailers.

© Copyright 2011 Diane Nielsen.
All rights reserved. No part of this publication may be reproduced, stored in a retrieval system, or transmitted, in any form or by any means, electronic, mechanical, photocopying, recording, or otherwise, without the written prior permission of the author.

Printed in the United States of America.

ISBN: 978-1-4269-7912-5 (sc)
ISBN: 978-1-4269-7913-2 (e)

Trafford rev. 12/09/2011

www.trafford.com

North America & international
toll-free: 1 888 232 4444 (USA & Canada)
phone: 250 383 6864 • fax: 812 355 4082

To my editor, friend and sister Cynthia Heilbrun, thank you for the many hours you put in, ideas you added and the ear for me to talk off. To my sons Dean and Brandon, and my sister Cathy, all my love for your support and believing in me. You too Sherry. Thank you!

PROLOGUE

The heavens erupted with thunder that growled, lightning that burned, and boiling clouds that were black with anger. The fates were mad. More then mad. They were furious. They hissed their rage and stirred chaos, as they let their anger be known to the guardians that lived amongst the stars.

One of the guardians had changed the course of destiny that had been written for a mortal on earth. A destiny that the fates had written themselves, when the human had been born. Guardians were not allowed to interfere with a human's destiny, only charged with giving guidance, bringing the mortal back to the path it was to follow if it strayed. To change the course of a destiny could cause a ripple effect that had the power to change other lives, other destinies, and unleash chaos on the earth.

As the fates twisted in anger, their voices joined as one to summon a powerful guardian to do their bidding. "Saul," they shrieked into the wind, "Appear before us!"

In the blink of an eye, the mighty guardian stood where the dark clouds had just been. They parted for the immortal, but did not disperse, their wind lifting his dark hair, making it dance around his handsome head. The lightning that still forked did not touch him, and the might of the thunder did not frighten him. He was more than all of it put together, he was immortal, powerful and impressive to behold.

His dark eyes scanned the expanse, until he found the fates assembled before him. In a deep voice that was meant to sooth and settle, Saul addressed the beings before him.

"Why have you summoned me?" he asked. He did not demand but showed respect as the fates deserved.

"One of your kind," their voices responded, "has broken the cardinal rule of the immortals. One of your kind has foolishly interfered and changed the course of a written destiny."

Saul's dark eyes flashed, "Have you called on me to destroy another immortal?" he growled in anger.

"No," the collective voice answered. "We are giving you the task of going to this immortal and showing him the error of his ways. You will find him standing at the Window to the World. The window that shows the seeker anything and anyone they wish."

"But I too am not allowed to interfere in destiny's path," he replied. "How can I right the wrong that has been done?"

"You will find a way," they answered, calming now that their champion had been chosen.

Saul was left alone as the fates disappeared in a twist of smoke. Wasting no time he unfurled the mighty wings that rode his back, and flew with the speed of light to the Window, before slowing and folding his wings behind him. He saw before the Window a small boy standing with his hands upon his knees, absorbed at the scene in front of him.

"Leonard, what have you done?" Saul asked quietly, moving to stand close behind the boy.

Jerking up straight, the dark haired, brown eyed boy turned with guilty, down—cast eyes to face Saul.

"I didn't mean to do anything," Leonard said with innocence in his voice. "I only wished for her to be my friend."

"Yes, I know," answered Saul, trying not to let censor creep into his tone. "Your wishing for her to be your friend has caused her to be taken before her time. Because of this, her human soul will not be able to learn its lessons in this lifetime. The course of destiny has been changed, not only for her but for others as well."

Saul let this information sink in for a moment, using the silence that followed to ponder Leonard's motives. Leonard had come to join them at a much too early age. He still greatly missed his human family, and because of his loneliness had turned his longings on a mortal woman. He badly wanted to be friends with her, and had wished for her to join him.

At Leonard's continued silence, Saul reached out a hand and lifted the small chin, until dark eyes met darker eyes. "Do you understand what I am explaining to you?" Saul asked.

"I should not have wished for her yet?" replied Leonard.

"Yes," said Saul nodding his head. "She would have come to us when it was her predestined time."

"Can you fix this?" asked Leonard, once again dropping his eyes to stare at his feet.

"I don't know if I can," Saul said with honesty. "I have to follow the same rules that you and all immortals are bound to. I am not allowed to interfere in the destiny of my charges. Come," Saul said, holding out his hand to take the smaller one. "We will go find another to help with your training. Until the time that you are deemed ready, you may not approach or use the Window to the World again. Do you understand?"

"Yes," replied the child.

Placing his hand in Saul's, Leonard let himself be led away through the clouds that still rolled and clashed. As Saul led him, he was deep in thought trying to find a solution to the problem Leonard had caused. So deep was his concentration, that he didn't notice the reluctance in Leonard as he was led farther and farther away from the window. Nor did he notice the crossed fingers behind the small back, hidden from sight by small wings.

Immortals were unable to read the minds of other immortal beings. If it were different, Saul would have had reason to pause, as Leonard was wishing with all his might that Saul would fail. He wanted a new friend, a new toy and if wishing did not work, then he would just have to find something that would.

A sneer, that was much too old for his face, curled his lip and a spark of defiance was born in his eyes. Tantrums from a mortal child were irritating, but tantrums from an immortal were deadly, and Leonard was working up to a big one.

CHAPTER 1

Spring had finally come to the mountains of Colorado, where the sun shone down from the mile high sky warming the air that still carried a bite to it. The grass was green and wildflowers were starting to open, making the clear mountain air smell like a new beginning was possible. Birds sang as they built their nests for their upcoming young in fragrant pine trees that moved lazily, whispering to each other, as if telling stories of the winter past.

Time slowed down with peace and quiet being abundant, allowing troubles to melt and flow away with the spring thaw. The Rockies restored and refreshed all visitors that took the time to linger and relax.

On this late May day, noon had come and gone before the lump under the covers showed any signs of life. Ten delicate fingers slowly appeared from under the quilt, gripping the edges, lowering it inch by inch to reveal the treasure it had protected during its slumber.

Waves of thick dark brown hair appeared, covering the pillows and providing a perfect frame for the face emerging to be gently kissed by the golden sunlight coming in through the open window. Dark slashes above closed eyelids emerged, followed by thick black half-moons that lay on smooth cheeks, showing the light blush of rose from sleep. A slim nose with slightly flared nostrils and a mouth that was maybe a tad too wide completed the unveiling. All that remained hidden were the eyes that had yet to open.

Little by little they opened revealing color that was the deep, dark green of a man—made emerald. With happiness, they glowed with green fire that snapped and sparkled, but with anger, they deepened in color until they were almost black—smoky and cold.

This morning they appeared veiled and flat, as twenty eight year-old Ashton Rider let memories rush in as to why she had fled half-way across the country to her family's cabin in the Rockies.

Ashton had a good life, more money then she could ever spend, beauty, health and good friends. So what was wrong with her lately? She used to have hopes and dreams but lately her dreams had dwindled and faded until they were no more. She cried without knowing why, and felt empty and restless. Try as she might, she could not figure out what was wrong or how to fix it.

Then, two nights ago, a strong feeling had washed over her. It was as if a voice in her head, and in her heart, had told her to drop everything and travel to Colorado. Go to her family's cabin in the mountains. Go now. Ashton had packed a few things, left a note saying she needed some alone time, got into her car, and without a backward glance, left everything behind.

Something was there, something she needed badly, and whatever it was pulled at her very soul.

A slight frown marred her clear brow. For the most part she remembered her trip, just not arriving and crawling into bed. She remembered being bone tired, not having stopped to rest, so she guessed she must have finished her trip in a fog of exhaustion.

Still feeling tired and worn out, Ashton closed her eyes, trying to decide what to do next. She finally sat up, flipped the covers back, and swung her long legs out of the bed, letting her warm feet touch the cool floor.

Standing up, she turned to make the bed, remembering what her mother had taught her all her life. "Never leave your room without making your bed". Even now, four years after her parent's deaths, she could still hear the gentle voice in her head. Running a final, smoothing hand over the blankets, she decided a shower was what was needed to chase away the lingering cobwebs.

Ashton made her way into the small bathroom, where as a child she had perched on the counter with her feet in the sink, watching her mother lightly apply her make up. She remembered wondering why she did not look like her mother, five feet two, blonde hair, green eyes the color of true emeralds. But her wonderings stopped the moment her father entered the room, encircling his wife's waist with his loving arms. The same dark brown hair, the same deep green eyes, and a smile that was just a little too wide, left her little doubt as to where she got her looks.

For just a moment Ashton let her self wallow in the grief that, after four years, still felt fresh and raw. It seemed like yesterday that they had died unexpectedly. Releasing a final sigh, she put her grief away.

Ashton studied her reflection in the mirror, trying to see the person she had known all of her life. What she saw was a tired and worn down stranger staring back at her. Who are you, she wondered?

Turning her back on the image, she peeled off her clothes and stepped into the shower. The hot water beating down on her, caused goose bumps to cover her body in pleasure. She opened her eyes and watched the water swirl down the drain, hoping and wishing that her troubles would go with it.

Letting her mind wander, as she shampooed, conditioned and rinsed, Ashton tried to plan what was left of the day. Her stomach gave a rumble, and she decided that food was the first order of business. She took that as a good sign, as she had not had an appetite for days.

Stepping out of the shower, Ashton remembered a beautiful lake about a half-mile away. After eating, she decided, some exploring might be fun. "Yep," Ashton thought, "that sounded like a plan to her."

Hair combed, dressed, and with canned soup in her belly, Ashton stepped out of her back door. Her first look at the scenery nearly took her breath away. God it was beautiful! Mountains all around, covered with tall pines and the pure scent of fresh air had her mood lifting and a heavy weight falling from her shoulders. A small spark came back into her eyes and a slight smile touched her lips. She said a quiet "thank you" out loud, to no one in particular, just to everything for being there for her.

Seeing a path almost overgrown with brush, Ashton's memory came back, and she knew without a doubt that this was the way to the Lake. With a spring in her step, she stepped off the porch, and made her way to the edge of the trees, entering their shadowed depths.

It was cooler in the forest and Ashton had forgotten to bring a coat, but she was not going to turn back now. Instead, she walked faster to keep warm, and in no time at all found the trees parting to give her the much awaited first look at the Lake she and her father had considered it theirs.

Time stood still, and it was as if her father stood at her side gently laughing at her as she insisted the lake looked like a big foot print, rounded at the back, narrow in the middle, and opening up wide at the other end. He always said she had a wonderful imagination, and had hugged her close. "See Dad," she whispered "it does look like a foot print just like I said."

Ashton moved to the very edge of the trees, and stood looking at the lake before her. Everything was perfect. Her shoulders relaxed, and without being aware, she let go. Let go of all her worries, unhappiness, loneliness, and troubles that she'd had to carry over the last four years. Her head fell back and her arms rose out from her sides. Palms up, her hands appeared ready to receive the gifts that this place had to offer. Was this what had drawn her to Colorado, this place of calm and quiet?

Closing her eyes Ashton decided that this was where she was meant to be, where she belonged, and where she would stay.

CHAPTER 2

The woods were quiet and sleepy. Birds and small animals flew or scurried through the thick growth, seeming to follow no path, but with purpose. They were always, watchful for the bears, hawks and big cats that shared their home.

Sam Barnhart listened to the sounds around him, enjoying the familiarity of them. He had come to know the sounds of this mountain, which had been his home for five years, and had learned, sometimes the hard way, to enjoy himself but to stay alert. Especially when he was by the lake, as he was today, fishing.

The lake was the central watering hole for all the animals that lived in the area and those just passing by. Sam loved the peace and quiet, the slow pace, and the hint of danger his home offered. It was isolated, and perfect for what he needed. It was a good place to disappear.

Sam's line of work had made him a ton of money that allowed him the freedom to choose whether to work or not. Since moving to Colorado he had chosen to ignore the offers for the particular talents he possessed, and just relax.

Hard to find? Yes he was, and he guarded the secret of his whereabouts ferociously. But those who needed his talents could reach him by placing ads in a few obscure publications.

Whether he contacted them or not was up to him. His decision, his choice.

On this late May day, Sam stood on the shore of what he thought of as *his lake*, and lazily cast his line into its glassy surface. He didn't care if he caught a fish or not. He just liked the solitude and laziness of being outdoors by himself. Besides, when he did happen to snag a fish, he just let it go anyway. Sparing its life felt good to him.

After all, in his chosen line of work taking life was an ordinary event. It's what he had been trained by the government to do, what they still used him for. He was quiet but effective, and that is why they still called on him. Get in, do the job and get out without causing a ripple, that was his specialty. He worked only for the government, and took only work that he felt was warranted. Only a few high-ranking government agents knew of him, and even they knew him only by his code name The Messenger. All other records of him and his services had been erased years before when he had been recruited to be an assassin. Now all that remained was his reputation and the fear it caused in the circles that used him. Should your name be chosen by The Messenger, your days on this earth were numbered. No matter how hard you ran or how deep underground you went, he found you and with quiet dispatch, put you down.

Sam had long ago made peace with what he did, and had no doubt that when his time came he would not be going up but would be going the other way. So be it. He would do what needed to be done, and deal with the consequences later.

Today Sam had no worries. Life was good and he was at peace, although sometimes lonely. By choice Sam could not bring a woman into his world and worry about her getting hurt because someone was trying to get to him. Likewise, he didn't want to risk hurting her himself by the lies he would have to tell about what he did for a living when he left for an assignment.

Really, what could he say, "Honey, I'll be gone for a few days because I've been assigned to kill someone who seriously deserves it". Hell, it was just easier to be alone.

Still, he had needs like every other man and on occasion he found companionship, going far from his home to do so. It was safer not to play in his own backyard, so to speak. So he kept these meetings few and far between.

Sam had resigned himself to the fact that he would never have love, a family, or a normal life. Even friends were a luxury he could not allow himself. So Sam learned to live with his isolation and had even come to enjoy it. On rare occasions, like today, thoughts of what life could be like if he had someone special to share it with crept in unbidden and caused a dull ache near his heart.

Sam let his mind wander and dreamt of a woman who would stand by his side, touch him, and love him. Someone who would be there when he woke up and share his day with him. He let himself feel the ache he usually kept buried deep inside, and just for a moment made believe he could have a normal future. Sam opened up his heart and let his yearnings for a mate and a family wash over him. Just for a moment he wished.

The far away look in Sam's eyes faded as he pulled himself back to the present. Tucking his dreams and fantasies away in the small corner of his heart where they belonged, Sam reeled in his line and began gathering up the few things he had brought to the lake with him. As he slipped his arms into the old, faded button down shirt, he caught a flash of light out of the corner of his eye.

With reflexes brought about by years of training, he dove behind a nearby tree, at the same time pulling out the small gun strapped to his ankle. Sam remained silent and listened for any sounds out of the ordinary.

Staying low, Sam peered out from his hiding place, sweeping the lake and its surrounding area. What he saw made his eyes go round and his mouth go dry. There at the edge of the forest was the most beautiful woman he had ever seen. Arms outstretched, face turned up to the sun, she stood perfectly still. The light Sam had seen seemed to be coming from her. From her whole being. Its golden glow bathed her from head to toe, radiating a light so bright it caused the late afternoon shadows to retreat before its intensity.

Sam continued to watch the woman for a full five minutes, making sure all was as it seemed to be. Who was she? Was she sent to find him? Was she alone? What was she doing here? All these questions whipped through Sam's mind as he continued to observe her from the edge of the trees.

Detecting no other presence, he slowly made his way back to his forgotten gear. Placing the gun in the back of his waistband, he gathered his things and slowly made his way towards the woman, keeping his eyes moving at all times. Slowly and quietly, Sam lowered his gear to the ground and waited for her to notice him. He was curious to see what her reaction to him would be. He figured if she was not surprised or frightened, he had a problem. She would have been sent to find him and then he would have a decision to make, live or die. Time would tell. So he waited and watched.

CHAPTER 3

Ashton stood at the edge of the trees basking in the warmth she felt around her. She felt light and airy, and knew she had finally come home. Lowering her arms and taking a deep breath, she opened her eyes and screamed. Stumbling backwards two steps, she promptly tripped over a branch and landed on her butt.

Tipping her head back, she looked up at the man standing in front of her. Tall, broad shoulders, narrow waist, long legs, and an acre of taut, tan skin covering a chest that was visible through the opening of an old shirt that looked soft and faded from age. She couldn't seem to take her eyes off that chest, as her eyes followed a lone drop of moisture that travelled slowly downward till it reached the top of his jeans and was absorbed there. She sat for what seemed like an eternity, with her gaze locked on the gorgeous hunk of male before her.

A clearing of a throat, that rivaled a roll of thunder, broke the spell and had Ashton's eyes flying upward. Her eyes met and were held by serious teal blue orbs with sinfully thick, long ebony lashes. Lashes that never blinked as the hunk held her stare. In awe, her green eyes slowly pulled away and traveled in a daze over the rest of his face. Strong cheek bones, a thin nose with flared nostrils that seemed to be attempting to draw in her scent, a lean jaw that held a shadow of a dark stubble of whiskers. She knew that her hands would fit perfectly along that jaw if she were to cup it in her hands. All this was completed by a mouth that was made by the Gods, she was sure, to drive a woman crazy with images of what it could do. Over all, Ashton decided this man had the look of being made for love, but underneath there seemed to be a stillness about him, of control not easily lost.

Mentally giving herself a shake, Ashton brought herself back to reality and tried to regain her composure, which was not easy as she was sprawled at the feet of this stranger.

"If you're done staring, maybe you would like to try to get up now. Or, if you'd rather, I could join you down there." The raspy, deep voice seemed to pour over her. The hint of sarcasm and arrogance it held had Ashton trying to stand as gracefully as possible, while ignoring the hand held out to assist her.

Sam watched as she turned that very cute butt towards him, dusting the dirt and pine needles from it. She was unaware of the needles clinging to the mass of dark hair hanging down her back. Sam could no longer see the glow around her but he definitely felt the pull on his senses caused by a beautiful woman. It must be way past time for one of his trips, because that was the only reason he could find for the strong and immediate attraction he was feeling.

While her attention was elsewhere, Sam quickly ran his eyes up and down her looking for any strange bumps or bulges that could indicate a hidden weapon. But the only bumps he could see seemed to be in all the right places. Places that for an instant in time he could picture himself holding, caressing, and burying himself in.

Frowning, Sam decided it was time to do a little prying to see why she was here and if she was a danger to him. "Who are you and what are you doing here?" Once again the deep raspiness of his voice reached out to Ashton, causing goose bumps to cover her arms and legs and to pucker her nipples until they were small pebbles pushing against her light t-shirt.

Jerking upright as if she had been touched by a hot poker, Ashton wondered what in God's name was wrong with her. She had never reacted to a man this way before. Especially one who looked like this one. Usually the good-looking ones with great bodies were stuck on themselves and could care less about anyone or anything that did not center on or around them. Those were the ones to steer clear of. The man before her was just that kind. Hot to the point of smoking.

"Well," he asked again? When Ashton still didn't answer, Sam shifted his feet and bent at the waist until his nose was almost pressed to hers. "I've always been pretty good at reading people, but I skipped school the day they taught us how to read minds. So, again, what's your name and what are you doing here?"

A small pink tongue crept out quickly to moisten dry lips before retreating into her expressive mouth. But not before Sam saw it and wanted to pull her to him and have that tongue warring with his.

"Ashton, Ashton Rider," she finally got out. "And I'm staying in my family's cabin about a half a mile back that way." "Your turn," she countered. "What's your name and why are you at my lake?"

"Sam," came the reply along with a hand that was extended for her to shake. "I live around here, and I've been thinking this is my lake since I've been the only one fishing in it for the past five years. I haven't seen you since I moved in."

Ashton looked down at the hand still extended between them and knew if she touched him, even his hand, things in her life would never be the same. So Ashton looked at the hand, nodded her head, and stuffed her hands in her back pockets.

At her movements Sam tensed and moved his hand to grab the gun in his waistband. Ashton didn't see Sam tense and slightly crouch as he prepared for trouble. She moved past him until she reached the edge of the lake and stood looking at it for a moment before turning back to him.

"I haven't been here for a long time. The last time I was with my parents. Since no one else lived anywhere near here and we were the only ones to come to the lake, I've always thought of it as our lake. Guess that's not exactly true." Ashton had no problem telling others when she was wrong. Had she been delusional to think her family had dibs on this peaceful place? This had always been her and her dad's special place where no one had ever intruded on their time together. No harm though, the lake was big enough for both of them to enjoy and still maintain their privacy.

Turning back to face Sam, who had only come a short distance toward her, Ashton gave him a slight smile. "Well Sam, it was interesting meeting you, but I think I will be heading back before it gets any darker. See ya around."

Ashton walked past Sam and he let her, fully intending to follow her to see if she met anyone or was even truly staying nearby. If she was telling the truth, then he could go back to his isolation with a few memories of a short time spent with a beautiful woman. If she was lying to him, then he had no choice but to handle things the best way he knew how.

For the first time in many years, Sam crossed his fingers and sent out a little prayer asking the Gods to let Ashton be everything she said. For the first time in a long time Sam wanted to protect, wanted something to be as good as it seemed. Sam squared his shoulders and entered the woods.

Let the game begin.

CHAPTER 4

Ashton plunged into the ever-increasing shadows of the forest as she started her trek back to the cabin. The beauty of the woods was lost to her, as her mind turned over the brief meeting she had just had with Sam. The last thing she had expected when she had decided to come back to the mountain, was to find someone else in this remote area. And to top it off, she had not expected her reaction to him to be anywhere as strong as it had been.

Ashton had dated men before and considered herself to be a good judge of people, but she had never been attracted to one at first sight before today. She did not believe in love at first sight, and would not believe that that was what had just happened. She knew nothing about him and had no intention of finding out either. She hadn't come here to get involved with anyone. She had been drawn here, hoping to find peace and to get back on track. She needed some alone time. So, with a squaring of her shoulders, she pushed the image of Sam to the back of her mind.

Ashton wrapped her arms around herself and kept walking, becoming aware of the temperature change as the sun sank behind the mountain peaks. She would have to remember to take a jacket with her the next time she ventured out. It wasn't safe to trust the weather in the high country. Even in the midst of summer it could change in an instant and take a life with no qualms. Keeping her eyes on the almost hidden path, she finally emerged from the trees and walked across the small clearing to the steps leading into the cabin.

Once inside she decided that it was not much warmer inside than out, and went to the fireplace in the living room to build a fire with the logs she had seen earlier. Her dad had left a small stack of logs arranged in the fireplace, and a few stacked alongside with a pile of newspapers that were now yellow with age. Kneeling down, Ash crumpled up the papers, grabbed a box of matches from the mantel, and touched the flame to the dry paper. She sat back on her heels and waited to see if her efforts would work. It wasn't as if she built fires every day, so she was pleased when the paper crackled, catching the logs on fire, giving an instant warmth to the chilly cabin.

Staring into the flames Ash wondered what she was to do next. She was sure that the TV service had been disconnected long ago, and she had not yet taken the time to explore the house to find a radio. No one in the mountains went without at least a radio. Not only did it provide noise, it also was a way to keep track of the weather and the outside world. She made a mental note to have the television service restored as soon as possible.

Sitting back and wrapping her arms around her legs she decided to just enjoy the fire, the warmth and the quiet for a few minutes. The fire threw shadows across her face and danced in a hypnotic rhythm that lulled Ashton into a semi dream state. She let herself float as she became entranced with the dancing of the flames as they licked at the sides of the logs.

The silence was deep except for the crack and pop that was the symphony the fire provided. Ashton lowered her head to rest it on her raised knees, and it wasn't long before her eyelids followed. It was a few minutes before she noticed a small persistent sound intruding into the quiet of the evening.

Raising her head Ashton concentrated on locating and identifying the sound. She could hear a low humming but could not decide where it was coming from. It seemed to be all around her, and yet no one place at the same time. She wondered if she should be worried as she was alone and had no means to call for help if she needed to.

Turning slowly to face the room, Ashton caught her breath and froze.

For the second time that day she came face to face with a strange man. Only this one was in her house and was one of the strangest sights she had ever seen. A long flowing white garment that Ashton thought was a robe but wasn't sure, hung down to the floor and seemed to be moving with a breeze that she could not feel. It covered him from neck to toes and had long wide sleeves that covered all but his fingertips. A sash of shinny material, she could not put her finger on what it was, cinched the waist and hung down the front to where his knees should be. For that matter, she could not quite make out the type of material the robe was made out of either. It seemed to be going in and out of focus and the outline of the man himself was constantly changing. He did not move but seemed to be in constant motion, kind of like looking at a reflection in water with the ripples blurring the image. Long dark hair hung to his shoulders and, like his clothing, seemed to be lifted by a breeze.

Ashton rubbed her eyes, blinked them, and even tried closing them for a few seconds to erase the image that she was sure was a figment of her imagination. But when she opened them again, there he was.

Leaping to her feet Ashton backed away until she felt her back hit the roughness of the cabin walls. "Who are you, what do you want?" she asked. She had no weapons and nothing at hand to defend herself with, if the need arose. The pulse in her ears was so loud that she had to strain to hear the soft, soothing, musical voice that seemed to be coming from inside her head answer her.

She shook her head and tried to refocus her attentions on the man in front of her. She must be dreaming, or even hallucinating, because she could have swore she heard the person before her say he was her guardian angel and that he was here to help her.

"I must be going crazy. This is not happening. I must be losing my mind," she told herself.

A slight smile curved the lips of the man, as before her disbelieving eyes a pair of wings the color of opals appeared from his back and stretched across the room. Taking up most of the space from floor to ceiling and from wall to wall, the wings held for a moment and then began to slowly retreat to wherever they had come from.

Ashton did not think her eyes could get any wider or her brain more befuddled and she was correct. With a soft sigh, Ashton slid down the wall and with no effort on her part, and for the first time in her life, fainted.

CHAPTER 5

Sam gave Ashton a one-minute head start, then began to follow along the same trail she had disappeared down. He moved steady and quiet, being careful where he placed each step. He did not want to alert her to the fact that she was being followed, by stepping on a fallen twig or by rustling the dead needles laying in wind blown piles on the ground. Sam caught glimpses of her as she passed from shadow to sunlight and from between trees growing on either side of the forest path. He kept his eyes moving from side to side, making sure there was no one else spying from the trees. It wouldn't be wise to be caught unaware, as any mistake in his line of work could be fatal.

Sam was good, anyone who knew him would say he was the best, which was evident as stealthy he followed his target. He was patient and stayed far enough away from her to keep her in sight, but not be detected. He saw Ashton wrap her arms around herself for warmth and had to smirk to himself. If this was the best they had to send after him, then he didn't have too much to worry about. It was obvious that she had not done her homework very well when it came to Colorado weather, as she shivered in the chill of the mountain air. A good tracker would have come prepared for the elements.

When Ashton reached the edge of the woods that

surrounded the cabin, she didn't hesitate or look around, but went straight to the stairs and entered the back door, closing it immediately behind her. He imagined the lock falling into place on the other side of the cabin door.

Sam waited for a few minutes, taking his time to look over the area with a practiced eye. As he looked, Sam noticed there was no car in the drive behind the house. Keeping to the trees, he made a complete circle around the house and found no car, anywhere. How had she gotten to this place without a car? No cabs were going to drive all the way from Denver to drop her off at her doorstep. Keeping low, Sam exited the tree line and made an inspection of the short, curvy driveway. No tire tracks there either, which added to the mystery of how she had gotten here.

Sam made a mental note of where each window was, and the vantage points he would use if it were him inside watching. After his reconnaissance of the area, Sam crept to a window on the side of the house closest to the trees, and slowly raised himself until he could just see over the windowsill. Even though the glass hadn't been scrubbed in a long time, he had a clear view of the living room and into the kitchen. He decided to settle in and watch from this vantage point for as long as it took him to find out if she was alone or if she posed any danger to him.

It did not take long before Ashton came into view. She knelt in front of the fireplace settled in between the two rooms, and appeared to be trying to start a fire. Sam had to admire this mystery woman, who got the wood crackling on the first try. Maybe she wasn't as fragile as she appeared.

Sam still had not seen signs of anyone else in the house, and began to relax just a little as his sense of danger was beginning to abate. Things seemed to be as they appeared, except for the question of how had she gotten here. It was as if she had dropped out of the sky and landed on the porch of this cabin high in the mountains.

Sam was just about ready to back away and return to his house when he noticed Ashton stiffen as she knelt before the fire. Making a sweep of the room Sam saw nothing out of the ordinary, but just the same he reached behind his back and retrieved the pistol hidden there. He watched as Ashton leapt to her feet and backed toward the wall until her back was against it. Then, seemingly without cause, her eyes rolled up and she slid unconscious to the floor.

Sam's eyes darted back and forth but he could see nothing. Something was evidently wrong, but he couldn't ferret out the source of her fear. What had spooked her and frightened her until she passed out?

Then slowly Sam rose to his full height, as his eyes focused on someone or something inside the house. He was afraid to look away, or even to blink, because what he was seeing could not be real. During his life, Sam had figured he had seen just about everything there was to see, and some things he had even seen twice. But this, this was not possible.

The hand that held the gun now hung down at his side, and was all but forgotten with the new turn of events. Sam swallowed hard but could find no spit in his throat to relieve the dryness that had overtaken his mouth.

Slowly, with his eyes on the house, he backed away and kept going until he was once again hidden in the trees. When he could no long see the cabin, Sam turned and walked hastily to his cabin. He hurried up the weathered steps until he was secured inside. He pulled out a chair from his kitchen table, laid his gun down, and finally let his legs give out.

This was not possible, he thought. Turning what he had witnessed over and over in his mind until he was almost numb, Sam finally had to admit to himself that maybe he was not crazy. Maybe what he had seen had really happened. But who would believe him? Shit, he still could not believe it, and he had been an eyewitness. It was burned into his brain.

As he had crouched outside the window, Sam had seen Ashton rise up off the floor and lay down on the couch. Only she had not gotten up and walked. She had floated.

CHAPTER 6

Ashton came swimming slowly up from the dark void into which she had fallen. Lying for a few seconds with her eyes closed, she tried to remember where she was and what had happened. It came back to her in a rush. The strange man in her living room, the unbelievable sight of him sprouting wings and saying he was her guardian angel.

Her eyes flew open and she bolted upright, finding herself sitting on the couch instead of on the floor where she remembered having fallen. How had she gotten there? A slight sound to her right, caught her attention. She slowly turned her head and recoiled as the stranger from before came into view.

Holding up a hand as if to stay Ashton from bolting from the room, the stranger began to speak, "Do not be afraid, I mean you no harm. In fact, as I said, I am here to answer your questions and to help you."

Shaking her head violently from side to side, Ashton tried to bring herself back to reality. "This is not real, you are not real," she repeated over and over to herself.

With a look of sad reality, the vision tried to calm Ashton as he said, "I can assure you, I am very real and you are not dreaming."

"More like a nightmare," she said under her breath, closing her eyes and shaking her head again as if it would make the images before her disappear.

With a smile that was warm and welcoming he sat down on the end of the couch facing the young woman beside him. "My name is Saul," he said in a low soothing tone. "I know this is all very hard for you to take in, but I am real and I am here for a reason. That reason is you," he said as he pointed his finger at her. "I need for you to open your mind to something that you may believe impossible and to listen to what I have to say before you make any decisions. Can you do that"? he asked in his melodic voice.

Ashton had no reason to believe him and many reasons not to trust his intentions. But whether because of his gentle voice or just plain curiosity, she settled back, looked Saul straight in the eye, questioned her sanity, and nodded her head timidly in agreement.

"Very good," Saul said. With what seemed to be a squaring of his shoulders and much determination, he began. "As I said, my name is Saul and I have come to you because something has happened that I must explain to you. Because of an unfortunate occurrence yesterday, here on earth, you had a car accident and you did not survive.

Ashton jerked as if she'd been physically stricken.

The angel continued, "However, it was not your time to be taken, and because of this upset in "the plan" you have been given a time span of two months in which to fulfill your destiny here on earth. During this time you will be allowed to live as you want, go where you want, and do as you please." He paused for a few moments, then staring into her disbelieving eyes, continued, "But be aware, that at the end of the two months you will be taken from this earth. No traces of your presence here will be found. It will be up to you if and when you should tell anyone of your situation. Do you have any questions?" he asked coming to the end of his unbelievable monologue.

Ashton's face had taken on a look of disbelieving horror as he made his speech. *Did she have any questions? Was he out of his mind*? she wondered. *Of course she had questions! Of course he was out of his mind*!

Clearing her throat she tried to force a sound to come out, but nothing but a slight squeak could be heard. Her tongue seemed to be sticking to the roof of her mouth, and she had to work for a moment to get it back in place. So many thoughts were flying around in her head that she felt like she was in a whirlpool being sucked down to disappear into some unknown drain.

Finally finding her voice, Ashton began to speak haltingly in a small voice. "Why should I believe anything you have said? It is just too far fetched to even consider." She looked warily at him, then away again, shook her head in disbelief, then went on. "Let me see if I understand what you've said. Your name is Saul. You claim to be my *guardian angel* and were sent here to *help me*.

Her voice was gaining strength as she continued, "But your idea of help is to tell me I died yesterday in a car crash that wasn't supposed to happen? To top that off, I have been given two months to fit a whole lifetime of living into, because of some *heavenly* mistake?"

By this time her face had become flushed and her voice almost angry as she confronted the angel seated casually in her living room. "During this time I have the choice of telling people what has happened to me, at which point they will lock me up in a loony bin for being crazy! Does that about cover it?" she finally asked, running out of breath.

Saul smiled at her with patience and understanding as he answered, "In a nut shell, yes."

Ashton came to her feet and faced him squarely, "Get out of my house!" she said in a tone that left no doubt of her anger. "I do not know who sent you, why they sent you, or what they plan to get out of this but it isn't funny. Jokes over. Now there's the door, use it". Standing rigidly in the middle of the room, Ashton pointed to the door and waited, breathing heavily through her nose.

She really expected him to get up and leave as requested, or jump up laughing at the practical joke he'd been hired to deliver. Instead he remained sitting, looking up at her with pity in his eyes.

"I understand this is hard for you, and I am sorry to have to break the news to you in such a blunt manner, but I am willing to spend as much time with you as you need to help you come to the realization that everything I have said is true and will happen as I have said it would."

"You're not real are you?" she asked abandoning the idea that this was a practical joke. "It must have been the soup. Yes, that's it. It was old and had gone bad and I am hallucinating because of it." She pressed her eyelids tightly together and shook her head as if to clear the images from her mind and sight with the simple action. She pressed her clenched fists to her ears to block out the words that were coming from the results of a bad dinner.

Saul stood up to join her. He reached out and took her clenched fists and placed them on his chest. "I am real. You can see me, hear me, and now, even touch me."

Her knuckles rubbed against the silkiness of his robe and she could feel his powerful chest beneath its folds.

"What I have said to you is true," he emphasized each word as he looked straight into her eyes, which were now wide open and set upon his face. "I would change this if I could," he continued in a more gentle tone as he gathered her closer to his chest. "I would spare you the pain of knowing your future, of knowing that death is coming at you like a freight train."

He held her gently for a few seconds, as a father would a daughter, before extending her to arms length again, and looked straight into her eyes as he said, "Your time is short, do not waste another second, but live it to the fullest."

They looked at each other for a full minute, she searching for the truth and he for her understanding. Then he led her to the couch where they sat together, still holding hands. He reminded her, "You had a very strong urge to come to this place, didn't you Ashton?"

Her face took on a quizzical look as she nodded.

"Something unseen seemed to be pulling you to your old home, do you remember, Ashton? Saul searched her face for confirmation.

A look of agreement crossed her face, as he nodded his head and assured her, "You will find what you need in this place. Just look for it, be open to it, and when you figure out what it is, cherish it and hold it close to your heart for all time," he said as he once again placed her hand upon his heart.

"Take this gift of time, and make no mistake it is a very special gift not often given, and use it wisely, my dear Ashton," the angel said.

They sat for a few minutes in silence as he waited for her to come to acceptance of his words, then he rose and spoke to her one more time before leaving the cabin, "Good bye, Ashton. We will meet again."

With that, Saul began to fade before Ashton's eyes. She could no longer feel the solidness of his body before her, and, in the space of a few heartbeats, she was left alone with her hand still raised to where it had rested on his chest. Slowly Ashton let her hand fall to her side.

What had just happened here in her old family cabin, where ghosts of her family could still be felt in the familiarity of the furniture, the pictures, and the love that still filled the walls? Could what the angel said be true? How was she ever to believe what she had seen and heard?

In a daze, Ashton made her way to the kitchen and took a soda out of the fridge. Popping the top she drank as if she had just crossed a desert, the cold liquid immediately quenching her dry mouth and throat.

She pushed through the screen door leading to the porch and sat in an old rocking chair that her father had built from the wood of an old tree from the nearby forest. She had spent many a day sitting on his lap rocking in this chair, naming birds that landed in the trees and playing *I Spy Something* for hours at a time. She began rocking gently, trying to digest this new mystery, which she suddenly found herself smack dab in the middle of.

She looked out over the yard, the woods just beyond with the majestic beauty of the mountains as their backdrop. Everything looked undisturbed, just as it should be. Nothing had changed, had it? For some reason she had a nagging feeling in the back of her mind that seemed to indicate something was off. But the harder she looked, the more elusive it was to find.

It was dark by the time Ashton decided to go inside. She had watched the sun set over the mountains and the stars come out in a clear night sky. They appeared so close, she felt she could almost reach out her hand and touch them with her fingertips.

She got up, cold and stiff from sitting so long trying to figure out what to do next. She really needed to find her jacket if she intended to sit outside for any period of time again. She began to picture a pair of soft warm flannel pajamas she had packed for sleeping on nights such as these and couldn't wait to jump into them to take away the chill that had settled in her bones.

She turned to enter the house, and again the nagging suspicion that something was not right hit her. Mentally shrugging it off, Ashton decided to get a good night's rest and tackle the day ahead. She would definitely need to make a trip into town and pick up some food, no more canned soup that caused hallucinations for her, and maybe a couple of paperbacks on the paranormal would be fitting.

As she reached for the doorknob it finally came to her what had been nagging at the back of her mind. Where was her luggage and outdoor gear she had brought with her? For that matter, where was her car? Wildly turning around, her eyes searched the area around the cabin. Oh my God, how had she gotten here?

CHAPTER 7

Morning was just a mere thought when Sam awoke. He flung a bare arm across his face as he tried to work the grit out of his eyes and the cobwebs from his brain. He had spent most of the night turning over in his mind what had happened, or what he thought had happened at the Rider place.

That is what he now called it since he had fired up his computer to do a little digging on the woman he had met and the cabin she said belonged to her family. What he found confirmed what she had told him. The land had been bought by the Riders almost twenty years ago, and a very nice cabin had been built and used by them as, what seemed to be, a summer-get away. She had told the truth about her parents being deceased and about who she was. She had left out though that she was somewhat of an heiress, having been left a small fortune upon her parent's death. Both of them had been very prestigious lawyers and had made names for themselves in the field.

Still, having a cover that checked out was not to say that she still had not been sent here to find him or even to do more. Having great looks and a lush body was also a good thing to have as it usually proved a distraction to the target. People with less to offer had been recruited to work undercover and had been very successful because no one would suspect them of being anything other then what they appeared.

Sam still had some resources he could use to dig a little deeper, but last night the words had begun to blur and his mind had shut down. So he had packed it in and caught a few hours of sleep.

Sam crawled out of bed and made his way to the bathroom. Passing the mirror he caught a look at his reflection and had to do a double take. His hair was standing up in spikes, his face had a scruffy growth of dark whiskers, his eyes were only opened about half way, and he detected a small crusty spot by his mouth caused when he had drooled during his short sleep. He smirked at his reflection, sure he would scare animals and small children with his current appearance. Not to mention a beautiful woman like Ashton. Since meeting her the day before she seemed to be the only thing on his mind.

Scratching his chest, Sam entered the shower and turned it on full blast. He rested his hand on the wall and let the cool water wash over him, finishing the job of waking him up. After a few minutes of sheer bliss he turned the water off, grabbed a thick towel, made a halfhearted attempt at drying off, and walked naked to the mirror. Running a hand over the dark stubble on his cheeks, Sam decided to shave for the first time in a week. No one was around to see him, so shaving was a hit or miss situation on most days. He did not want to admit that the reason he was taking extra pains with his appearance today might be because of the possibility of running into Ashton again. He lathered his face and began to scrape the tough growth from his lean cheeks. When he was finished he picked up the comb and actually ran it through his thick, ebony locks. He had not had a haircut in months so the mink soft hair hung almost to his shoulders. He chose to ignore the fact that on most days he did not bother with a comb but just ran his hands through it and called it good.

Giving his image one last look in the mirror, Sam walked back into his bedroom and approached the closet. He looked over his wardrobe and spent a moment trying to decide what to wear, until he realized what he was doing. For Christ sake, since when had he become concerned with what to wear? Convincing himself he was not trying to look better today than any other day he grabbed a clean pair of jeans and pulled them on. The fact that they fit him a little tighter then his everyday baggy ones was just a coincidence he assured himself. And just because he pulled out a shirt that did not look like it belonged in the ragbag was only because all the rest of his clothes were dirty. Well, maybe not all of them were dirty, as he was a fairly clean person when it came to keeping house and not letting things pile up.

Satisfied that he was finished with primping, Sam made his way to the kitchen and grabbed a soda from the fridge. He had never acquired a taste for coffee so a pop was his choice of a wake up call in the morning. He took his drink to the table and opened his small stack of newspapers and began to read the want ads.

It took him little time to find the messages that awaited him. Three in fact, asking for his immediate attention. All business now, he looked over each one gleaning the clues left within the text. Two would require overseas travel and one was within the States. Not interested in the travel, he turned on his computer and entered the site indicated in the paper. Using his own code, Sam was instantly linked to a page where the details of the job were very briefly described. Name of the target, what the desired results were, time frame, and price, were all that was listed. The name on the page made him raise his eyebrows in question as he recognized it as a CEO of a major oil company. Well, well, it seemed someone was not happy with the price gouging at the pumps by the oil companies and had decided to send them a message. This might be worth looking into, he decided. He typed a response that he would be considering the job offer and would let them know within the week.

Having finished his breakfast, Sam decided he'd take a trip down to the lake today. Purely for fishing and relaxing purposes, or so he told himself. If he happened to run into someone, say his new neighbor, then so be it. He packed a bag with some munchies, grabbed his pole and walked out the door. Leaving his gear on the porch, Sam took his time making a complete inspection of the outside of his home and the edge of the woods. He never left without looking for tracks and/or signs that someone had paid him a visit during the night. He also made mental notes of the placement of rocks and piles of pine needles to check later to see if they had been moved or disturbed. He never took his safety for granted, and made sure he would not be caught unaware of any trouble that might be coming his way.

He was all business, cold and sharp as he made the tour of his property. He'd seen this terrain a thousand times and would not allow himself to become complacent and miss any telltale signs that could get him killed. Satisfied that all was good, he returned to the porch, gathered his fishing equipment, and set off for the lake.

Taking his time, he moved quietly through the trees until he reached the lake. Before stepping out into the open, he once again took his time and scanned the area looking for any danger, whether it was on two legs or four. The only other occupants of the lake were two deer that had stopped to drink and grab a bite of the grass at the waters edge. As the last preparation before walking out into the open, Sam bent down and double-checked the pistol strapped to his ankle. He took it out, checked the bullets, made sure the safety was on, and held it in his hand for a moment. Testing its weight and balance he stopped and looked at it for a moment. He never went anywhere without it, shit, he even slept with it under his pillow. It was his friend, and the only thing he put his total trust in. Satisfied that all precautions were in place, Sam tucked the gun away at his ankle and moved into the open.

Appearing at ease, but with eyes on the move, he made his way to a spot on the opposite end of the lake from where he was at yesterday. Don't be predictable. Change your routine. Good advice to live by. Sam set his equipment down in the grass, fed a worm onto the hook at the end of his pole, and cast his line into the water. He sat down in the shade with his back to a tree, and prepared to wait. She would come, he was sure of it. As sure of it as he was his own name. For the first time in years, Sam felt anticipation. Anticipation for something personal and pleasurable that he wanted just for himself.

It felt good.

CHAPTER 8

Shadows began to retreat and give way to the pale morning light that would not be denied, as a new day began. Ashton sat in a rocking chair on her porch, wrapped in an old patchwork quilt, watching the new day being born. She had spent the night pacing the floors of the cabin, and had finally ended up on the porch, where she could breathe the fresh air and try to make sense of what had happened to her since arriving at the cabin.

All through the night she had struggled with the information that Saul had given her. Did she believe it? She had come to the conclusion, after much crying, cursing and denial, that she didn't have any other choice. There were too many things that could not be explained for her to doubt the visitor and what he had said. For instance, where was her car and luggage? How had she gotten to the cabin, and why couldn't she remember arriving?

Still, she did not feel dead. She still felt hunger, hot, cold, happiness, and sorrow. She ate, slept, and even peed like anyone else, but she was, for all purposes, dead. And now, because of some mix-up in heaven, she was being given two months to live a lifetime in. Some consolation prize.

She contemplated what she should do. Should she travel and try to see as much of the world as she could fit in, or should she just remain here at her family's old summer cabin in Colorado? After debating this for quite some time, Ashton decided that she had been brought to this place for a reason. So she would give it some time and wait to see if the reason would be revealed to her.

It was not in her nature to dwell on depressing thoughts, but she had wallowed in self-pity for a good share of the dark hours before dawn. After all she reasoned, she would not be getting married, having children, or growing old with grandchildren sitting at her feet listening to her life stories. She had so little time. Two months were nothing when it came to doing everything she had always figured she had time to do.

She had decided not to waste anymore of her time feeling sorry for her situation, so she had pulled the quilt from the bed, wrapped herself in its warmth, and sat on the porch to watch the sun come up. All the colors were there for her to see, and she'd sent a small thank you skyward that she had been awake to see it. She refused to feel resentful that she would only have a few more of these peaceful, glorious moments.

Would she still be able to watch sunrises after she was gone? Actually there were a million questions she would like to ask her angel, now that she had been given the time to think. But he wasn't here and she did not know how, or even if, she could contact him. She had tried calling his name, it worked on TV right, but the room hadn't become suddenly bright with heavenly light and no one appeared out of the blue, leaving her feeling stupid for trying. She had not suddenly been given the knowledge of secrets only the dead knew, so she knew no more today then she did yesterday. Well, except that there were angels and she was dead. She kept circling back to that fact. It was hard not to.

Letting out a big sigh, Ashton wiggled her backside more firmly into the rocker and tried to find something positive about this whole mess. Let's see, she could now eat whatever she wanted, after all how much weight would she gain in two months, and she did not have to worry about taking it back off. Bonus! She would not have to work out every day just to look the way society thought she should. Double bonus!! No more worrying about cancer, colds, or catching the flu or any other sickness, she was already dead right? She would still try not to get sick in the next two months, as it would make her remaining time very unpleasant. Best of all, she thought and if what she heard was true, was that she would get to see her parents again. She had missed them terribly since their deaths and that would make it almost worth it in her book. *Ok*, she thought, *I can deal with this*. Not that she had a choice.

She stuck her tongue out at the sky and finally rose to her feet. She was tired but now was not the time to be taking naps. She went into the house and climbed the stairs to the bedroom she was using. Putting the quilt back on her bed she went to take a shower and start her day.

She took pains with her appearance, deciding to go back to the lake to see if there might be a gorgeous man fishing there. Would it be fair to get involved with Sam when she knew she had so short a time left? She wanted to feel love and, sorry Saul, have hot, wild sex a few more times before her time was up. Good for her, bad for him. Well, maybe she was putting an awful lot of faith in the fact that he might want her. Time would tell.

Getting dressed in a light sweater, faded jeans that fit her rear nicely, and her favorite pair of comfortable tennis shoes, Ashton rummaged through the cupboards and came up with a few things she could make a light picnic out of, including a few chocolate bars, one of which she ate with no guilt whatsoever before she loaded everything in a backpack she'd found hanging behind the door, and started out her back door.

Slipping her arms into the straps of the backpack Ashton turned to pull the door closed behind her. When she swung back around, she instantly screamed and slammed into the door at her back. There, standing at the top of the stairs was

Saul, looking exactly as he had last night when he had visited her in her living room.

"Good morning, Ashton," he said. He spoke in the same soothing tone, same understanding look in his eyes, same smile lightly curving his lips. Ashton was getting a little tired of having the crap scared out of her every time she turned around lately, and she let a little of the ire show through as she faced Saul with her chin raised.

"Would you stop doing that? Can't you make some noise instead of sneaking up on me? You are going to give me a heart attack and my time left will be considerably shorter than it already is," she scolded the figure at the top of the stairs.

Saul had been worried about how she would react, after having a night to process everything he had told her. He could have watched her without her knowing, but had decided it was a private time and had given her space to try and adjust. Bowing his head slightly he said, "I'm sorry. It was not my intention to frighten you. Shall we sit down"?

He moved to a chair beside the small wooden table in the kitchen and sat down waiting for Ashton to join him. She did so reluctantly, removing the backpack and taking the chair on the other side of the table.

"Why are you here now? Don't tell me you have more surprises for me"? Ashton challenged the angel across the table.

"No," he said, "I have come to answer your questions, which I am sure you have for me. Please, ask me now," he said as he folded his arms in front of him and looked patiently at her.

Ashton leaned forward, resting her arms on the dusty tabletop and looked intently into the angelic eyes across from her. "Why me? You said there had been a mistake, what did you mean by that? What happens after my time is up? Where will I go? Will it hurt? Will I just cease to exist, or what? That ought to do for a start". She leaned back and took a deep breath, as her questions had been delivered in one steady stream.

Saul had anticipated all of these and more so he was ready to try and soothe her as best he could.

"As I told you last night, due to an incident beyond my control you were taken before your time. This incident did not happen on purpose, nor was it done as punishment for anything you have done. You have led a good life, Ashton, been kind and loving to those you've met. It's because of your goodness, that you are being given this extra time to try to find your purpose here on earth."

He paused to let what he had just said soak in for a few minutes before he continued. "When your time is up, you will begin to fade and finally disappear, as I did last night. It will not cause you any pain. You will then join me and others, such as your parents, in a place that is beautiful, quiet, and peaceful. With time and training, you will be able to look down upon earth and see what you wish."

Again he paused and reached across the table to take her small hand in his large one. "I sense that you have begun to accept what has happened to you. Am I wrong?" he asked.

"No," she replied with resignation, "as off the wall as it sounds, there are just too many odd things happening that have no other explanations."

"If I may ask, what will you do with your time" he asked, knowing it was none of his business, but curious none-the-less.

She replied, "I have decided to remain here for the time being and see what happens next. I plan on enjoying each day to the fullest and, I guess, to try and store up as many memories as I can. Is that what you wanted to hear?" she finished with a touch of anger in her voice.

Ashton did not want to blame Saul for her circumstances, but since he was the only one here he would just have to grin and bear her attitude. "If I have any more questions, will I be able to contact you or not?" she asked him.

Slowly shaking his head no, Saul came to his feet, walked around the table and laid a hand on her shoulder. "No," he said, "I have done all that I can for now. The rest is up to you. I have faith in you, Ashton, you will choose wisely," he said preparing to leave her again.

"Wait!" Ashton spoke urgently grabbing for him as if to prevent him from leaving before she was done with him, "I have one more question before you disappear again. You said I was to fulfill my destiny. What is that exactly? What happens if I can't figure it out?" she asked with a hint of desperation in her beautiful eyes.

Saul began to fade from her eyes and grasp, but Ashton could still hear his voice as he left her with one last piece of advice. "Just live Ashton. Take nothing for granted and look for the beauty in everything around you."

With that he was gone, and once again she was left alone to try to fit the pieces together. What was real and what should she do next.

The idea of the lake was not so appealing any more, as Ashton just wanted to be alone for a while. Still, taking the backpack and throwing it over her shoulder, she started out in the opposite direction. With eyes that were now open and taking in everything as if it were brand new, Ashton started to walk. Today really was the first day of the rest of her life, and she intended to fill it with all the beauty she could find. Fill herself until she could hold no more and then begin again. She would make memories. Memories to last a lifetime.

CHAPTER 9

Ashton began walking with no real destination in mind. Her only purpose today was to explore her world and try to capture, and hold close to her heart, all the beauty around her, before it was too late. As she wove her way through the trees, going deeper into the woods, she viewed all she saw with eyes that were as wide open and naive as a new baby.

She took in her surroundings, as if for the first time. The trees seemed to be taller, greener, and more fragrant then she ever remembered them being. She noticed the nests that most of them held, picturing them filled with the voices of new baby birds, their barely feathered heads raised, beaks open in anticipation of the next meal their mother would deliver.

As she passed through the forest, she reached out many times to feel the trunks of the trees. She used to think that all trees were alike, but was discovering that there was a uniqueness to each one. As she ran her fingers over them she felt the texture of the bark, many times coming away with sticky sap on her fingers. Another sign of life growing around her.

She noticed the color of the leaves ranging from the deep green of the pine needles, to the soft green, vibrant oranges, and golds of the scattered aspens. They appeared to have been lightly dusted over the pines to add garnish to the never-ending deep green landscape, much like a floral bouquet of roses with the wispy white babies breath added to soften the arrangement.

As she compared the trees she noticed that one was a darker brown then its neighbor. The next had an unusual knot that whorled in an ever-tightening circle. The next had lines in the bark as if a large animal had used it for a scratching post, whether it had been recently or not she could not tell. Some had thick sprouting of needles while others looked more like the Christmas tree on Charlie Brown. Ashton liked those the best, as they seemed to need more love and attention then their fuller more beautiful neighbors.

Whenever she came to a clearing she would stop to enjoy the warm sun on her head and shoulders. She'd look up and take in the crystal blue of the sky, and watch the clouds chasing each other across the expanse, until they disappeared over the treetops. She remembered looking at clouds when she was young and trying to find shapes in their design. As she now watched, she could again see wonderful, fanciful images within their masses.

Ashton smiled as she realized she felt good. Free and young again. Everything around her filled her with a new wonder. She couldn't help feeling a little sad that it had taken her all this time to find the treasures her world had held because she had been to busy to notice.

As she walked she noticed all of the spring flowers that were in bloom, lavender, white, and yellow dotting the landscape and giving unexpected vibrancy and color to the greens and browns of the woods. She stopped many times, as she noticed each new variety, to crouch down and smell the fragile blooms. Some were spicy, some were sweet and, as she found out, some smelled like a skunk had used them for its own personal marker. But to each new experience she smiled and stored the memory in her brain and in her heart.

When she was hungry she stopped at a dry spot in a cozy clearing, took out the light jacket she had placed in her backpack, spread it over the ground, and sat for over an hour eating the simple sandwich and fruit she had packed, enjoying all the activity around her.

She had sat very still as a mother deer and her two fawns entered the clearing in search of their own lunch and perhaps an afternoon nap. They had looked a bit startled when they first spotted her in the clearing, their eyes large and round in their beautiful faces, but after a moment must have decided she posed no threat to them, and lowered their heads to chew on mouthfuls of tender, young spring grass. For over an hour Ashton kept watch over the doe and her young, admiring the way the mother kept one eye on her young while going about the business of feeding on the grass in the clearing.

When Ashton finally left the clearing, she felt richer for having shared a moment with nature. Another treasure for her bank of memories.

She continued her walk, winding her way again through the trees with no direction in mind. She noticed shiny things peaking through the needles and grass that covered the forest floor like a carpet, and stopped to peer closer. What she found were the shiniest rocks she had ever seen. Each new discovery was packed full of mica and quartz in every color she could imagine. Gold, silver, pink, smoky, white, and even some greens could be found like forgotten treasure for her to pick up. She became so engrossed in hunting for the sparkles sprinkled over the ground, squealing in delight at each new find, that she was sure she had been a Magpie in a previous life. She found rocks that looked unassuming and plain until she picked them up, turned them over, and found great hunks of crystals in their underbelly and middles. She could see shapes of mouths with teeth hanging jagged and lethal. Each new discovery was a ray of joy going straight to her heart. She was having the time of her life and it cost her nothing but time and the willingness to seek out the beauty Mother Nature provided every day.

Ashton loaded her backpack with all her treasures, picturing in her mind where she would put them when she got home. She would make a lovely rock garden in the backyard so she could look at them in the mountain sunlight every day and remember the joy finding them had brought her. She also hoped that they would brighten everyone's day when they visited her home, while she was there and even after she was gone.

Stopping for just a moment after she had hoisted her pack onto her back, Ashton looked around her and with a peaceful smile on her face said "Thank you," out loud to Nature for allowing her the pleasure and the privilege of her wonderful finds.

As she raised her face to the sky, Ashton noticed the sun was hanging lower in the western sky, and figured it was time to head home. She knew she had walked west during the day, as the sun had been to her back almost all of the way. So, if she headed east, in the opposite direction she had come, she should be back to the cabin in time to enjoy supper on the porch, with the stars shining overhead. She smiled at the prospect and began her journey back through the woods.

The going was slower and took more effort, as she had the added the weight of her discoveries in her backpack to contend with. She kept moving at a steady pace through the same trees she had recently explored. Even having been this way just that morning, she still noticed new sounds and scents as the nocturnal animals came to life in darkening woods. Ashton wasn't afraid, but rather a feeling of contentment traveled with her as she drew closer to home.

The sun was just setting when her cabin came into view. It looked inviting to her and she realized she was tiring from her day of exploring and her night before with no sleep. She rounded the corner of the cabin and mounted the stairs to her back door. She lowered the backpack gently to the floor, and then had to smile while shaking her head in wonderment. She had set the pack down as if there was something breakable inside, instead of hearty rocks that could take abuse and never show a scratch.

Ashton opened the door and walked inside, turning on the lights as she went. She left the door open to let in the cool, clean evening smells and went to clean up before settling down to make her supper. In her contentment, she had no idea she was being watched by a pair of intense teal blue eyes.

CHAPTER 10

Sam sat with his back to a tree enjoying the cool morning air. He crossed his legs out in front of him as the peace and quiet of his lakeside retreat worked its magic, and let his eyelids slowly lower. One by one his muscles finally relaxed. Sleep had eluded him for most of the night, as he'd spent it thinking about and investigating Ashton Rider. Not really meaning to, he slid effortlessly into a light doze. He could still hear the droning of the bees, the chirping of birds, and the lapping of waves, in other words the music of nature. He did not sleep heavy enough that he would not hear approaching danger, but just slightly below the surface of wakefulness.

He could see Ashton standing across the lake, looking as she had yesterday. Lovely, breathtaking, and alone. She glided towards him with a smile of seduction on her lips and an invitation in her eyes. Those eyes, those dark green eyes. They haunted him. They taunted him. They held promises of delights to be found in her arms and in her body.

He watched her as she came to stand before him, wearing a thin flowing robe in the same shade of green as her eyes. The color was perfect for her, making her skin appear ivory white, creamy and satiny smooth. His eyes roved up and down the perfection before him. His hands clenched in an effort not to grab her and greedily find out for himself just how she felt.

A light breeze touched her hair and lifted it in a lazy dance of come hither seduction. She licked her lips, making them wet and glossy and showing him a teasing glimpse of her tongue as it slowly circled before retreating back inside her mouth, making him want to follow and taste.

She raised her hand to slowly expose one smooth shoulder, drawing his eyes, willingly, upwards as he watched her fingers follow the edge of the robe as it slid down and caught at her elbow. She folded her arm and brought her hand to rest between her breasts as she allowed the other sleeve of the robe to slide silkily down her shoulder. If not for her hand holding the cloth up it would have slid all the way to the sand.

Sam swallowed hard as he wished she would put him out of his misery and let the cloth fall. His eyes roamed over the exposed tops of her breasts, and he looked his fill as she stood statue still in front of him. When he finally raised his eyes to once again stare into hers, he was rewarded with the same hunger mirrored back at him.

Her nostrils flared and her breathing became heavy as she drank in the wanting she could feel rolling off of Sam in thick, hot waves. It reached out to her, exciting her. Then, as if in slow motion, Ashton let her arms lower to her sides and the robe pooled around her slender ankles.

She stood before Sam in her naked glory hiding nothing from his hot eyes. Giving Sam all the time he needed to look his fill, she remained standing tall and straight. The cool morning air washed over her fevered skin, cooling it, making her nipples stand out like diamond studs, hard and beautiful. The breeze sent slight waves across the tight, sable curls between her legs carrying her scent to Sam. He knew that scent, dark, mysterious, and all women.

Sam's breath came in heavy pants and he wanted her now, right here, with no walls or secrets between them. Sam watched as Ashton seemed to float to him, until she was standing over him, her feet on either side of his thighs. She slowly lowered herself until her eyes were level with his and the most intimate part of her was resting on the rock hard bulge in his pants.

Sam slowly raised his hands until they were entangled in her dark brown tresses, the hair wrapping around his forearms until he was her captive. He pulled her face to his, and with a groan that he felt deep in his soul, got his first taste of her.

It was all he imagined, hot, rich and spicy. His lips could not get enough of her taste. He felt her wrap her arms around his neck and work her body against his to the time of the thrusting of two tongues.

Pulling his mouth away, he let his lips travel where they wanted, and they wanted to be everywhere, taste everything. He kissed and tasted her neck, licking and sucking his way down until her back was arched and her breasts, heavy with desire were quivering before his eyes. He took one hard nipple into his mouth, washing it with his tongue before sucking it deep into his mouth. He suckled her breast as a newborn would, tugging on the sensitive tip and nipping it with enough force to cause electric jolts to course through her body.

Sam moved to the undersides of each breast, giving each the attention he knew would drive her crazy. So often these luscious, sensitive spots were overlooked by being in too big of a hurry, and Sam aimed to take his time, his fill.

Sam continued to run his lips over every part of her body, until he heard her whimper with her need, a need that matched his own. Raising her hips slowly, Sam undid the buttons on his jeans, no small feat as he was straining against their confines. Releasing himself so his full, hard length could stand between them, he raised his hips to tug the unwanted barrier down and out of the way.

The muscles in his arms bulged as he lifted Ashton up until his tip was touching her, inviting her to lower herself and take him inside. With slow movements, she did just as he wanted, slipping him inside her until she was flush against his thighs. Sam filled her to over flowing, and still tried to get deeper, become part of her with every thrust they made together.

They rode together in harmony each feeling and knowing what the other needed and wanted. Sam felt the pressure build in his body and he felt hers tighten around him, as both were ready to fly apart and be reborn together as one. *One more second,* he thought, *one more deep thrust.*

Just as he was about to let go, Sam heard a twig snap. His eyes flew open and he came face to face with a raccoon standing on its back legs looking at him. After a moment, the raccoon lowered itself to all fours and lumbered back into the forest.

As he came awake, Sam's heart was still pounding and sweat was standing out on his forehead as he looked around trying to figure out where he was. He looked at the lake and the still forest around him. He remembered.

Letting his head fall back, eyes tightly closed, and clenched fists raised to the sun, Sam howled.

CHAPTER 11

Sam knuckled his eyes and wiped the sweat beads from his forehead. He could feel the moisture running down his back and took a deep breath to calm himself. The dream was so vivid. He could still taste Ashton on his tongue, feel her body as if it still surrounded him, could remember the minutest detail of their encounter. He was having a difficult time believing it had all been just a dream. He had never had a dream like that. That's not to say he had never had sexual dreams before because being a normal, healthy male, he, of course, did. Just not on this level.

Finally collecting his scattered wits, he heaved himself to his feet and made his way to the water's edge. Squatting down he splashed water over his face enjoying the icy coldness that lifted the fog from his brain. Still balancing on the balls of his feet, he shook his head like a dog and let the clear droplets fly where they would.

Now that his senses had returned, Sam was disturbed that he could have been so engrossed in his fantasy, that his guard had been let down so completely. He had always prided himself on his ability to sleep light, wake up sharp, and, if the need arose, deadly. Not this time. This time he had been foggy and disorientated. Major mistake in his line of work.

Sam's eyes turned flat, cold, and the lids lowered until only a sliver of turbulent blue could be seen. He would not let some woman get into his head until he became vulnerable and open to attack. What had he been thinking anyway? He had only met her the day before and he still did not know enough about her to rule her out as a potential danger to his safety.

Sam looked at the dark face of his watch, nothing shiny to catch the sun and give him away, and noticed it was almost noon. A slight frown creased his brow as he expected her to be at the lake by now. If she was not here, then where was she? What was she doing? Deciding to give her one more hour, Sam tended to his fishing line and removed the fish that had been snared there. He gently lowered it back into the water and watched it swim away to live another day. He tossed the line back into the water and, moving back into the trees, began a slow circuit of the lake to check out the immediate area and make sure all was safe and secure.

The only tracks he could detect came from animals moving to and from the water. Taking all the time he needed, Sam made his way back to his fishing gear and, once again, picking out a tree to lean against, sat with his back to the old trunk. He brought out the backpack he had packed with food. He rummaged through it until he found what he wanted and slowly ate his fill, all the while keeping his eyes moving and his senses sharp.

He was on the lookout for danger, he told himself, not trying to catch his first glimpse of a slender, dark haired, green eyed beauty. Sam finished his meal and carefully put all the remains and trash in his pack to take with him for disposal. He knew not to leave scraps out that would attract the bears and big cats in the area and give them a reason to start hanging out by the lake, expecting an easy source of food.

Sam brought his mind around to the message he had seen in the paper that morning and began to turn the idea of his next possible mission over in his mind. Beginning to make a mental list of the pros and cons, possible reasons behind the request, and the ramifications of his actions should he accept, he began the process of making his decision. It could take a couple of weeks for him to feel comfortable and sure that he had all the information he needed to make his choice.

Once his mind was made up, and he decided to go ahead, he would form his plan carefully and check it many times and from many angles to make sure everything would go off with out a hitch. No mistakes, no surprises, no regrets. Sam could afford none of these. He would not allow anything to stand in his way, nor thoughts of the act afterwards. That's the way he worked. At least for now.

He knew his time in the business was coming to an end. He was still a young man, in his prime at thirty-five years of age. He would not wait until age, including all the aches and pains that came with it, slowed him down enough to get caught, or worse get him dead. So maybe, this would be his last job.

He still enjoyed the aspects of his work, which probably made him sick in most people's minds, but he was not done living yet and wanted to be around for a while longer. So maybe, who knew, this could be his last job.

Putting these thoughts away Sam again glanced around wondering if Ashton was even going to show up at all. He would have bet anything that she would, but there was always a fist time for him to be wrong. Sam smirked at the arrogance of that thought, and figured if he did not say it out loud to anyone he could get away with it.

Again he glanced at his watch, looked up at the sun, and decided to pack up and call it a day. He hoisted his pack, reeled in his line and started the trek back to his home.

When he arrived he hid his gear and made his customary circuit of the land, missing nothing as he made his home secure for the night. Entering his back door Sam dumped everything in the washroom and made his way to the fridge to grab his favorite soda, diet cherry vanilla Dr. Pepper. He drank it, paced his house for about an hour and finally gave up and faced what was making him so restless. He wanted to find out where Ashton was and what she had been up to all day.

Sam changed from the clothes he had put on that morning, to an all black outfit. Black jeans, black tee shirt, black shoes, and a black jacket for the cool weather that still came to call when the sun went down each night. Sam made sure the door was locked and the area clear before he turned his attention to his goal. Finding Ashton.

He made his way into the trees, and was about to set out for the Rider place when he thought he heard a faint laugh. Immediately diving behind a tree he became perfectly still, as he strained all his senses to pick up the sound that had seemed to float to him on the breeze.

Sam never doubted his instincts and they were screaming at him right now that he was not alone. He was sure he had missed nothing earlier so he wondered, but only for an instant, where the threat had come from. He cautiously moved from his hiding place and moved, with only a whisper of sound, through the woods, alert and armed, ready for anything.

He looked everywhere but couldn't find anything out of the ordinary. No tracks, no broken branches, and no footprints leading to or going away from his property. Sam slowly backed deeper into the woods and stood stock still, blending into the shadows, waiting for any movement to show the hiding place of the intruder. But no movement was seen, no sound heard, and no more laughter reached his ears.

Slowly placing his gun back in its ankle holster, Sam began to relax, one muscle at a time. He finally turned to continue his hike to Ashton's, but could have sworn there were eyes still on him. He slowly melted into the shadows and finally disappeared from sight.

Sam's instincts had been correct for there was a pair of eyes on him. Watching him, but not just as he left his house, but all through the day. They had focused on him never letting him out of their sight. They had made him drowsy, had planted the dream in his head while he slept, and made sure thoughts of Ashton were never far from his mind.

After Sam had gone from sight, Saul materialized out of thin air and stood by the edge of the woods. He dusted his hands off feeling quite pleased with the results of his days work. Ashton did not have time to waste, so he had decided a little help had been in order. He was sure that a small push in her direction was all that was needed to bring the two of them together. He had read Sam's thoughts and knew he was attracted to her and he knew they were meant to be together. So, a push here, a thought there, and then leave the rest to the humans.

Saul paused and tilted his head to the side as he remembered how Sam had picked up the merest thread of a small chuckle that had escaped him when he was gloating in the fact his plan was working so well. Very odd. Beginning to fade from sight, for now, Saul once again let slip a small chuckle. Should he or should he not pay a visit to Ashton and see how things progressed? Hmmmmmmmmmmm?

CHAPTER 12

Sam didn't like the feeling he had felt when he started the trek to Ashton's cabin. Someone was close to him, watching him. He knew it. He was never wrong when it came to instincts regarding his safety. That he was not able to locate the source of his suspicions, did not sit well with him. He would have to pull out all of his tricks when he returned, and put the mystery to rest, along with the person or persons who was foolish enough to invade his domain.

He made sure to not take the same path he had used the last time he had scoped out Ashton's place. No matter where he walked, the woods never failed to relax him and melt away his stress. Today was no different. Instead of his senses being on high alert, he found his mind wandering to the woman that he was going to see. As he wound his way past trees and bushes that he would not remember later, a smile tugged at his lips while he thought about his dream from earlier in the day. How shocked would Ashton be if she knew the content and the details his sleeping imagination had come up with? Hell, he was shocked himself. Sam wondered if dreaming about Ashton was such a good thing. What if she did not live up to his dream? Would he be disappointed? He supposed it was not fair to either of them to compare their love making, for there would be love making, to his fantasy.

Sam felt good, not only because the day was beautiful and the weather was perfect, but also because he was on the hunt and hunting always made him come alive. This time the hunt was personal and he had a feeling deep down inside that everything was riding on this one.

Sam came crashing back to reality when he heard a twig snap up ahead of him. He stopped where he was, covered in the deep shadow of an old pine. Slowing his breathing until he could no longer hear it himself, he brought all of his senses to bear on the area where he had heard the tell tale sound only a second before. Something or someone was there. He could still hear the movement. Whoever was there was not trying very hard to be silent.

Sam slowly crouched down to balance on the balls of his feet. He felt the need to be small, but ready to move. He waited and listened until he could no longer hear any sounds. Slowly unfolding his body one muscle at a time he rose to his full height. Taking one cautious step at a time, he slowly moved into the waning sunlight. He stopped and again listened. Hearing nothing he moved on. He rounded a group of trees and froze in his tracks. His heartbeat doubled, sweat popped out on his forehead and began to run down his back.

There on the grassy edge of the path was the biggest black bear he had ever seen. His mind was working overtime as he assessed the situation. He still had his gun strapped to his ankle, but the damage it would do would only piss off the big guy and make him attack. He had been so full of thoughts of Ashton when he left he had forgotten to strap on his hunting knife when he left. He knew better then to leave his home without being prepared for trouble.

Damn, damn, damn. Maybe if he moved very slowly and quietly he could back out of the clearing and give the bear a wide berth. This was the only option he could think of that had a snowballs chance in hell of working. So, with all the stealth he could muster, he placed one foot back a half step and then the other. His progress was slow but seemed to be working, as the bear did not raise his head from the berries he was eating with such relish. Only a few more feet and he would be safely under the cover of the shadows again.

As Sam took his last step his foot came down on a twig. The snap echoed through the forest, sounding to his ears like a cannon shot. Sam froze. The bear had come alert with the sound, and its small eyes rested squarely on the man standing ten feet away. It stopped chewing and sniffed the air, trying to tell if the strange being was a danger or not.

Time slowed and Sam could hear the sight breeze winding its way through the treetops. Seconds slipped by and neither of them moved. The bear must have decided that the berries were more important then Sam, because he lowered his massive head and, once again, began to strip the berries from the bush in great mouthfuls.

Sam released his breath and took one more step back. At that moment the bear shook its head and gave a great bellow that sent the birds settled in the trees flying into the sky. It rose up on its hind legs to stretch well over 6 feet in height. It pawed the air and shook its head from side to side, as if trying to dislodge some object. Its mouth hung open and great strings of spit flew through the air with the wild movements of its distress. Bellows of rage followed one after the other, and its eyes, burning red with anger, settled on the only strange thing in its world. Sam.

Sam bunched his muscles and got ready to move. The bear lunged even before it had landed on all fours, and tore across the short distance between him and Sam. Sam dove off the path and ran zigzag through the woods, looking for an avenue of escape. He could hear the crashing beast behind him knowing it was getting closer by mowing its way through bushes he had to go around. He ran as fast as he could but he knew it would not be enough in the end. He could almost feel its hot breath on his back as this freight train of death closed in on him. He would not think of the three inch claws that were reaching for his back, or of the teeth that could and would sink themselves into his flesh like hot knives through butter. Sam's mind was clear and he did not take the time to feel fear. All of his efforts were focused with crystal clarity on survival.

He came bursting out of the woods and found himself on the edge of a ravine. Without a second's hesitation, he gathered his legs under him and leapt the 6 feet to the other side, landing, falling and rolling. He got up and made the cover of the trees before he stopped to look back. He saw the bear skid to a stop and stare at the spot where its prey had disappeared. It pawed the ground, rose up on its back legs and let out one more deep, soul-chilling roar before it gave up and wandered back the way it had come.

Sam let out his breath, bent over at the waist, and rested his hands on his knees. He took deep breaths, and only then did he allow himself the luxury of stopping to think about what had just happened. He had encountered bears before in the woods but never had one reacted the way this one had. Usually they were more interested in eating and exploring than in attacking. This one was just crazy.

Sam wiped the sweat from his face with the hem of his shirt, took several deep breaths, then turned and headed towards the Rider place. After all he was almost there and he figured he should warn Ashton about the bear. He escaped but he was sure, should she come across it, she would not be so lucky. Slowly and with care he entered the forest and disappeared from sight.

Where the bear had stood not two minutes before, there now stood a small boy dressed in a white robe. He seemed to be floating a foot off of the ground. The small head of dark hair was turned looking at the spot where Sam had entered the woods. The seemingly innocent small figure remained still for a moment, before turning his head to stare off into the distance. The expression of disappointment was clear on his angelic face, mouth turned down, lowered lids, and slumped shoulders. With an effort, he finally squared his narrow shoulders and raised his bowed head. Lids lifted to allow his eyes to once again stare off into the distance. Should anyone have been around to see, they would have run. Run for their lives, as the eyes that peered out from the beautiful face burned black as sin.

CHAPTER 13

Leonard stood at the edge of the ravine and vibrated with a rage that no six-year-old boy should ever feel. But then he was no ordinary six-year-old boy. Oh no, he was an angel with powers. He had been learning how to use his powers on his own, since "they" all thought he was too young, too weak, and too little to be entrusted with the knowledge of the extent of his abilities. So he had been working in secret, watching the older angels, experimenting to see what he could do. Controlling the bear had been easy. Its brain was so small and so manageable. It had taken very little effort to make it charge and want to rip apart the human body before it. And not just any human, no, Leonard wanted it to be Sam.

Leonard knew what Saul had planned for Sam and Ashton. He was working to get them together, to fall in love, and to make it happen in two months time. Well, a few days shy of two months now.

Leonard felt that was not fair. He had seen her first, had wanted her for his friend. He was the one who had made her die in the first place, when he looked upon her from the Window to the World. If Saul had not interfered, she would be with him already. So Leonard watched Saul in secret as he worked to plant thoughts, dreams and ideas in Sam's head. Saul was manipulating Sam for his own purpose. So why couldn't he, Leonard, work to have the outcome swing his way? He wanted Ashton for his own, and didn't want to share her attention and her time. So, he'd decided to try a little manipulation of his own.

It had almost worked, too. It was just dumb luck that the ravine had been there and Sam had made the jump. Leonard kicked at the dirt that he hovered above, looking like a small boy in the midst of a tantrum, and wished that Sam could at least have broken a leg when he landed, so he would not have been able to walk to Ashton's.

Leonard rubbed his small hands together and seemed to pace in the air, as he tried to come up with another plan. He needed to think, he needed to be creative, and he needed to act soon. A flame began to burn deep in his eyes as a new plan came to him. He would have to think this new idea through carefully, so that finally Sam would be out of the way.

A smile began to turn up the corners of his sweet mouth and soon became a full-blown grin, a grin that had a touch of malice as it grew in intensity. His eyes again turned black, but this time they had a slight red tint to the once brilliant whites.

Leonard felt different, strange. Every time he thought about Sam and what he was taking away from him, he burned a little bit more, a little bit hotter, and found he liked these feelings more and more. They felt good, they felt right, and they felt like power. Leonard was learning that he liked power a lot. Power was what it took to get what he wanted, and power was what Leonard was going to get. One way or another.

CHAPTER 14

Sam walked the rest of the way to Ashton's cabin without incident. He kept his senses on alert, not wanting to be taken by surprise again. He should have remembered the bears were just coming out of hibernation and they were hungry. It was always a good idea to give them a wide berth, because when they were hungry or had new cubs, they were deadly.

He made it all the way to the edge of the Rider property before he stopped, crouched down and began watching. He wiped everything else from his mind and concentrated on the area before him. It was just approaching dusk and the sky was brushed with purples, pinks and grays. There was no wind and sounds traveled far in the still mountains.

Sam watched the house but could not detect any movement within. No lights were coming on, no radio or TV could be heard through the cracked windows. He assumed that Ashton was not at home. Where was she? Could she have had an accident in the woods on her way to the lake? Was she off meeting someone? Time would tell.

He settled in to wait, zeroing his eyes in on the house and the immediate area. He did not have to long to wait, as Ashton came walking out of the trees from the west. She was not quiet and he knew she was there long before she came into view.

She looked good. Maybe a little tired, dirty, and had a few needles and twigs caught in her hair, but her eyes and her whole face glowed with contentment and pleasure. She was carrying a backpack over her shoulders and it seemed to be heavy. Sam was going to have to get a look at the contents, maybe it held the clues he needed to figure out the questions that were Ashton Rider's purpose here in Colorado.

He watched her climb the back steps, set the backpack down and enter the house. A light came on, but she did not come back out for the pack. Keeping low, Sam ran across the yard and, without a sound, climbed the steps. He kept his eyes on the back door as he felt the pack he had cradled between his knees. He felt neither wires nor anything he could connect to a booby trap.

With as little sound as possible he unzipped the bag and only then did he take his eyes off of the door. He cautiously peered inside and relaxed. Inside he found rocks. "Rocks? Was she crazy? She had rocks all over her yard, why would she have to go pick up more?" Hard to say what was in the mind of a woman. Sam rezipped the pack and made his way silently back to the trees to wait a few more minutes before he'd march right up to the door and knock loudly. If she ducked or dove for cover, it would be another sign that she had something to hide.

Sam waited until the light on the second floor went out, before he moved the distance to the back porch. He climbed the stairs, stood at a right angle to the door and knocked one, two, three times. He could see Ashton in the kitchen, with her head stuck inside a cupboard, jump at the sound. She did not react like a person sent on a mission, but like someone startled by an unexpected knock on her door. She drew her head out of the cupboard, giving Sam a view of her thick hair piled on the top of her head. She must have just gotten out of the shower because damp tendrils hung down her back and curled around her ears.

Ashton looked out the door and tried to make out the figure standing on her porch in the dark. The light from the kitchen did not reach far enough to illuminate the porch, so she moved slowly towards the door and flipped on the outside light. A wide smile covered her face and lit up her eyes as she recognized the tall man who had come to visit. Pulling the door wider Ashton gestured him in. "Hi Sam. This is a surprise. What brings you here?"

Sam took one step inside the door and looked her straight in the eyes and replied, "You." He could not help returning her smile with one of his own, and the effect it had on Ashton was immediate and unexpected.

A warm flush covered her cheeks, deepening the green of her eyes. Seeming flustered she moved farther back into the house allowing Sam to come further in. "Well, come on in," she said gesturing for him to enter the kitchen. "I was just about to scrounge something up for supper and you are welcome to join me if you don't mind pot luck."

She turned back to her cooking while Sam took a quick but thorough look around. All seemed to be in order. "You don't have to go to any trouble on my account," he said. "I just stopped by to say hi and to warn you that there is a big bear roaming around not too far from here." He gave her a brief accounting of his earlier experience with the bear as he warned her, "If you plan on going out, you should stick close to your house. It was not too happy when I saw it, so just be careful."

His deep voice poured over Ashton's senses. She had forgotten how rich and dark it was. Like the first bite of chocolate that melted in your mouth and coated everything with hidden pleasures, giving satisfaction and promising more to come.

Ashton turned wide eyes back to Sam and lost a little of the color in her cheeks. "I just came in from a walk in the woods. I spent most of the day just wandering around, exploring." She shuddered a little thinking of his close encounter with the unfriendly bear, and what would have happened to her if she would have been in a similar situation.

Then on a lighter note she told him, "I found some great rocks and even brought them back with me. I can't wait to add them to my rock garden." Sobering again she said, "I forgot about the wild animals in the area. It's been a long time since I was here. I just didn't think." Ashton realized she was babbling and closed her mouth to stop the rush of nervous chatter.

Standing in awkward silence Ashton pushed a piece of stay hair behind her ear. Waving a hand towards a kitchen chair Ashton invited Sam to sit down.

"Let me just look in the cupboard and see what I've got. I haven't had time to shop so the pickings are pretty slim," she said as she rummaged around in the pantry for anything edible.

"I didn't see a car when I came up. How did you get here?" Sam asked in a conversational tone.

Ashton paused for a heartbeat not knowing what to say. "Oh, well, I died and was sort of transported here by an angel," was hardly the answer he would believe and Ashton was pretty sure the visit would come to an abrupt end should those words leave her mouth. She grabbed the first thing she saw off of the shelf and turned back to Sam. "Peanut butter and jelly on crackers is about all I have. Care to join me?" she asked with a tilt of her head.

Being on his own for so long now Sam had eaten that meal too often and thought he could do better. "Tell you what," he said, "How about you and I walk over to my house, pick up my truck and I'll take you into town to eat?"

Ashton held the jars to her chest and a flush again rose in her cheeks. "I wasn't fishing for an invitation to dinner and I apologize if it came out that way. It was just that I wasn't thinking when I asked you to stay. I really need to stock my cupboards with some decent food," she caught herself once again rambling. He seemed to have that effect on her.

Sam rose to his feet, took the jars from her hands, placed them on the counter and crossed his arms over his chest. "I did not make the offer because I felt obligated to. We both have to eat, I would enjoy the pleasure of you company, and my place is only about a half a mile by road from here. It's no trouble and we could have a chance to get to know each other better. So, say yes. I'm starving," he finished and flashed her a hundred watt smile.

Ashton relaxed under the warmth of that smile. "What could dinner hurt? You're not a serial killer or anything, are you?" she asked only half kidding.

"No," he replied with a hint of humor in his voice. "I gave that up for lent."

Ashton looked at him for one more moment and nodded her head in agreement. Let me get a jacket," she said, "I'll be right back." She left the room and got a light jacket out of her closet. Slipping it on she returned to the kitchen and headed for the door with Sam behind her.

She stopped suddenly and Sam actually ran into her back, so close was he following her. Turning back to Sam she voiced a question that had just popped into her head, "What about the bear? Is it going to be safe walking to your house if it is still in the area?"

"Well, I made it past once, I figure we could do it again if we have to," he teased, watching her eyes grow wide with worry. "But my guess would be that it has moved on to find food somewhere else." He reassured her gently placing a finger to her cheek, "I would not put you in danger. I already thought about the bear before I made the suggestion. Don't worry," he said protectively, "I'll keep you safe."

Having no real reason to trust him, but doing so any way, Ashton walked out the door.

CHAPTER 15

The night was cool, the air was still, and the stars more brilliant than any Ashton remembered having seen before. Maybe it was because she was seeing everything from a new point of view. The knowledge that she had such a short time to appreciate all the world had to offer, had opened her eyes to beauty, fragility and the gift that was life. She pulled her coat more tightly around her body, trying to trap all the feelings rolling inside her. How could she store up all these sights, smells, and feelings to take with her? Was that even possible? She hoped so.

Sam was quiet as he led the way up the driveway, then pointed to the left as they came to the gravel road connecting their two houses. Their footsteps crunched loudly as they made their way to his cabin. He kept an eye on Ashton as they walked and wondered at the silence of the woman beside him. She seemed to be deep in thought, and from the expression on her face she was trying to work out a problem. Her concentration was deep, and Sam wondered if it had anything to do with him.

Once again a smile tugged at the corners of his mouth as he considered the arrogance of the thought. Curiosity got the better of him and he finally broke the silence, "You're very quiet, can I ask what are you thinking about?" He kept his voice low, to match the night that was dark and quiet. It just seemed a shame to disturb the peace.

Ashton turned her head to consider the shadowy figure beside her. Shrugging her shoulders she replied, "I was just thinking how beautiful the night is up here," she said gazing up into the starry sky. "The quiet is amazing compared to the city noise. After a while you get used to the noise of the traffic, neighbors, police sirens, and the people passing outside your door, until you don't even hear it any more. But being up here makes me realize just how different the two are." She turned her face to his as she asked, "Do you like living here alone?"

"Yeah," Sam replied. "I used to live in a city, too, until I found this place about five years ago. I came for a visit and never left." He paused and glanced around into the darkness then continued, "This place seems to feed my soul." Now why had he said that? He did not open up to strangers and he had never said anything so *girly* as that in his life. Feeling slightly embarrassed and a little defensive, he braced himself for Ashton's laughter or criticism. But it never came. He glanced over and saw her nod her head in agreement.

"I know what you mean. This place seems almost magical compared to every where else I have been."

"And where is that?" he wanted to know. "Have you traveled a lot? Tell me where, what have you seen, what did you like best?" Now she was going to think he was being too pushy he told himself, but he wanted to dig a little into this woman who had captivated him since the first moment he saw her.

Ashton smiled and began answering his questions. She found him easy to talk to or maybe it was because it was dark and things could be said in the dark that you would not say in the bright light of day. She was engrossed in the telling of her travels, when she stumbled over a rock sticking up in the road. Sam reached out a hand to steady her and felt a current go up his arm and lodge in his chest. It was not a bad feeling, in fact he liked it. His hand moved down her arm and easily linked with hers. She didn't pull away and they finished the walk to Sam's cabin silently hand in hand.

When they reached Sam's driveway he nudged her shoulder to get her to change direction and walk down the slight hill to his back door where his car was parked. Sam unlocked the door to the SUV and helped Ashton into the seat. He walked around and climbed in shutting them inside the vehicle.

"What do you feel like eating?" he asked her. "Italian, Mexican, American, I can find you almost anything you want." He turned sideways and laid his arm along the back of her seat. Ashton rolled her eyes up and thought of all the food she had denied herself forever. So many choices now. Where to start?

"How about a nice big pepperoni pizza dripping with extra cheese?" she said with a smile on her lovely face. "That sounds heavenly right now." Ashton looked at Sam for his reaction and was met with a big grin of delight.

"It sounds like you're my kind of woman." Sam straightened around and started the car, put it in reverse and pointed it towards town. He put the heat on low and kept the chatter light, pointing out places of interest as they drove.

Ashton gave a laugh of delight and said, "You know, I can't see a thing in the dark right?"

Sam grinned back and promised her, "We'll do this again in the daylight."

The invitation hung in the air for a heartbeat before Ashton replied, "I'd like that. I'd like that very much. It's a date."

Sam was hit by the realization that he had just made a date with a woman. He avoided dates, and the inevitable sequence of events they brought about that always seemed to end badly, but this one was going to be one he would look forward to with relish. He caught Ashton, out of the corner of his eye, wiggling her butt more firmly in the seat and knew she too was happy about the upcoming adventure they were going to share.

It seemed that in no time at all they reached the outskirts of the small town of Nora Falls. Sam drove down the main street and again pointed out to Ashton all the small home-owned stores, and relating an amusing antidote about each one. Ashton was charmed and loved each new sight. Sam was good with words and kept her attention riveted on her new surroundings.

At the far end of town Sam pulled in to the parking lot of a small restaurant called "Come and Get It." Ashton turn doubtful eyes in Sam's direction and he had to laugh. "I know," he said, "but just wait, you will love the food. This place is one of the best-kept secrets in the whole state. Everyone passes it by because of the name, but the locals know what is good and this place is it. Come on," Sam said, getting out of the car and coming around to collect Ashton. He tucked her hand in his and led her to the door.

When he opened the door to the café, the smells that wafted out caused Ashton to almost drool with anticipation. It smelled so good. Ashton walked into the warm, fragrant interior and stopped short when all eyes turned to her and Sam. All conversation seemed to have stopped. For a moment you could have heard a pin drop, so total was the silence.

Ashton stood frozen on the spot. She had no idea what was wrong but she was uncomfortable and immediately self-conscious. Sam took her arm from behind and gave it a reassuring squeeze. A large women came from the back and gave a great, loud,

"Wooee," as she spotted the pair at the door.

"Sam!" came the booming voice, "I haven't seen you in a coons age. Come on in and sit anywhere you like." She gave Sam a huge hug that all but made him disappear. Sam laughed and let the stuffing be squeezed out of him. Pulling back the woman patted his arm and turned her keen gaze full bore on

Ashton, looking her up and down and not hiding the fact. "Well Sam, who have you brought with you? Speak up boy," she prodded him with an elbow to his ribs.

Grinning, Sam again took Ashton's hand as he explained, "Ashton, this beautiful hunk of womanhood, and the best cook this side of anywhere, is Laura Mae." Then turning to the large woman on his other arm he completed the introductions, "Laura Mae, this is Ashton. I've tried to get Laura to run away with me, but she just laughs at me. She broke my heart." He placed a hand to his chest and let out a sigh that would have made Hollywood happy with his acting abilities.

Laura pushed at him playfully, but her attentions were all for the woman standing at the side of a man who always kept to himself. It had taken her years to get him to be comfortable and open in her presence, and now, for the first time, he'd brought a woman with him. And Laura approved of his taste. She was exquisite. Laura liked the way she didn't squirm as she took her time looking her over.

Looking at Sam she winked grabbed his arm and gave it a squeeze. "You done good Sam, by god you done good. I was beginning to worry about you, but I'm happy now. Come on in and sit down."

She led the way to a table to the right of a large stone fireplace where a blaze crackled in invitation. "Sit down, sit down. I'll be right back. You both just warm yourselves for a minute." Again patting Sam on the shoulder she left them, humming to herself as she disappeared into the kitchen.

Sam looked across the table at the firelight dancing across Ashton's face and lost himself in her eyes. "Welcome home Ashton, he said in a deep whisper meant only for her ears." He raised her hand and kissed the back of it, lingering over the feel of it on his lips. Ashton was lost.

CHAPTER 16

The next three hours passed in a happy blur for Ashton. She ate slice after delicious slice of the gooey pizza, until she was so stuffed she thought they would have to roll her out the door. Her eyes sparkled as she talked, laughed and just plain enjoyed Sam. He had been quiet at first, but Ashton was able to draw him out with her lively chatter until he finally joined in without hesitation. Both had shared stories of their youth and laughed at the others pranks as children. They found they had a lot in common and were well on their way to becoming lasting friends as the night wore on.

Somewhere, about half way through the evening, their hands had found their way into each other's. Their chairs had moved closer together, until they finally sat side by side, their dark heads nestled together. Bursts of laughter could be heard coming from their table, and Laura Mae, who peeked often in their direction, found tears coming to her eyes. She was touched to see the two lovely people enjoying themselves so much. It was about time that young man found himself a young lady. And the one he had picked was as near to perfect as she could have hoped.

Laura Mae, feeling it was her duty to help Sam find a girl, had sent every pretty, single girl from town in his direction over the past five years. Much to her disappointment, he had been polite but firm, letting them know that he was not interested. She had begun to worry about that boy, but with the turn of events tonight he had restored her faith in him. Wiping her damp eyes, Laura Mae waddled her bulk over to the table to offer the couple coffee before she presented them with their final ticket.

"So, could I interest either of you in a cup of the best coffee in town?" She asked, stopping by the table.

"Hmm," Ashton said smiling up at the woman, "if it truly is the best in town, I guess I'll have to try some."

"Coming right up." Laura Mae smiled as she patted Ashton's shoulder and moved away.

Ashton turned her eyes back to Sam, looking at him with a soft smile.

"What are you smiling at?" he asked with a slow smile of his own.

Ashton took a moment to answer, as she was not really sure why she was sitting there with a big, stupid grin on her face. "I guess it's because this has been the most unpredictable night. I'm having such a good time and I didn't really expect to."

Sam raised his eyebrows at the answer he had received. "Just what did you expect the evening to be like?" he challenged her with a teasing smile.

Trying to cover her choice of words so as not to offend her new friend, she explained, "It's just that I've only spoke to you that one time by the lake and you seemed rather defensive and aloof," she offered with a questioning raise of her eyebrows. "So I figured tonight would be kind of stilted, and we would just talk about the weather or something like that." Ashton looked Sam in the eye and a slight blush touched her cheeks because of the crinkle of humor around his eyes.

Sam put an arm over the back of Ashton's chair but left his hand dangling loosely.

"I guess I didn't give a very good first impression by the lake, did I?" he questioned with a guilty look on his face. "I don't have many friends and I usually am not looking to add to the list," he explained away his lack of manners. Then he smiled warmly at her and continued, "You're so easy to talk to and amazingly this old grump likes talking to you." His expression softened as he told her, "I like watching you, the expressions that dance across your face, the way your eyes glow when you are amused, and way you get so animated when you are talking about things you are interested in. Memories make your eyes go all dreamy and deep, and when you are thinking hard you get a little line right between your eyes." He brought up his free hand and with one finger, lightly traced between her brows, down her nose and over her lips, catching her bottom lip and pulling it down slightly as he went.

Ashton's whole word was reduced to that one finger and the path it was making over her face. She licked her lip as the finger was removed to come to rest on the table.

At that moment Laura Mae arrived with the cup of coffee. Ashton moved to sit up straighter in her chair in anticipation just as Laura Mae bent to set the cup in front of her. As if by magic the cup flew through the air and landed upside down square in the middle of Sam's lap.

"Oh shit!" Sam yelled, and with quick reflexes he jumped to his feet, spilling the now empty cup onto the floor. All three of them grabbed napkins and began to wipe at the effected area. Sam nearly did a jig while he was trying to get the hot coffee off of him. When his lap finally cooled down he thought enough to push the helping hands away, and gingerly pull his jeans away from his crotch.

Laura Mae was in tears as she apologized over and over. "I don't know what happened. One minute it was in my hand and the next it wasn't. I'm so sorry Sam," she apologized rubbing and patting his back.

Sam shook his head, held up his hand and reassured her, "It's ok, Laura Mae. No permanent damage was done I'm sure. Relax there, ok?" Sam sat back down gingerly and asked Ashton if she still wanted her coffee.

Ashton shook her head no as she began to stand up, "I think we should get you home and out of those pants," she replied innocently.

Sam's head flew up and Laura Mae immediately stopped talking.

Realizing her slip of words, Ashton blushed as she stammered, "That came out all wrong. What I meant was you need to get cleaned up." She was now self-conscious and couldn't seem to bring her eyes up to his.

Sam smirked and Laura Mae began to fan herself.

"I think we will just be going Laura Mae, we've had enough coffee for one night," he kidded. "If you could bring the bill we'll be on our way," he said rising from his chair and taking Ashton's elbow.

"Nonsense, your dinner is on the house. It's the least I can do after what just happened," she insisted with a wave of her hand at his attempt to pay for the meal. "And I'd be glad to clean your pants for you, too," she told him.

Sam bent over and planted a sweet kiss on her face. "I'll accept the offer of the meal. Thanks Laura Mae, and please don't feel bad about the coffee. It was just an accident. No harm, no foul," he finished with a hug for the flustered woman.

She put her hand to her check and said to Ashton, "You best be watching this man of yours or I might just have to move in on you."

The comment lightened the mood, and before Sam left with Ashton he placed a tip on the table big enough to cover the meal, and then some.

Taking Ashton's elbow they turned to leave. Sam realized that every head in the place was turned their way watching as they prepared to exit the restaurant, some with smiles on their faces, some with concern, and some with envy. Of course all of the attention came from members of the female persuasion who would love to have been in Ashton's place.

Sam looked at Ashton, shook his head, and turning back to his audience lifting a hand of good night to everyone watching. Giggling together, arm in arm they walked into the night.

CHAPTER 17

If the patrons of the café would have been listening closely, they might have heard the sound of a small child laughing as the couple exited the building. Leonard was so pleased with himself that he laughed with glee and did a little happy dance.

He had watched and listened to the two of them during the meal, anger building inside him with every look, every laugh, and every seemingly innocent touch. She was not for him! She was his! How many times did he have to show them that they were not meant for each other?

It had been child's play controlling Laura Mae's mind, as she flung the hot coffee into Sam's lap. It was almost as easy as getting inside that bear's head had been. Laura Mae had been as surprised as Sam at her actions, wondering what had come over her. Little did she know that Leonard had come over her, he chuckled to himself.

He dusted his small hands together, assuring himself that any ideas Sam had for himself and Ashton tonight would be put to bed for the time being. He floated off into the shadows at the side of the building and watched as Sam opened the car door for Ashton, then got in himself, and drove away. Jealousy burned so hot in his small body it threatened to consume him.

He smiled darkly as the beginnings of a plan formed in his mind. When the time came he would show them, he would show them all. His eyes were fierce, the red glow more pronounced than before.

Then the air shimmered as Leonard faded away, returning to his home in the clouds to watch and wait.

CHAPTER 18

Sam pulled out of the parking lot, but instead of turning right to head home he went to the left. Ashton looked over at Sam and raised an eyebrow at the direction he was going. Sam caught the look out of the corner of his eye and shrugged his shoulders. "I thought you might need a trip to the store to stock up on a few items," he answered the question in her eyes.

Ashton was surprised that he had thought of this, and glad as it had not occurred to her to stop while she was in town. "That's a great idea!" she smiled in appreciation. "Thank you for thinking of it."

Sam shot her a quick look and smiled. "I had a purely selfish reason for making this little side trip. The next time you invite me to stay for dinner, I would like to say yes and stay home with you instead of going out." He quickly added, "Even though I enjoyed tonight, I think we would do fine by ourselves without the prying eyes of the whole town." She nodded in agreement as he continued, "I'm sure that we will be the talk of the town gossips tomorrow, if they can wait that long."

Ashton thought about what Sam had said. She was not too concerned about the people of Nora Falls talking and speculating about the two of them. In fact she liked it. She was totally okay with her name being linked with his. She was also very okay with Sam coming over for dinner. She felt a small nagging guilt over what she was doing with Sam. How fair was she being to him when she knew what he didn't, that she had less then two months before everything ended for her? Literally. If she were him, she was not sure that she would be all that appreciative of falling in love with someone who was going to rip her heart out by leaving him suddenly alone.

But then who said he was going to love her? To Ashton, grabbing all that life offered to her now was the only possible thing to do. She wanted to be special to someone, to have them love her, and she wanted to take that feeling with her when it was time. She did not want to die feeling regret that she had not completely embraced all that she could. But, again was it fair to Sam? What if she told him what was coming and let him decide where to go from there? Ashton felt her pulse quicken and her mouth go a little dry as she thought of what could happen. He would probably think she was a wacko and run as fast as he could away from her. After mulling it over in her mind, she decided that's what she would do, let him make the choice.

"What are you thinking so hard about?" Sam asked glancing over at her studious expression. "You look far too serious right now." At her continued silence Sam quietly said, "You can tell me you know. I'm great at keeping secrets and I'm pretty good at solving problems. I could be your sounding board while you air things out. Come on, what have you got to lose?" he coaxed. This was a great opportunity for Sam to find out a little more in depth information about Ashton, providing he could talk her into trusting him.

Ashton hunched her shoulders and bit her lip to keep from blurting out what she had been contemplating. *Not now,* she thought, *I'll tell him soon but right now I just want be like everyone else and enjoy the feeling of being with a man.* She shook her head and turned a slightly forced smile on Sam. "It's nothing really. Maybe I'll share later."

Sam let her have her way, this time, but he was sure his time would come to have her open up to him and maybe he would be able to wipe that worried look off of her face. He did not know why but he felt protective of Ashton, but he did. Since when had he become so wishy-washy that he cared what anyone else was thinking, and why should he get involved with problems, and he was sure there was problems, that had nothing to do with him?

Sam's hands tightened on the wheel without him consciously willing them to. He turned into the lot of the convenience store, the only store open at this late hour, turned the key off, slid his arm along the back of the seat and looked Ashton square in the eye. "Someday you're going to have to trust me," he told her with a gentle smile. "I won't pressure you, but I'm willing to bet you've never met anyone like me? I promise you, Ashton, that you can take my word and that I'll help you if you need it." He gently touched her cheek trying to win her trust.

Ashton hoped the darkness was deep enough to hide her hesitation and the fear that came into her eyes when she thought about what she was getting them both into. Her only response was a slight nod of her head, after which she turned and got out of the vehicle. Sam followed and reached for her hand as they made their way across the almost deserted parking lot.

Coming in from the dark night, the bright white glare of the store lights made Ashton squint and hesitate just inside the door as her eyes adjusted. A slight tug on her hand drew her forward and they began the sport of shopping. Up one aisle and down another they moved, each adding items to the cart. Their treasures ranged from one end of the spectrum to the other. From healthy foods like veggies, chunks of sharp cheddar cheese, and whole grain breads and crackers, to junk items including a tub of rich creamy ice cream and hot fudge syrup, that were for pure comfort and pleasure. They laughed, joked, and sampled food as they went, popping grapes and cherries into their mouths. They were in no hurry to finish shopping, as it would mean their evening together was coming to an end.

Sam found himself glancing at Ashton occasionally, thinking that he was crazy to even, for one instant, consider continuing whatever it was they had begun. The idea of deepening their new friendship into a relationship both scared him and at the same time seemed to be the only thing that made sense. His mind seemed to go off in a direction that his instincts told him not to. He knew the reasons he made a habit of keeping to himself, but the harder he tried to bring these arguments front and center, the farther and fuzzier they seemed to get. He wasn't drunk and not on anything, but he felt out of control, like a puppet being used for someone else's agenda.

Sam dug in his heels mentally, and just to show he was in control, he placed the most, in his opinion, disgusting thing he could get his hands on into the cart. A can of red beets. A food guaranteed to make him barf. He glanced over at Ashton for her reaction and gaped at her. Ashton was almost doubled over with silent laughter. Her shoulders shook and she was holding her sides as tears leaked down her cheeks unchecked.

"What is so funny he asked? Ashton could hear the challenge in his voice but could not make herself stop laughing.

"Beets?" she finally got out between gasping for breath. "You like beets?"

At his defiant stance, Ashton tried to pull her self together, but failed miserably. Slowly her legs gave out and she sat on the floor almost rolling with mirth until her sides were on fire. Giving one last hiccup of laughter she got herself under control long enough to wipe her streaming eyes and rub her cheeks. She was sure they were now permanently frozen into a smile. Her mother used to tell her that if she made faces, her face would freeze into that position. She was beginning to believe that old wives tale as she tried to bring her smile into a sober position on her face.

Ashton managed to remain in control until she looked up at Sam towering over her with a rather stern expression on his handsome face. *Oh crap*, he looked offended, and she just couldn't keep a lid on her emotions as she shrugged her shoulders and hid her face behind her hands and once again rocked with laughter.

Sam finally gave up and squatted down beside the woman in the middle of the deserted grocery store. Waiting until one brilliant green eye peered out from between slightly spread fingers he asked, "Care to share the joke?"

Ashton cleared her throat, and with an effort, swallowed another round of laughter. "The beets just brought back a childhood memory that I had not remembered in years." At Sam's silence, she continued with her story. "Once, when I was about eight, my mother decided to try serving my father and I beets because she had heard that they were supposed to be good for you. Well, she cooked them up and put them in the middle of the table. This big bowl of red, bloody looking beets. Both my dad and I just kept looking at them because neither one of us wanted to try them, and we kind of hoped they were a figment of our imaginations. But they stayed there no matter how hard we stared at them. My mother insisted we try them and, to keep the piece, we took a small amount and put them on our plates." Laughter again began to crinkle the corners of her eyes as Ashton looked back in time. "The rest of the food on our plates just sat there and after much fidgeting and stalling we all took a bite together." She gave a little shudder as she continued, "They were, without a doubt, the most awful things we had ever tasted. But, we swallowed them and looked at each other to see the others reaction. I seem to remember we were all a little green around the edges, and then my father smiled. He had not swallowed his and he had those blood red beets squishing through his teeth. He looked like a vampire who had just finished, rather messily, a full meal. Mom was so shocked she let out a little scream, I started laughing and ended up with milk coming out my nose. Dad was laughing with red juice running down his chin and globs of beets hitting the table. The meal was a bust, as none of us could eat anymore with those things sitting on the table. When you put the beets in the cart, I could just see you eating them and all I would be able to think of was how you looked like a vampire sucking those things down."

By the time she had finished with her story, Sam was smiling and could just picture the scene as she described it. He had enjoyed watching the animation on her face and the sparkle in her eyes as she related the amusing memory shared with her mother and father.

"I'm sorry Sam, but there is no way I can fix those things for you," Ashton told him in a serious voice.

Sam looked up at the ceiling and then back at Ashton as he confessed, "Well to tell you the truth, I hate beets as much as you do. I only stuck them in the cart to see what you would do. I guess you could call it a test because I don't think I could be with a woman who ate those and liked it."

Ashton gave Sam a shove that had him toppling over on his butt for the joke he had just pulled on her. She pushed a stray strand of hair behind her ear and with mock outrage said, "Jerk!" Her eyes still sparkled and her cheeks were rosy. Sam had never seen such a beautiful sight, and in that instant he fell.

CHAPTER 19

Saul wiped a hand across his brow. Angels did not sweat, but he had had to work hard to get by Sam's defenses and bring his feelings for Ashton along quicker then nature would have. Sam had fought him every step of the way, with the need to be so careful for self-preservation. He was a tough nut to crack.

Even though Saul had achieved the results he desired, he had a feeling that something was not quite right. For instance, why had the cup gone flying from Laura Mae's hand? Saul had not seen anything, but had felt the power surge the act had taken sizzle in the air. Just because he had not seen anything, did not mean there were not forces working as hard as he was, only working against Ashton and Sam. Why? What was special about these humans that would warrant interference from the other side? The bad side.

Maybe it was the work Sam had chosen that attracted unwanted attention. Saul knew that having an assassin working on your side, was a big plus for the bad guys. That's the way he thought of his opposition, the bad guys. After all, who would want to go *down* instead of *up* unless you were a bad guy? Anyway, Saul was going to have to find out why the other side wanted Sam and Ashton apart.

Saul began to fade, planning one last peek in on Ashton and Sam before he could find the answers to his questions.

Suddenly an unearthly scream rent the air and Saul hung suspended, arms flung wide, head thrown back, with his body arched. He tried to finish fading, but was stuck half way in between the two worlds. Slowly releasing his wings to their impressive width, he attempted to draw power into himself and escape whatever force was holding him in limbo. Another stab of pain hit him between the shoulders and sent a second scream of agony into the night. Saul was having a hard time concentrating, but realized the only thing that could give him this kind of pain was an attack by another immortal.

Bolts of lighting shot from the fingertips of the person behind Saul. They crackled and danced in the air before they again made contact with the frozen angel. Putting everything into one last blast, Leonard let fly the final bolt and thought, *Die you interfering bastard. Just die.*

CHAPTER 20

It was Sam's turn to fall quiet as they made the short trip to Ashton's cabin. He turned the knowledge over in his mind, the knowledge that he had fallen in love with her. How had that happened, and so quickly? This just did not happen to him, had never happened to him. He turned this new discovery over and over in his mind, worrying at it like a sore tooth. Trying to pry it apart so he could rationalize it. But no matter how hard he looked at it, it stayed rock solid and shone bright as a star in the darkness of his mind.

He knew he had been acting differently since meeting her, more carefree and happy than he could ever remember. She made him feel as if he could tell her anything, could share everything. Every secret he held close to him wanted to come out and be shared. He cringed inwardly at the thought of telling her all the things he had done in his life. She would think him a monster, a killer, and if she had any sense at all, she would fear him. He could not bear to see her shrink from him, look at him with condemnation in her emerald eyes. He wanted what he had had in his dream, her— warm, loving and open in his arms and by his side for the rest of his life.

He took a chance and looked into his future, a future with her in it. Imagined what it would be like to come back to her each night and spend every day with her. Touching her and having her turn into his arms for warmth and shelter. How caveman was that?

Sam ran a tense hand through his hair as he pulled into her driveway and rolled around to the back door. He shut off the engine and reached out to open his door. A slender hand reached out and lightly grabbed his right arm, halting him more effectively then any restraint could have. "What is it Sam? You have been so quiet since we left the store," Ashton looked at him with a worried expression. "Is it me?" she asked as she apologized, "I usually don't lose control like that, at least not in public, very often. Did I embarrass you? Tell me please," she asked gripping his arm tighter.

Sam looked across the seat at Ashton sitting in the moonlight and ached to take her in his arms. He was so close to the edge, an edge he was not sure he should approach, let alone cross over.

"There are just some things I feel we need to talk about," he reassured her. "Secrets that need to be told. I was just thinking about that." He watched her face for a reaction.

Ashton felt a cold shiver run up and down her spine. *Did he suspect something*? she wondered to herself. *Of course not, that was impossible. No one could ever guess what she was keeping inside.*

Ashton got out and shut her door. She moved to the back of his vehicle and started to unload the bags, taking all that she could manage, and headed up the stairs. She set the bags down and opened the door, turning on the light, then turning back to pick up the bags. With that simple movement, she found herself pressed against the rock hard chest of Sam who had come up behind her carrying the remainder of the groceries from the car.

Awareness hit her right between the eyes. Where she touched him, she burned, she ached, and she wanted. In that one brief instant, Ashton made up her mind.

Moving aside, she silently gave permission for Sam to enter. When he was in, she shut the door, took the bags from his hands, and set them on the kitchen table. Pulling out a chair she again offered him a silent invitation to make himself at home.

Sam remained standing not sure what was coming, not sure he wanted to know anything deep and dark about her, feeling pretty sure that that was what was coming. A deep dark secret.

Ashton looked at him with a silent plea in her eyes, "Please Sam, I need you to sit down. Please?" she asked.

Not having a choice, Sam sat, but remained tense, not being able to relax. *Was she going to tell him she was sent to kill him? What would he do if that was the case? Would he have no choice but to kill her, before she killed him? Would he ever be able to trust her if he didn't?* the questions raced through his mind as she looked at him. Closing off his emotions Sam sat, giving the outward appearance of mild curiosity, while his mind and his heart were racing.

Ashton went to the fridge and pulled out a couple of pops. She knew she was stalling for time, and finally sat at the table, facing Sam. "I'm going to tell you something that you may find hard to believe, but I need you to hear me out before you say anything, before you ask any questions. Can you do that for me?" she asked of him. "I know we haven't known each other very long but I feel such a connection to you." she said as a slightly embarrassed smile touched her lovely lips. "However corny that sounds, it's what I feel." Squaring her shoulders Ashton began her story.

"The day I met you at the lake, I had woken up here at the cabin. I didn't remember arriving here, coming inside, getting into bed, falling asleep or anything," she said wringing her hands together. "What I did remember was driving. Feeling this place pull at me. I knew I needed to be here, that there was something here for me. I got up that morning and I went to the lake. I met you and something felt really good about that meeting." Ashton paused, took a sip of her pop and hesitated before revealing the rest. Ashton sat up straight in her chair and clasped her hands tightly beneath the table. "When I left you, I came home and was settling in for the night when I had a visitor show up. His name was Saul, he didn't come in through the door, he wasn't inside waiting for me, he just appeared. He scared the hell out of me!" she said with a look of fear on her face as she remembered the incident. "He told me he was an angel. He showed me his wings and I think I actually, for the first time in my life, fainted," she shook her head as she spoke. "When I came to, I was laying on the couch and he was still here. He talked to me. He told me things that I couldn't believe. He told me I had had a car accident on my way here, and although it had been a mistake, I had died in that accident," she watched Sam's face as she spoke looking for a reaction. She continued, "He told me I was being given two extra months, to live, to find my purpose in this life. I didn't believe him, couldn't believe him. He wasn't real. None of it was real. But then he took my hand and I touched him, Sam." She put her hand on Sam's chest as she had on Saul's that night, "I touched him. He was as solid as you or I. When he was finished talking he just faded away. One minute he was standing in front of me, I was touching him and the next, the next he was just gone. My hand was still raised where it had been resting on his chest."

Ashton paused and tried to read Sam's reaction. But she couldn't. He sat before her with nothing showing on his face. Nothing in his eyes. Ashton had expected at least disbelief or something, but there was just a blank wall looking at her. A shutter had fallen over his beautiful eyes.

Ashton almost lost her nerve but she had come too far to back out now. She removed her hand from his chest and clasped them together under the table, her nails biting into her palms as she continued with downcast eyes, "He gave me a day to decide if I believed him or not, to marshal my thoughts and to think of questions I wanted to ask. He came to me the next day and we talked some more. I spent a sleepless night, pacing, thinking, denying and rejecting what he had said. But some things did not add up to anything else, like, how did I get here?" she looked up at him with a questioning look. "My car is not here, I have no luggage, my purse, or anything I left home with. I have to believe him Sam. Nothing else explains what has happened to me," she looked into his face for acceptance.

She took his hand and looked him in the eyes as she finished her story, "So, before this thing with us goes any farther, I need you to believe me and to know what you are getting into. I think I'm falling in love with you Sam," she let the words tumble from her lips, "but I'll be gone in less then two months. Not to another town or another state, but dead. I'll be dead Sam."

CHAPTER 21

Sam sat as still as a statue. Of all the things he imagined Ashton telling him, this was not even in the realm of his speculations. It wasn't even something he would dream about. This was so far fetched he could not wrap his mind around any of it. He tried to dissect it so it would make sense.

Let's see, first she did not remember getting to Colorado, only that she had needed to be here. Then she had met him at the lake. He remembered that. How she had seemed to have a glow around her as she had stood on the shore, just at the edge of the trees. Ok, that had been a little strange but it was just a trick of the light. Things seemed different in the thin mountain air, crisper, clearer more vibrant. The meeting had been brief and he remembered nothing unusual about it, other than the fact she had seemed like the most beautiful woman he had ever seen. He remembered following her to her cabin, to see what she was about and if she was a danger to him. He had seen no one approach her, nor was there anyone waiting for her in the cabin. He knew this was true because he had looked in her window to see if she was alone. He remembered thinking it was strange that there was no car in the driveway, or anywhere else on her property.

He remembered then, with a slight jolt, how he had seen her crumple to the floor and then she had floated over to the couch, as if someone had been carrying her. How had he blocked that bit of information from his mind? He just now remembered it. Try as he might, he could not rationalize what he had seen. No trick of light could explain it away. Was she telling the truth? Of course not, how could she be? Things like this didn't just happen everyday. They did not happen any day. So, if he was to believe her, he would have to believe she was brought back from the dead to live for two months and then die again. Was she insane? Did she really think for one minute he was buying all this spooky crap?

Sam's eyes refocused and he looked at Ashton sitting across the table from him and he was again hit with her beauty, her sweetness and her appearance of openness. But he just couldn't believe her or trust her for that matter. Not now. Not if this was the best story she could come up with.

"Ok," he finally said, "let's pretend for one minute that I take everything you have said has happened at face value and believe you. I would like to talk to this Saul. Now," he emphasized. "If what you say is true, him being an angel and all, I should be able to see and talk to him, too, if he were to so choose. So, bring him here for me," he finished with a challenge to her story.

Ashton had been watching Sam trying to digest the information she had just dumped on him. All in all she could not blame him for being skeptical. If she had been told a story like this, she would have been on the phone trying to have the men in white coats coming to her rescue.

"I can't, Sam," she said, "he seems to come and go whenever he wants and not on my command. I've tried to call him, summon him, whatever you want to call it, but it just doesn't work like that. I would if I could, but I can't," she said letting the helplessness show in her eyes. "I know this is all hard to digest and believe, but I swear it is true and I am begging you to give it a chance, give us a chance," she begged him. "Spend what time I have left with me, Sam."

Sam sat still, trying to decide what to believe. She had no proof, nothing tangible and no witnesses. He wanted to believe, he wanted to trust her, but he was almost positive she was either a liar or a complete nut case. What should he do?

Sam got up from the table and looked down at Ashton. He needed time to think and he could not do it while she sat and watched him with those big green eyes, so full of trust and expectations. Her emotions swirled in the depths of those eyes as she waited, holding her breath for Sam's reaction.

When he stood up, her heart fell to her feet. He was leaving, and she was sure he did not believe anything she had said. Could she blame him? She rose also, on wobbly legs, to face Sam. "You're leaving," she said. It was a statement and not a question.

"I am," said Sam, "I need time. I will tell you now that I am inclined to think you are taking me for a ride. But I will give it a day of two and think things over. That's as good as I can do for now," he tried to let her down as easily as he could.

Ashton had to be ok with his decision. After all he had not come right out and told her to buzz off and take her tall tales with her, had he? She could cling to a small ray of hope and maybe he would come around to her way of thinking. If she could get a hold of Saul and convince him to visit Sam, maybe she would still have a chance at sharing love with him. Maybe.

Ashton followed Sam to the door and watched him through the screen as he walked stiff legged down the steps and got into his vehicle. She watched as he drove out of her driveway and disappeared from sight. She had a sinking feeling that she would not ever see him again. The realization that this could actually happen caused a pain to shoot straight through her chest. She shouldn't have felt so strong about him, as they had only known each other for a few days. But she did. The pain of losing him was soul rending. Ashton felt paralyzed by it. She could not move and could hardly breathe.

Her hands gripped the side of the doorframe as she watched her driveway, willing Sam to turn around and come back. Come back and tell her that he loved her and would believe her on faith alone.

For what seemed like an eternity she stood looking out into the night. Finally, she turned back into the house and closed the door on the crisp night air. She made her way back into the kitchen, moving like an old woman, slowly, feet shuffling and hunched over. She looked at the sacks of groceries waiting for her to put away. The same ones she and Sam had just bought. They had had a great time buying things they both liked, and it was hard to imagine that it had only been a few hours ago. It felt like a lifetime since she had laughed with him. She had ruined it all by trying to be honest and spare Sam the hurt of not knowing what was to come.

Slowly she began to store the packages, finishing all too soon as she had not wanted to think and wanted to keep busy for a time. A time to forget. Ashton tried to remember that Sam had not totally left her, he had only left to think he had said. So she would cling to that small thread of hope. If she didn't, she feared she would fall apart.

Half way across the kitchen, Ashton stopped dead in her tracks and stood with her eyes wide and her mouth agape. She knew. She knew without a shadow of a doubt what her purpose was here. It was Sam! She was meant to meet Sam and fall in love with him. If there had been more time would she have bore his children? She again ached because of all the life she would miss with him. It wasn't fair. It wasn't fair! She was to be cheated out of loving the man she was destined to be with. Their love, if he came back, would still be in the fledgling stage when it would come to a crashing halt.

Ashton could feel herself flying into a thousand pieces at the pain that roared through her. She did not think she could hold it together knowing what she had finally come to realize. Her legs crumpled and she rolled into a ball on the floor, almost mad with the knowledge of what she felt and what was to come. She rolled onto her back, faced the ceiling and with clinched fists raised, she yelled out to the only person she could talk to and blame. "Saul, she roared, her voice booming with its rage. "SAUL!"

CHAPTER 22

Sam drove out of Ashton's driveway without looking back. He did not know what to do or what to think. Why was it the only woman he'd ever really had any interest in was turning out to be a kook? With all he had heard tonight, he still wanted her. This was not good, he decided. Maybe it was time to put some distance between them before things got any deeper. Yeah, that was it. He would look into his next job and lose himself in work. It would take him away from home and give him something else to focus on. His work would allow no other thoughts to interfere and that is just what he needed.

Reaching his home, Sam made his nightly rounds, checking the parameter around the cabin. Seeing nothing out of the ordinary, he went inside with a feeling of security as he prepared to settle in for the night. He opened the frig and got out his usual soda, then headed for his computer to fire it up.

Once his mind was made up, Sam gave all his attention to the chosen task. He opened his saved files and reread the information on his next target. He'd made up his mind to take the job and wasted no time in placing his response in the same publication where the offer had been placed. *Offer accepted. Task completed in two weeks. Watch.*

This done, Sam pulled up the name of Jared James, CEO of Global Fuels. He surfed the web until he came up with a picture of the man who was now on his radar. Jared James was 57 years old, 6 feet 4 inches tall, brown hair, brown eyes, single, an international playboy, huge bank account, cheated on his taxes, arrogant, liked the press, and he had powerful enemies. Sam read the last interview Jared had with the press and was not surprised that someone wanted him gone.

Jared was full of himself and unsympathetic to the plight of the public regarding the outrageous gas prices. His view was that if the consumers did not like the prices, stop driving. In his arrogant mind, it was their own fault that their bills were so high. They should wear more clothes and turn down the heat in their homes, ride bikes or walk to work, or better yet, stay home to save money. If they wanted to drive, then they shouldn't go out to eat, or to the movies, and they should stay home instead of taking expensive vacations they couldn't afford. His last ridiculous solution to their plight had been a whopper, how about getting a better paying job instead of being on the bottom of the business food chain, or just plain stop whining about their pitiful little lives.

He was cold and condescending at every turn, and the press had had a field day with the bullshit that had come out of his mouth. The public was outraged and protests had been started against his company. Still, Jared had been very much out in the public eye. Posing with beautiful women, sailing his boat, eating at the most expensive restaurants, and basically thumbing his nose at the world. Since he was not in hiding and only travelled with two body guards, Sam figured this was going to be a piece of cake, and he would probably get a standing ovation from the American public for wiping this asshole from the face of the earth. Times were tight and if you were not willing to do everything in your power to help them out, this is what you got. Dead.

Sam spent the rest of the night studying all the available information at his fingertips, hacking into personal schedules, learning the routine, likes dislikes and hangouts of his prey.

Because that was what Jared was to him. His prey, nothing personal. Sam studied his notes and turned over different scenarios as to how to do the job in his mind. He would have to follow the man around for a few days to decide how close he could get to him. Sam had no intentions of having his picture taken by accident, so he'd make it a priority to find out how much press hung around, and if James really was as public as he seemed.

Since Sam could not decide exactly how to complete the job, based on the information he had, he would just have to pack a few of his *toys* to take along. With airline security the way it was since 9-11, the issue of whether he would be driving instead of flying was decided. He would begin packing his vehicle and head out as soon as possible in the morning.

Sam shut down his laptop, stretched his arms over his head, and arched his back. He had been bent over in concentration for hours, and had to work the kinks out slowly as he stretched his pent up muscles.

He was satisfied with the information gathered so far, and felt he had a good base to work from. He remembered the one detail he had forgotten to check while in his computer so, once again, he booted it up. Once he was again connected to the world of cyberspace, he typed in the number of his bank account which was located in a country that did not tax him to death and was virtually untraceable. Looking at the bottom line of his bank statement, he could see that four million dollars had been transferred into his account not more than a half hour ago. That was half of what was owed to him for this job. Half now and half when the job was completed. Not bad for two weeks work.

Sam looked at the amount. The abundance or zeros no longer sent a thrill through him as it once had. He had enough money to last him forever. *So,* he asked himself, *why did he keep doing it, if not for the money.* It was just a job now, with no big excitement for the payoff. The lack of excitement was the first clue Sam had that it was time to retire. When you did not enjoy what you did, no matter what you did, it was time to change directions. That was exactly what Sam was going to do after this job. He had nothing else to prove, enough money for even God, an exemplary reputation, and now maybe even someone to come home to. Damn it, how had she gotten in his head again? He had been all business not one minute before, and now Ashton was once again front and center in his thoughts.

Sam shut his computer with a snap and rose to his feet with an irritated jerk. He headed to his room and pulled a bag down from his closet. Placing it on the bed he began to fill it with a variety of clothing. The standard black clothes went in first, then there were clothes a tourist would wear, loud colors and stupid shorts, clothes for sailing, evening, daytime and night. Sam made sure to take along everything he'd need, so he wouldn't leave a paper trail buying clothes to blend in to any situation. Pulling a smaller bag out, Sam filled it with his shaving gear, fake facial hair, colored contacts and makeup. He did not plan on looking the same way twice. He did all of his observations in person, taking great pains to change his appearance not only every day, but for every occasion. He packed a camera with different lenses, and last, he took a bag and filled it with knives, ropes, pistols, and a long-range rifle broke down for easy camouflage. He planned for every contingency.

Satisfied with his preparations he went into the bathroom to take a quick shower that would help him have a relaxing night of sleep. He wanted to be fully awake and ready to travel in the morning. He stepped out of the hot shower, toweled the beads of water from his body, and donned a well-worn t-shirt and gym shorts, his favorite bedtime attire. Slipping his feet into a pair of loafers, he took his bags out to his SUV and loaded them into the back. He clicked the lock on the vehicle and made his way back into the house, setting the security alarm that would awaken him if anyone tried to breach his parameter, as he secured himself for the night.

Sam slept soundly, waking just as the sun was coming up to paint the sky with a wide brush of color. He dressed in the clothes he had laid out the night before, grabbed a bag of chips and a soda, breakfast of champions, and paused for one brief moment to take a last look around before he set out.

A feeling came over him as he paused to survey the scene before him. He did not know why, but he felt the need to memorize his home. Lock it into his head. He didn't ever remember doing this before, but stood still to drink in the sights and gather in the fresh mountain air.

Squaring his shoulders, he pulled the door shut, then walked to the SUV and slid in behind the wheel. Sam put the car in gear and pulled out of his driveway. Without looking back, he headed his car west. The deep growl of the engine faded along with the red of his tail lights, leaving the uninterrupted silence of the early dawn. The Messenger had been unleashed.

CHAPTER 23

The miles stretched into a long gray line as Sam made his way west. The drive to Vegas was not that far, only about ten hours by car, which gave Sam time to think and to continue planning.

Jared James, his target, was in Vegas. He was staying at the Top of the World Casino. The casino, in which he was a major stockholder, was opening a new nightclub, and he was there to attend the opening. Even though the opening would not be for another week, Jared had hit town early. He was a party boy elite, which gave the gossip rags something to write about. He seemed to be making the best of his time by staying out late each night, a beautiful woman on each arm, spending money like it was water, and playing the party circuit with all the big stars and jet set.

Sam had made up his mind that this was not going to look like an accident. This was going to appear like what it was, a hit, out in the open and messy. There would be no doubt that a message was being sent to anyone involved in *big oil.* Get in line, or be next.

As the hot miles of pavement raced past his window, Sam cranked up the air conditioner in the vehicle and mulled over several options on how to achieve the desired results, giving each one a short consideration before moving on to the next. Driving did not give him the opportunity to fully concentrate as he considered each option, but he would narrow down the possibilities by the time he reached his destination. Sam would be staying at the Empty Coin Purse Casino, where he would set up camp. It was located across the street from the Top of the World, and despite its name, was one of the most popular casinos in Vegas. Sam wanted to be close but not in James' back pocket during the time he was there.

Keeping his mind busy worked well for Sam, and before he realized it, it was time to stop for gas and for a little refueling for himself as well. He pulled into a lone, dirty little station and shut off his engine. The place looked dry and dusty, like the ones in old westerns that had tumble weeds blowing through them. Sam didn't have a good feeling about the place, but it was the only show in town for miles. So he calmly opened the glove box, took out the pistol nestled inside, placed it in the back of his jeans, pulled his tee shirt over the butt of the gun, and got out of the vehicle.

There was a sign on the pump that said you had to pre-pay before pumping gas, so Sam casually made his way into the station. As he opened the door, a bell jingled overhead and a blast of cold air hit him in the face. The place smelled stale and bad. Not bad like sweat or rotting food, but bad like mean.

Sam kept his eyes moving as he made his way farther into the store. It took him only a second to size up the man behind the counter. He had greasy black hair, a weeks worth of scruffy beard, stained, crooked teeth, breath that Sam could smell even standing ten feet away, dirty shirt and jeans, that had, from the looks of them, not seen the inside of a washer in weeks, and small beady, bloodshot hazel eyes. Those eyes looked calculating, flat, and hard, as they looked Sam up and down.

"Can I do something for you mister?" a gravelly, smokers voice came out of the man's mouth to fill the empty store.

Sam turned his own flat, hard but calm eyes on the man, and with a slight nod of his head replied in a nonchalant voice, "Need gas and maybe something to snack on."

"You have to pre-pay here, go out and pump your gas, then you can come back and get the eats," the man told Sam.

Sam walked up to the counter, and pulling out his wallet took out a hundred dollar bill and laid it in front of the man. Putting his wallet back in his jeans pocket he said, "I'll fill up and be back."

Sam had not missed the way the man's small, greedy eyes had lit up at the bills in his wallet. He had a suspicion that trouble was about to knock on his door, but he let it take its course as he went outside to tend to his gas. As he filled up, he looked at the attendant through the dirty glass of the station window, and wondered what he should do. To dispatch the man would bring unwanted attention.

Sam looked around for security cameras but could see none, feeling sure that what happened in this out of the way place was not something anyone wanted a record of. He put the nozzle back into the pump, capped his tank, and made his way back inside, steeling himself on the inside, but keeping his poker face on so as not to appear any different than any other traveler stopping for a fill-up.

Sam again made his way to the counter, only this time he noticed, in the back of the store and on his right stood another man, just as filthy and seedy as the one behind the counter. Sam made his way around the store, picking up a few candy bars, chips, nuts, and a couple of sodas that he figured should last him until he reached Vegas.

Stopping in front of the counter, Sam kept his body angled to the right so both men were in his sights. The man behind and to the right of him moved closer trying to crowd Sam and box him in. Sam put his food on the counter and looked at the man he had talked to before. "This will do it, along with the gas," he said, one hand on the counter, one down at his side.

"Well," came the same shitty voice as before, "me and my brother here have kind of done some calculations and we think it is going to cost you more than the hundred dollars you have laying here." He paused looking Sam in the eye, "In fact it's going to be a lot more. Let's say about a grand in all," he challenged moving a dirty chewed up toothpick around his crusty lips.

With this said he pulled an old, worn baseball bat from under the counter and laid it out in plain view, so Sam could not miss the meaning of what would happen if he refused to make the payment. The man to Sam's right folded his arms over his chest and grinned with malice.

Sam sized the men up deciding that neither of them were really ready for a fight, and confident that he could take them out without ever really breaking a sweat. They must have done this many times before and got away with it to feel at ease with the outcome. Scaring travelers must be a daily business for them, and was probably quite lucrative as well. But then they had never come up against Sam.

"Well, demanded the first man, "what are you waiting for? Unless of course you are thinking about refusing payment, which me and my brother there would not recommend," he said puffing out his chest and hitching up his pants. "You better be digging for that fat wallet of yours right about now," he finished, bouncing the bat on the counter to once again draw Sam's attention to it in a meaningful way.

Sam looked from one man to the other, smiled, and slowly shook his head. "You don't want to do this. I don't want trouble and I'm sure you two don't either. So how about if you just ring up my stuff, and let me be on my way? We'll forget this happened and everyone goes about their day. No harm, no foul"

Sam noticed the tightening of muscles as they drew themselves up, realizing he was not going to pay up and leave with his tail between his legs, like all the others victims these two thieves had terrorized.

"Hand over your money mister, or we're going to each have a turn at you until there won't be enough left of you for even your mama to recognize," brother one threatened.

Sam looked down and slowly shook his head, "You don't want a piece of this," he said again in a low, ice cold voice, "Just let me be on my way and no one gets hurt," he said giving them one last chance to back down. The tone of his voice, the ice-cold deadliness gave the brothers pause, but they had come too far to back down now, and the greed in their eyes would not be denied.

Smashing the bat on the counter brother one yelled in rage, "Give us your money you dumb fuck. We won't ask again!"

Sam took a deep breath, figuring he had given them every chance to back out and let him leave. So be it. With one smooth motion he drew his gun and had it between the eyes of the vocal brother. "Now," he said with deadly calm, "I'll ask you one more time to ring me up and let me be on my way. You do not want a piece of this," he promised. He paused to make sure he had their attention then continued, "Listen as if your life depends on it, because it does. You have no idea what you are getting into. You do not want to piss me off," he warned. "Now why don't you move real careful like over to the register and let me see you do as I've asked." He motioned with the pistol at the man behind the counter.

Not turning his head he addressed the brother to his right, who had backed up just a little at the previous exchange. "You, come on over here and join the fun. Now." Sam's voice left no doubt that this was a demand and not a request. He waited until both men were side by side behind the counter before he let a cold, mirthless smile lift his mouth. He pushed the hundred-dollar bill closer to the register and looked, without blinking, at the men. Sweat popped out on their brows without him saying another word. Sam saw the one reach for the bill at the same time the other made a move to come over the counter and wrestle the gun from him.

With the barest of motion, Sam moved the gun to point between the two greasy heads and calmly squeezed off a shot. The retort rang in the small store, and the smell of smoky sulfur hung in the air. Sam had not moved an inch, letting his snake cold eyes move from one to the other of the men, while an evil grin danced over his handsome features.

"More?" he asked into the sudden quiet that had overtaken the room.

There was a scramble as the items were rung up, money exchanged, and change given. Sam then motioned for the brothers to raise their hands into the air, picked up his bagged items, and then backed out of the door, smiling to himself. The little encounter had not been planned, but had put him in the right frame of mind for the job to come.

Trouble was coming, and its name was death.

CHAPTER 24

A whirlwind whipped through the empty parking lot of the lone gas station, as Sam drove away. The dust flew and bits of trash spun through the air, heading west like a flock of birds in formation. In its wake, a dim, small figure could be seen standing in the middle of the deserted highway.

Leonard had tried his best to control the actions of the two dim-witted oafs that ran the place. Being small, he had not been able to overcome their fear of the gun pointed at them, or make them swing the bat to bash in Sam's head. It had been an opportunity to get rid of the tiresome man, and Leonard had tried to cash in. But it had not worked.

Frustration could be seen in the tense lines of the small angel. He clenched his small fists, frustrated at the missed chance and at the lack of strength and power that was needed to make a human bend to his will.

At least that is what Leonard blamed it on. He told himself that it could not have been Saul standing invisibly between Sam and Leonard's devious plan. Leonard had not seen Saul since he'd ambushed the older angel, giving him confidence that he had taken care of that obstacle the last time they had met. That victory had been sweet. Even though Saul had not seen his attacker, Leonard knew it was he who had taken down the older, stronger angel, and that was enough for him for now.

Leonard figured that if he continued to shadow Sam, opportunities would present themselves, and eventually he would find a way to destroy the man. With each encounter, Leonard grew a little stronger, a little smarter, and a little meaner. He no longer felt any guilt towards his actions, and even felt a rush of pleasure during the attacks. He justified his actions telling himself, *he was an angel, a superior being, and therefore he should get what he wanted.* Having once been a human himself had no influence on his disregard for these mortals. He would use them to meet his needs, and if some of them lost their pathetic lives in the process, then so be it.

Learning to be selfish and hard was coming way too easy for Leonard, and if it had been happening to an older more experienced angel, there would have been red flags raised in the heavens. But not so with this young one.

Leonard felt nothing but anger and determination. His attention was wholly centered on one goal, having Ashton for himself. He began to fade, invisibly trailing the unsuspecting Sam, intent upon staying close enough to act when an opportunity presented itself. By the time his body was gone from sight, all that remained floating above the lonesome highway, were two red-hot glowing eyes, focused and intent on the destruction of one man.

CHAPTER 25

Sam rolled down the highway, sunglasses reflecting the barren, hot, dry landscape. Daytime was not the ideal time to drive through the desert, but he wanted to reach Vegas and get settled in before night fell. Not that there was a rush on the job, but he wanted to put as much distance as possible between himself and the two brothers back at the gas station. What had ever possessed them to try anything with him, was beyond his comprehension. He looked like he could take care of himself, and had never projected the image that he was an easy mark. Greed made even the most honest of people think twice about doing wrong. But no one did wrong by him.

The miles flew by, boring and uneventful, as he drew closer to the *oasis in the desert.* He sat low in the seat, and could feel sweat crawl down his sides, despite the air conditioning in the vehicle. He did not move to wipe it away, as it provided a distraction to the business of completing his journey and getting down to business. He was patient and did not go over the speed limit, cruising along, eating up the miles with every passing minute.

The sun was still high in the sky when he caught his first glimpse of casinos against the skyline. Their peaks and towers had the look of mountains from a distance, man-made mountains that came into focus as the distance grew smaller between them and the lone car on the desert highway.

Sam slowed as he entered the city limits, and flowed with the now heavy traffic on the strip. He pulled into the self-parking garage of the Empty Purse Casino, not trusting valet with his luggage, and not giving them a chance to be able to identify him in the future. Valet was a lot more observant then most people gave them credit for. They remembered hot cars and their drivers, good tippers as well as the bad ones, and just about anything that made you stand out from the crowd. Sam had the looks that made people turn their heads for a second look. Women looked because they wanted to taste, and men looked because they envied. It was his burden to bear and Sam did it with style.

Sam parked his car and pulled a baseball cap over his hair before getting out and pulling his bags from the hatch. He would carry them himself, check in, and get a shower to wash off the road grime, before hitting the strip.

Sam made his way to the front desk and asked for a room on the ninth floor. Nine was his lucky number, and it was high enough to provide a good overall view of the strip outside his window.

He paid in cash, then boarded the elevator that would take him to his room. Once inside the room, Sam checked inside the bathroom before opening the barely ample closet, where he hung up his clothes. He made sure to hide his other bags in different places throughout the room. Hanging the *Do Not Disturb* sign on the door, he proceeded to take a cool shower. It revived his tired muscles as well as his brain, readying him for a night on the town.

As he dressed he decided that tonight would not be for working, but rather for playing the tourist and checking out the town and the sights. He figured that while doing this he would make a mental list of places and things that might be useful later. He had no destination in mind as he left his room.

The sun was setting but the temperature remained warm. After coming from the cool mountains, the temperature was almost too warm for Sam. He was used to the chill that settled in over the mountains after the sun dipped behind them. He had changed his clothes to blend in with the foot traffic moving on both sides of the street. A screened tee shirt, baggy shorts, and, again, a ball cap rounded out his attire. He kept his sunglasses on providing him a shield against the bright lights, as well as a slight cover, as he wandered the strip.

He stopped in front of various casinos and watched the street shows being presented on the sidewalks to draw in the crowds. The neon lights blazed in the dusk, and the dirt and trash on the streets faded in the covering of night, giving the illusion of wealth and splendor.

Sam watched people as they passed by him, some with hope, some with awe, and some with growing desperation on their faces, as they came and went from the gambling halls. He could almost taste the fear of failure in the air around him. It hung like drying laundry, visible to anyone willing to look. He passed hundreds of hungry faces, all hoping that they would come away winners, big winners. After all, why else would anyone come to this town, if not to get rich?

Sam had a good head on his shoulders and knew that these places were in the business to make money. It was called gambling, after all, not winning. If everyone came away a winner, where would the incentive be to build these "monsters" or even go into the business?

Sam kept walking, his eyes constantly moving, taking in the sights. Without conscious thought, he was storing information, locations, people, advantage points, and access to escape routes. He could not help it, occupational hazard. Sam spent hours just wandering where he would. He stopped to eat when he was hungry, enjoying the buffets with their wide variety of foods to satisfy every appetite. He stayed on the strip and did not wander down the back streets, knowing that he was likely to find trouble there. Unwary tourists were often mugged, and sometimes worse, when they went too far astray. As he said, greed made people do stupid things.

The time was creeping towards midnight when he finally completed his leisurely circuit of the strip. He was approaching the Empty Purse when he looked across the street and saw Jared James coming out of *his* Casino, heading towards a limo parked on the street. He had a blonde on one arm and a dark haired beauty on his other. The press was gathered between him and the car, snapping pictures and yelling questions in the hopes he would lower himself to stop and give them a few moments of his time. Even from where Sam stood he could see the aloofness and self-importance on James' face.

Sam stopped to lean back against the building and watched the scene unfold across the street. Other tourists followed suit, pulling cameras out and snapping pictures, even though some were unsure of who the guy was across the street. Sam heard one woman say, "I don't know for sure who he is, but he must be somebody. Look at all the press around him."

A balding, older man with an impressive paunch sneered at the crowd as he passed by. "He's one of the bastards that are getting rich by gouging prices at the pumps. Why are you all taking his picture? Somebody ought to run him over." He shook his head and spat on the street before moving on, disappearing in the throng that had gathered.

Sam had watched the exchange, and, taking a camera out of his pocket, had snapped a few pictures of the man who had been so vocal in his dislike of James. He also snapped a few pictures of the man now getting into his car across the street, and of the security around him. As he had learned in his preliminary research of his target, there were only two personal bodyguards, joined by three casino security guards. Not a problem there.

Sam waited until the car had smoothly joined traffic and the bodyguards had gotten into a black SUV to follow, before he returned his camera to his pocket and moved inside his casino. He was going to call it a night, and get a fresh start in the morning.

He had to walk through the casino to reach the elevators, a clever way for the casinos to get you to play a few more coins before you retired for the evening. The true diehards never slept while they were in Vegas, trying to cram unlimited fun and excitement into the short amount of time they were in town.

Sam had almost reached the elevators when he felt a hand on his arm. A slightly slurred voice reached his ears, but not before the smell of alcohol hit him first. "Hey baby, what's doing? How about sitting over there with me and buying me a drink?" she gestured a long red fingernail toward the bar area. Then she leaned into Sam with a promise of something more, "We could be friends, really good friends."

Sam's gaze slid over the woman attached to the hand on his arm. She was in her early thirties, he figured, maybe once attractive but not so now. She didn't look like a hooker, but rather, Sam figured, someone who had run out of money and was looking for a sugar daddy for the evening. People in these type of places would sell their body and soul for their next hand of cards or glass of courage. Her hair was messed up, makeup smeared, her eyes red, watery and unfocused. She was toasted, Sam decided. A blind man could see that from a mile away.

Taking her hand from his arm, Sam placed it at her side and shook his head, "Not this time, thanks."

He turned to walk away and again his arm was grabbed, this time with more force as the long red nails bore into his flesh in a death grip. "What's the matter, you gay or what?" The voice now had a sneer in it, and Sam knew that his rejection was not going to be taken well.

He quickly looked around to make sure they were not drawing attention, before turning eyes, that had taken on a hard glaze, back on the woman. Getting into a verbal battle or worse was not on his agenda, so he took a breath, reached in his pocket, and handed her a $5 bill. "Call a cab," he said, "Go home before you do something you will regret."

"Who are you," she slurred, "my father? What happens in Vegas stays in Vegas, baby, or haven't you heard?" She looked down at the bill in her hand, calculating what it could buy her, then unsteadily turned on her stiletto heels and sloshed her way towards the nearest barstool. She'd have her drink then move on to her next mark, or John, whatever the case may be.

Sam shook his head, climbing onto the nearest elevator, and made it all the way to his room without further incident. He took off his cap and glasses, laying them on the dresser, and pulled the camera from his pocket. Scrolling through the photos, he stopped on the ones of his target. He studied them for just a brief moment, then closed the camera and tossed it on the dresser, too. He moved to stand before the window, looking out on the lights of Vegas and thought, *Tomorrow, James, tomorrow you get my full attention. Your clock is ticking.*

CHAPTER 26

Saul had no concept of time or space as he floated on a wave of never ending pain. He knew that he had things to do and humans to watch over, but he could not get past the soul burning fire that rolled through his being. He remembered being attacked from behind by another immortal, but did not know who or why the attack had been launched. He was not even sure when it had happened. Time had no meaning for him at the moment. He knew he must heal himself and do it quickly but he feared his injuries were going to take some time and all of his concentration for a while to come.

This was not the first time Saul had suffered an attack and had to heal himself, but the extent of his injuries this time were more severe, severe enough that he had almost been destroyed.

Acting on instinct, Saul stretched out his wings to their greatest length and closed his eyes. He pulled all of his concentration inside and became quiet and still. Inch by inch he closed his wings until they wrapped around his body, enclosing him a cocoon of warmth, healing light, and power. A few small rays of white light could bee seen escaping from between the impressive feathers, but with one small adjustment of his wings, the rays disappeared trapping in the healing light, and Saul began the healing process.

One final thought was allowed, one final feeling felt, one final promise before he became dormant. Wrath was a terrible thing to behold in an angel, and Saul's would be unleashed on whoever had done this to him. *So*, he thought, *run and hide if you can. I'm coming, I'm coming soon and I'm coming for you!*

CHAPTER 27

Ashton had spent a long night after Sam left, pacing, crying, berating herself for sharing her secret with him, and angry at Saul. In desperation, she had called out to Saul, pleading softly at times and demanding loud enough to wake the dead at others, but he had not come. Finally around dawn, she had given up in defeat, falling into an exhausted sleep filled with dreams of never seeing Sam again, of spending the rest of her life alone and isolated. When she woke she had found her cheeks and pillow wet with tears, shed during her troubled dreams.

Slowly she swung her legs over the edge of the couch where she had fallen asleep, and sat cradling her head in her hands. Her head felt like it was splitting in two, as sharp pains, brought on by stress and unhappiness, pounded against her forehead.

She got up and moved towards the bathroom, hoping a hot shower would wash away the cobwebs and bring some ease to her aching body and soul. Her movements were slow and jerky, as if she were a puppet and some unseen hands were controlling the strings. She made it to the mirror and could only stare at herself in horror. Her hair stuck out in tufts, looking like she had tried to pull it out in frustration. Her eyes were red and puffy from all the crying she had done, and her skin was pale and sickly looking. She licked her lips and grimaced because her tongue, which was more sticky than wet, coated her lips with a slimy film. She was sure that if she was in a cartoon, her breath would be coming out in green clouds and killing plants and small animals.

Stepping back she peeled off her clothes from the night before and almost crawled into the shower. She had a fleeting thought about taking a long hot bath but she felt sure she would not be able to remove herself from the tub once she got in.

She turned on the hot water and let it beat down on her tired body. After a few minutes she began to feel better as her muscles loosened and some of the tension abated. She poured shampoo into her hand and began the labor of washing her long hair. Her arms ached by the time she was finished. She let them dangle by her sides, standing under the steady stream, letting the hot water do its work. When the room was filled with smothering steam, she shut off the taps and stepped out. The air in the bathroom was so thick, she had to feel around for the towel before wrapping herself up in its softness.

She opened the door to the bedroom and let the cool air rush into the room. Water began to run down the mirror as the steam turned clear and cool. She towel-dried her hair and pulled it back from her face in a ponytail. She decided to forego makeup as her cheeks had taken on a healthy pink blush in the heat of the shower. She brushed her teeth, ridding her mouth of the acrid odor that had settled in overnight.

Feeling almost human, she made her way to the bedroom. Reaching into her closet she pulled out the first thing her fingers touched, an old flannel shirt that had seen better days, and then thought better of it. Carefully she flipped through the clothes on the rack, realizing that she wanted to look especially nice today.

She had made up her mind to walk over and see Sam. She would plead her case with him and not leave until he gave her, and them, a second chance. She was not sure why Sam was so important to her, as she had only met him a few days ago and had only shared one dinner with him, but he was all she could think of. Maybe her feeling that he was the reason she had been drawn to Colorado in the first place, had been right. Whatever the reason, Sam was going to listen to her, and if she had to sit on him to get him to believe her she would. Maybe a night to process the information she had gave him had helped. She hoped so.

With renewed hope in her heart, Ashton finished dressing, grabbed a bagel as she passed through the kitchen, and walked out the back door, turning towards Sam's. As she walked, she began to enjoy the fresh morning air. In spite of her trying evening, she began to perk up and feel more optimistic with each step she took. *Yes*, she thought, *this was going to work*.

Walking with determination, Ashton reached Sam's house in less then an hour. She marched right up to the back door and proceeded to pound on it with vigor. "Open up Sam, I have to talk to you," she demanded to the closed door. "Come on Sam," she said, louder this time. "We have things to talk about." She stepped back and waited.

The seconds drug out and she began to feel anxious. What if he didn't come to the door? What if he was inside and just refused to see her? He probably thought she was a nut job, and was cowering with fear inside. She couldn't blame him, but she was not going to leave even if it meant camping out on his doorstep. He had to come out sometime, didn't he?

Ashton banged one more time and called out as loud as she could, "Damn it Sam, I need to talk to you, please." She waited again and finally came to understand she was not going to be let in.

Holding back a sob, she turned away and stared out into the yard. After letting her gaze wander around the perimeter of the yard, the realization came to her that Sam's car was gone. She jumped down the stairs and made a circle around the house. No car, no signs of life in fact, nothing. The blinds at the windows had been drawn, and no light could be seen coming through them. There was only silence.

"Where is he?" Ashton wondered out loud. Feeling relieved that he hadn't purposely ignored her knocking, the questions as to where he could be raced through her mind. Had he run into town to take care of an errand or something? Or had he just run? For some reason she could not explain, she felt the latter was correct. She sat on the bottom step and wrapped her arms around her body. Bending forward she began to rock slowly, keeping time to the waves of pain that washed through her heart at the prospect of losing this man she had known for such a short time.

"No Sam, don't leave me," she whispered to no one. "I need you, I need us to work. Please come back, please come back," she said, her voice getting quieter and quieter with each word she spoke.

She rested her head on her knees, not capable of deciding what to do next. Her eyes were so dry they burned, and her heart felt like it was broken in to a million pieces, like the sparks from fireworks falling and fading into nothingness, their purpose having come to an end.

Please, Ashton cried out inside, *don't let me be like that. Don't let me burn out and fade away, leaving nothing but a fleeting happiness behind when I go. Let someone remember me burning bright, bringing joy and happiness.* She knew that she had a gift inside her, the gift of love that she wanted to share with the one special person she was meant to be with

At that thought Ashton jerked upright. She was struck with the sudden knowledge that she was in love with Sam. The blood drained from her face and seemed to pool around her feet at the knowledge running through her mind and body. She was in love with a man and she had totally screwed it up. She had scared him away with her story of angels and death.

Ashton couldn't move, sitting still as a statue her eyes closed, not knowing what to do or where to turn next. She knew she had to find Sam and try to make him see things as she did. As she sat there she began to feel a warmth creep back into her. In fact she began to feel hot.

As she opened her eyes, her breath caught in her chest and she began to shake. Two feet in front of her was a small boy, dressed in white, floating off the ground as Saul had done.

"Who you are?" she asked in a trembling, breathless voice. "*What* are you? Are you an angel, like Saul? Did he send you? Where is Saul?" she threw the questions at him demanding answers.

The small boy looked at Ashton with kindness and something else. "My name is Leonard," he said, his sweet voice reaching Ashton's ears, soothing her fears. "Please, do not be afraid of me." He paused, then told her, "I am the one who has brought about your current circumstances. I have been watching you for a long time. I wanted us to friends, to be together for eternity, with no interference from anyone or anything."

Ashton kept staring at Leonard, trying to make sense of what he was saying. Realization setting in she asked, "You did this to me?" You are the one who "made a mistake" as Saul put it?"

"There was no mistake," he said shaking his dark head as he came closer to her. "I knew what I was doing. I saw you first, and I wanted you. I want to be your friend. All you have to do is take my hand and tell me that you want to be with me, too." He held out a small seemingly defenseless hand to her.

Staring into his eyes, Ashton felt a powerful urge to take his hand and go where he asked. She slowly stood up and moved, with out meaning to, towards the boy angel. She watched her hand begin to reach out to his, and knew that in another second she would be touching him, grasping the hand that she did not want to touch.

There is something wrong here, she thought. She did not know him, she did not want him, and she could not believe this was happening. She felt out of control, powerless against the force pulling her towards him. She shook her head from side to side and took a deep cleansing breath, fighting against the feelings warring inside her body. She regained some control and lowered her hand to her side.

"This is wrong," she told the angel who called himself Leonard, "this is not supposed to be happening. I don't know who you are, but I do know I will not go with you."

Leonard felt his control over Ashton slipping away and was filled with rage. How dare she refuse him? Had he not done everything for her, so they could be together?

"You dare to refuse my offer," he asked with a voice that grew in volume and dripped with distain? "You, a mere mortal, who should be honored that I have chosen you? Do you know what I have done to bring us together?" he asked moving forward as she continued to step backward away from him. "I have moved heaven and earth, I have changed the course of your life, and I will not be denied, even by you. You will obey me!" he told a disbelieving Ashton.

The sky cracked with lightning and the wind whipped around Ashton. She probably should have been afraid, but she was not. He was small and looked so unable to hurt her, even though the air was on fire and the wind showed his rage.

Ashton stood her ground and let her own anger have its way. "You dare to come to me and demand that I go with you, to fall in with your plans without blinking an eye?" She took a step toward him as she continued, "You stand there and admit that you have robbed me of my life and did so because of your selfishness? *Because you wanted?* What about what you have taken from me? ***WHAT ABOUT WHAT I WANT***? I had dreams. There were things I have not yet seen and done. I had a life, and you took that from me!" she challenged him, strangely unafraid. "I will never forgive you for what you have done to my life. I will not go with you, now or ever. Leave me alone! Don't ever come near me again!" she spat at him turning her back on him turning towards her home.

For a moment Leonard stood quietly stunned and frozen to the spot where he stood.

Ashton, hearing the silence, thought she had sent the boy back to where he had come from, until a wicked laugh behind her stopped her in her tracks. She turned around and the small, seemingly defenseless boy now seemed to be ten feet tall with eyes that burned with fire, with blood, and with the promise of revenge.

"You dare to tell me what to do? You think I do not know what you feel, or think or want?" Leonard asked in a booming voice that matched his transformed image. "Know this mortal," he warned pointing a finger at Ashton who was staring at him wide-eyed but yet unafraid, "because of your refusal, I will bring you more pain than you could ever imagine, and it will be a pain that will last for all time."

"What more can you do to me?" she asked, finding her voice amidst the chaos. "You have taken everything from me. Your threats are useless. Go find your mother." she threw at him with disdain.

It was as if she had slapped him. One minute Leonard was there and the next he was gone from Ashton's sight. Poof!

As she let out her breath, she heard a voice in the now still mountain air. A small child's voice, and the voice said one word. "Sam."

CHAPTER 28

Sam had gotten a good night's sleep, waking after noon, which was not uncommon for tourists enjoying the nightlife Vegas had to offer. He had enjoyed himself the night before, checking out the sights and getting reacquainted with the City of Sin. His brief encounter with Jared James had put him on the right track for gathering information and planning his strategy. His preliminary information had been correct, as far as he could tell, but he was leaving nothing to chance.

He dressed carefully for the day, deciding to get a closer look at the Hotel across the street, inside and out. He put on a dirty blonde wig, applied a mustache to his naked upper lip, and lightened his eyebrows to match the hair. His eyes were no longer the striking teal blue that drew attention, but had been changed to a muddy nondescript brown.

Satisfied with his appearance, Sam dove into his computer and hacked into the database of current employees for the Top of the World Casino. He searched through the file of picture ID's until he found an employee that looked similar to him. Scanning the personnel schedules he found that Bob was off for the day. Or maybe he wasn't. He was going to take Bob's place today, and he was going to make sure that he answered the pages that would take him up to the penthouse. That should get him a quick peek inside the suite and more information on the likes and dislikes of its occupants.

Sam hoped that a time schedule could be ascertained by pretending to work in the Hotel. He could determine when Jared got up, ate, left his suite, where he was going, and how he was getting there. If everything worked out as Sam planned, he could collect the clothes sent out for cleaning, and, before they were returned, place a small tracking and listening device inside them. This should help him narrow down the time and place of the hit.

So at 2:45, shift change for most of the casinos, Sam made his way across the street and walked around the Casino until he found the employee entrance. He kept his gate easy, watching the other employees as they came in for work. He carefully chose one man who was hurrying as if he was late, and cut him off.

"Hey man," he said in a nerdy voice. "Can you tell me where wardrobe is, I forgot my uniform."

A pair of impatient eyes glanced at him, and a hand was raised pointing down the next hallway. "Down there and to your left," replied the man as he barely glanced at Sam before hurrying into the building.

Sam moved in the direction indicated and soon found himself outside a window with the sign "wardrobe" posted on the glass. He waited behind a girl as she harassed an older female into giving her a cocktail waitress uniform. By the time it was Sam's turn the woman was not in the best of moods.

"Excuse me," Sam's nerdy voice came out, "I left home without my uniform and I would like to get a loaner just for today. Can you help a guy out so he doesn't get in trouble with the brass?" he asked with a wink and a pleading smile in the attendant's direction.

The woman hardly looked up as she asked what department and size Sam needed in a monotone voice. She didn't even ask for an I D or employee number, even though

Sam had gotten those in case someone was actually paying attention. No worries there though.

After five minutes Sam was walking down the hallway armed with a bellhop's uniform. He slipped into the first bathroom he could find and changed into the uniform, stuffing his clothes neatly behind rolls of toilet paper in a storage cabinet.

As he exited the bathroom he was stopped by a firm hand on his shoulder. "You must be new here," came a whiney voice from behind him. "Employees are not allowed to use the guests' bathrooms. We have to use the one in the employee break room."

Sam had stiffened for just an instant, but relaxed when he heard the reason for being halted. He dipped his head not looking the speaker in the eye as he said, "Sorry man, but I had to go and couldn't wait to get to the employee's john. I promise it won't happen again."

The security guard removed his hand from Sam's shoulder, nodding his understanding and motioned for Sam to get back to work. Sam moved on down the hall in search of the bellhop station. It didn't take him long to find his way into the busy area, where orders and requests were being called down from the guests. He busied himself straightening things, moving them from one location to another, waiting, until the call he had been waiting for came.

"Yes, we can have that sent up in less then an hour. Yes sir. Mr. James' suite. Oh, of course we can. The suit was brought back just a few minutes ago and will be brought right up. No problem. Thank you," said the dispatcher to the caller at the other end.

Sam moved into the line of sight as the woman looked up from taking notes and appeared ready to give the assignment to the first person she saw. "Hey," she looked down at his nametag, "Bob. I've got something for you to do." Sam stepped forward and nodded his head. "Take this suit up to Mr. James in the penthouse suite and pick up two more that need to go out. Then I've got a food order to go up, so get your butt back here pronto and don't dawdle," she shooed him on his way.

Without a word, Sam grabbed the hangers and made his way to the same bathroom he had used earlier. Slipping inside a stall, he closed the door and hung the expensive suit on the hook provided. He reached into his pocket and removed a small black case. Opening the case he took out a small dot, no bigger then a speck of fly poop, and placed it on the underside of the lapel. He pressed a button on a minute remote and activated the tracking and listening device. Smoothing down the collar, he exited the room without being stopped and made his way up to the penthouse.

Knocking on the door he waited until a man the size of a small redwood opened it, and looked at him as if he were dog shit on the bottom of his shoe. "Mr. James's clothing" Sam said. The man grabbed the hangers with beefy hands, turned them around inspecting the clothing. He grunted and digging in his pocket stuffed a five-dollar bill in Sam's hand before shutting the door in his face.

Sam was okay with this as he had accomplished what he wanted to do. He now had eyes and ears on James' whenever and wherever he went. He had also gotten a quick look inside the door, and planned on getting a closer look when he delivered the food that was waiting to be brought up.

Sam hustled back to the holding area, stepped up to the operator, gave her a shy smile, and held out his hand to receive the ticket. She barely looked up, as she handed him the meal ticket for the penthouse.

Sam took the slip and proceeded to the swinging kitchen doors to collect the meal cart covered with shiny silver domes and a bottle of bubbly chilling in a silver ice bucket. Once again he made the trip to the top floor. He knocked on the door and was again greeted by James' bodyguard. After lifting the covers on the tray to make sure there wasn't a surprise hidden under one of them, he waved Sam into the room.

Sam wheeled the food into the living area, removing the lids from the food as he prepared to serve James and his companions. James came out of one of the bedrooms and, looking at the cart, waved him away as if to say he would deal with the food later. Sam replaced the lids and made his way back to the door that was now open for him in an invitation to get out. He did as expected, stopping just inside the door and making a slight movement with his hand. For an instant he thought he was going to have to explain to the meathead what he wanted, but a dim light flashed on in the big oaf's head and again, with an annoyed frown, he was given a five dollar tip and rushed out the door.

Sam made his way back to what he thought of as *his bathroom,* and changed back into his own clothing, removing the fake hair and other remnants of his disguise. He whistled under his breath as he made his way back out onto the strip, heading away from his own Casino. He did not want anyone knowing he left one place, just to enter another across the street. You never knew who was watching.

He was satisfied with his work so far, pleased that things were moving along as he had planned. It had been way to easy to imitate an employee, and he'd found you could get just about anywhere or anything you wanted by doing so. Point in his favor.

Sam stuck his hands in his pockets as he joined the throng on the strip and went with the flow. He had forgotten what he had put in them, until his fingers came into contact with the objects. A smile touched his lips and he closed his eyes for an instant as he enjoyed the delicious sense of irony. Not only had he planted the device but he had gotten tipped for it.

CHAPTER 29

Sam took a quick walk up and down the strip before returning to his hotel room. He'd forgotten just how colorful Vegas could be. In what other city in America could a person be propositioned by a hooker on one corner and receive the promise of eternal forgiveness by a sidewalk preacher on the next? The people on the street ranged from your run of the mill tourist, snapping pictures of each new sight with the digital camera that hung around their neck, to the high-rolling gambler looking for his next hand of Texas Hold Em or a hot craps table, complete with a sexy blonde eager to blow on your dice for luck.

After he'd completed his tour of the strip, Sam decided it was safe to return to his hotel. He pushed his way through the spinning door and was immediately greeted by the music of the slots, beckoning him to become the next big winner. Here and there was a shiny new Hummer or convertible promising to be yours if you dared to play the odds. Sam knew from experience that many a tourist had lost all their money before they even made it to their room. The architects of these places knew what they were doing by placing the casinos in the path of the elevators. Sam didn't stop as he passed by the sea of lights and people. He wanted to get to his room and do a little homework.

Once inside his room, he checked to make sure nothing had been tampered with and that he didn't have any company. Settling down on the couch, his feet on the coffee table, he opened his laptop and dialed up the feed for thc dcvice he had planted in James suite. A satisfied smile crossed his handsome face as the picture came into focus and the audio, though somewhat muffled, was plain enough for him to hear what he needed.

From what he could see and hear, James and entourage were planning on going to a high profile nightclub, the Night Owl, leaving about midnight. It seemed that James did not want to get there too early, wanting to make a grand entrance, and getting maximum attention when he did arrive. He instructed his assistant to "drop the information" to a few reporters, making it sound like a secret to get him some media coverage.

What a media hog, Sam thought. He probably wouldn't even make the news if he did not manipulate the reporters to his advantage. Sam decided it would be a good idea to be at the club when James arrived.

He pulled up the Night Owl Club's website and found that it was a high end, expensive place where all of the uppity-ups hung out. If you were not well known, it was almost impossible to get in. Sam did not want to pose as an employee, but he did not want to draw too much attention to himself either, trying to pass through the bouncers at the door. This was neither the time nor the place for him to take out James, so he was going to have to figure out a way to get into the place and then fit into the crowd so he could observe his prey.

Sam began to formulate a plan. He looked through his wardrobe and disguises, choosing things that did not change his appearance that much. He was going to have to rely on his good looks and charisma to bluff his way in tonight.

Sam left his computer running, making a recording of the goings on in James' room, while he took a shower. He wrapped his wet body in a thick towel bearing the logo of the hotel, ordered up room service, and spent a quiet evening doing research and making notes on his target.

At ten p.m., Sam began to dress for the evening. When he finished he looked at himself in the mirror with an objective eye. He'd left his hair dark and long, but, with the help of colored contact lenses, changed his eyes to a deep, rich chocolate brown. In the dark of the night they would appear almost black, giving Sam a mysterious and almost sinister look. His clothing was all black, expensively cut and stylish. Black pants, black shirt open at the neck, black suit jacket, and butter soft black leather shoes, made Sam look handsome and worth a second look. The only color he wore was a gold chain around his neck and a gold Rolex on his wrist. Power was the look Sam was going for and power was the look he had achieved. Sam knew from experience that if someone was asked to describe him they would only remember the darkness of him and not the details of his face. This crowd would only remember his worth; they would judge the cost of his clothes, his accessories, the cut and style of his hair, and the money in his pocket. He would flash a modest amount of cash but not enough to make the greedy bastards sit up and take too much notice.

Sam splashed on a small amount of cologne, that made the one getting a whiff of it think of deep, dark nights and the promise of pleasures that could be had spending it with him. Sam called down to the concierges' desk and asked for a black limo to be ready in thirty minutes. Not a stretch limo but one of the smaller, more tasteful ones. He was assured it would be waiting for him. He walked over to the bar in his room and poured himself a weak cocktail. He did not want to be loaded when he got to the club, but he wanted to have just a hint of alcohol on his breath, as if he had had a drink with his evening meal. From past experiences he knew that the crowd he would be hanging with tonight were hard drinkers, hard partiers, egotists, and posers who became suspicious of anyone who did not fall in line and act the same. He would put on a show for them and let them see what they wanted, but he had every intention of remaining alert and in total control for the whole evening.

Sam set his glass down on the counter in the bathroom and looked at himself one more time. Liking what he saw, he moved through the room and out the door. He made his way across the lobby, seemingly unaware of the attention he was getting, just moving with easy unhurried strides out the door. He stepped into the car and gave the driver the name of the club, but no directions, as if he thought everyone should know where it was. He sat back relaxed and unconcerned. Drivers tended to hang together and talk about who they had as passengers while they waited for them. Gossip was a good way to spend an evening of boredom, and stories were passed around like the booze that flowed inside. His driver was not going to be able to contribute much tonight. His passenger would just remain the mystery guy that had enough money to party with the big dogs.

The limo cut a smooth path through the evening traffic, and before long was pulling up in front of the neon riddled entrance. The driver jumped out and held the door open for Sam. Sam counted to ten and then emerged into the night. There was a line snaking down the block with people waiting to get in, all trying to look bored and as if they belonged. Beauty could be seen everywhere, ordinary and ugly did not get a second glance, nor entrance.

Sam looked around with a lack of interest, slipped his hand in his pocket and walked right to the front of the line. Moving with confidence and ease he stopped in front of the thug guarding the door. No matter how he was dressed, in this case a suit and tie, the bulge at his side indicated he had the say on who got in and no trouble would be allowed. He did not smile as he looked Sam up and down. Sam did not squirm or fidget under the scrutiny, but stood his ground and looked the hulk straight in the eye. Both men stood the same height, which was well over the norm, so neither had the advantage in the test of wills going on. A couple hanging on to each other at the front of the line, who appeared to have visited a few other night clubs before landing at this one, smirked at Sam's balls in confronting the bouncer, and were sure he would be turned back with a withering look and a smart-assed remark. Their mouths dropped open as the bouncer, with a slight nod of his head, indicated Sam could enter.

"Hey man," the sloshed dude slurred loudly, "we were here first."

"Yeah," the girl chimed in, "what makes him so god damn special? We've all been waiting here half of the night. WE WANT IN!"

They turned to the waiting line and started chanting, "WE WANT IN," pumping their fists in the air, hoping to get support and have strength in numbers. Most just shook their heads and a few could be heard to mutter, "Tourists," before turning their backs on the seriously drunk pair. Still making a scene, the two turned to face front again and were confronted by a chest that looked a mile wide. Eyes, trying to focus, travelled upwards and were held by hard dark orbs. A rumble came from deep in the chest and the voice that came out was controlled but massive.

"Beat it scum. You're out." Tyrone, the bouncer, turned his back on the couple and was not in the least bit affected by the one finger salute given to him and all those left in line as they weaved their way, hopefully, to call it a night.

Sam had remained where he was during the brief exchange and now again looked the bouncer in the eye. "Nice," he said and held out his hand for the big man to shake. The three hundred dollar bills smoothly exchanged hands and no more was said.

CHAPTER 30

Sam moved into the Club. It didn't take his eyes long to adjust, as the inside was as dark as the night outside. Dim lights were set on each table and booths were arranged on the outer rim of what appeared to be a dance floor. People were milling around talking, drinking, smoking and making contacts. Sam recognized a few faces as movie and TV personalities, but was not impressed. He had had a few encounters with those types, and found the characters they portrayed were much more interesting then the real thing. Still he did not judge all at the expense of some.

He made his way slowly towards the bar, swinging one black clad leg over a stool and leaning down on one elbow until the bartender came for his order. She was a good-looking, young woman who like most, was probably trying to break into the entertainment business. A job like this could get her noticed by the right people, could get her "discovered". Long blonde hair was pulled back from a delicate face, where big blue eyes were busy roaming over the handsome man before her. He could see the calculation going on behind them, trying to size him up as being someone who could help her in her quest for advancement, or just some guy looking to rub elbows with the rich and famous.

He must not have looked like the movie type, for when she smiled at him it was not forced, plastic or hungry. It was relaxed and easy, showing him she liked what she saw. "Hey good looking, what will it be tonight?" Her voice was husky and completely at odds with her innocent peaches and cream looks.

Sam let a little heat creep into his voice as he said, "What would you recommend?"

Her lids drooped a little over her eyes and she licked her lips before answering. "Depends on what you're looking for. You want a buzz hard and fast, slow and easy, sweet, or just dirty and cheap?"

Sam did not miss the double meaning behind the words and smiled a little wider. Bartenders were information just waiting to be tapped. They saw and heard everything, and were told more secrets then a priest. Still Sam did not want to lead her on, and he did not want her remembering too much about him. With a sigh of regret Sam straightened up from the bar and said, "Just a beer for now, on the rocks."

She shrugged her shoulders as if to say, "no harm in trying." She got the beer and poured it over the ice with a flourish. She sat it on the bar in front of him and leaned in a little closer. "My name is Becca if you need anything while you're here. Just let me know."

Sam put a couple of bills on the bar and winked at the lovely barmaid. "Thanks Becca, I'll keep that in mind," he told her as her turned toward the gyrating crowd on the dance floor. He let his gaze roam over the shadowy room, finding an empty table a short distance from the floor. He made his way over to it, settling into the chair with his back up against the wall. He lifted his glass and drank, letting his eyes roam freely over the room. The music was loud, the beat heavy and deep, and bodies close as they leaned in to hear what was being said.

He made mental notes of the people there, noticing those who were looking at him. Not only women but men as well were checking him out. He did not roll that way and was careful not to make eye contact with any of them. The person he was looking for had yet to make an appearance, so Sam settled in with his beer to wait.

He didn't have long to wait, as the door opened and in walked Jared James. As usual, he had a girl on each arm and his two bodyguards following him like trained dogs on a leash. He made his way across the floor, snapping his fingers at the bartenders as he went. He sat down with a flourish and looked around the room to see who had noticed his entrance. Sam watched as people began to flock to his table. James sat as if holding court. He laughed, smiled, and lapped up the attention as if it were his God given right. He rudely dismissed some who came to his table as if they were of no importance and did not merit his time. The bodyguards stood, one on each side of his chair, arms folded across their chests, and waited for instructions from the pompous ass they guarded. Even the most famous of celebrities in the club did not have the entourage that James sported.

The night wore on and Sam watched, never letting his guard down as he gathered information. He noted the guards did not leave James alone at any time. If one left, the other moved to stand directly behind James' chair, keeping an eye on the crowd coming and going. He also noticed that James liked to drink, and the more he drank the louder he got, becoming more careless as the night wore on. He did not stick with only the girls he came in with, but moved his attentions elsewhere and often. He tended to grab onto any nice butt moving past him, and more than once pulled a woman onto his lap to grope and fondle her in public. These girls giggled and took it all in stride, giving James miniature lap dances before getting off.

Sam also noticed that the big named stars did not come over to the table, casting disapproving glances in the direction of the spectacle taking place. Jared seemed to preen with all of the attention paid to him, but once or twice Sam noticed him casting furtive glances in the direction of the patrons that snubbed his presence. *So*, Sam, *he wants to be accepted by the elite group and no matter what he tries, he's still on the outside.* Sam bet that that really burned his butt. His money could not buy him a way into that tight group.

Sam studied those in the elite group, a mixture of politicians, movie stars, and executives, and wondered who Jared was trying to impress. He bet that if he tuned in to Jared's room tonight he would get a name. Jared and his cronies would be rehashing the night when they got back to their suite, and he was sure to gather some useful information that he would be able to use to his advantage. A plan was beginning to form in Sam's head, and it was looking better by the minute. *Oh yeah*, he thought, *this just might be what I've been waiting for.*

Sam gave his attention one last time to Jared, and noticed him making his way to the bar. He motioned Becca over and was giving her a line of crap about being able to get her into the movies. He stroked her arm and whispered in her ear. Becca had a plastic smile pasted on her mouth, and didn't seem as relaxed as when Sam had talked to her. She nodded her head and took something from Jared's hand, some piece of paper.

Sam decided he had seen enough for one outing, and got up to leave. On his way out he made a detour to the bar and caught Becca's attention. She still had the paper in her hand, and was studying it, trying to figure out what to do with it. Sam looked her in the eye, reached across the bar, took the piece of paper out of her hand, looked at it, and crumpling it up, threw it away. It had been Jared's hotel and room number. "Don't," Sam said to Becca. "Don't even consider it. He's trouble and nothing that he says he is."

Sam took out a piece of paper from his pocket and wrote a name and number on it. "Call this guy," he said as he handed it over the bar. "Tell him I said to give you a shot. This is legit, and he won't expect you to sleep with him for it either." His dark eyes held sincerity, something not often seen in this kind of place.

Becca took the number, looking puzzled as she said, "I don't even know your name to tell him. Who are you, anyway?"

Sam did some quick thinking and chose a code name his buddy would recognize. "Tell him Sharp sent you. He'll know it's for real." He touched her fingertips and gave her a genuine smile. "Good luck, kid."

With that Sam walked out leaving Becca smiling widely at this turn of luck. He'd given her an important push in the right direction, but it was up to her from now on. Sam felt pleased at snatching one away from Jared. Smiling as he made his way out into the night, Sam figured it was Sam one, Jared nothing.

CHAPTER 31

Jared strutted back to his table feeling good about his latest conquest, because he was sure that was what it was. The fresh looking little bartender had been ripe for the picking, needing only a few half-truths to fall into his bed. He would get her to his room and tell her he could help her with her acting career. That's what all of the good-looking ones out here wanted. To be in movies and to make it big. Well, he had planted the seed told her he could get her what she wanted. But first, he was going to get what he wanted. He was getting tired of the women around him, and it was time to get some fresh meat. He had no qualms about using people to get what he wanted and he was conceited enough to think she would enjoy their time together. After he was done with her, he would kick her to the curb and think no more about it. He really didn't have any connections with Hollywood, but she didn't know that. Now if she was really good, maybe he could get her in some adult films. Hey, movies were movies right? So, he had not really lied when he said he could help her.

He sat down at his table and was feeling pretty good, when he happened to glance over at the bar, intending to give the little chippy a wink for good measure. The satisfied smile slipped from his face at seeing a man dressed all in black talking to "his girl". He watched him take the slip of paper he had given her from her hand, read it, and then give her another. His was thrown into the trash! He began to burn, slow and steady. How dare that upstart try and move in on his conquest. Who did he think he was anyway?

He took a closer look at the man. He had the good looks of a movie star, but wasn't someone Jared recognized as such. So, he must be a nobody, or a wanna-be. He watched the body language of the bartender. She looked relaxed and was leaning towards the man. She had not done that when he had been talking to her. The man's clothes were not better than his. Hell, he'd chosen a grey sharkskin suit with a dark grey silk shirt, and looked damned good. She could not be thinking that this guy had more money then he did. What was it then?

Leaning forward Jared rested his arms on the table and did not blink as he stared hard at the man's back. He watched the man leave, noticing that he walked with ease and confidence. Jared leaned back, and with one finger motioned to the bodyguard on his left. "Benny, see that man walking out the door, the one all in black?" Benny grunted his ascent and turned his beady, close-set pale blue eyes on the object of his employer's attention. "I want to know who he is. I want to know everything about him. Go find out." With a flick of his wrist, he dismissed his guard and returned his attention to the party around him.

Benny ate up the distance to the front door and walked outside just in time to witness Sam pulling away in his limo. He got the logo off of the door to the Hotel – Casino where Sam was staying. Benny was a lot smarter then he looked, and would do whatever his employer asked of him. Jared paid well and the work was easy, so he would not screw it up. Writing down the information, he returned to the table and gave a nod to Jared to let him know he was on it.

Jared stayed until the sun was coming up, throwing money around and eating up all the attention he was getting. He liked being the center of attention, making sure everyone knew he was a big shot in the oil business, and that he was paid big bucks to put the squeeze on the American public. If he noticed people start to move away from him as he bragged, he gave no indication. He just got louder and more obnoxious as the night wore on. When he got up to leave, the place was half empty, its customers having moved on to another party or finally to bed.

James walked by the bar and tried to catch the eye of the cute bartender, but she avoided his gaze. The man in black was brought back to mind. Jared did not like to be beaten, and he wasn't about to sit back and let it happen now. He had crushed better men than him, and was sure that when he had the information he needed, he was going to take care of this one too.

Jared left the Club and climbed into his long stretch limo, the two women he had came with once again hanging on his arms. Again his bodyguards got into a black SUV and followed him back to the penthouse suite. Jared got out and shrugged off the two clinging women, telling them to get lost. Odd as it was, he wasn't in the mood for sex games tonight.

He rode the elevator up to the penthouse, turning to his bodyguard, Benny, as he said, "Get on it. Now." He went into the bedroom that was the size of most people's apartments, and slammed the door. He flung off his suit, letting it lay in a rumpled pile on the floor where it landed. The maids would pick it up in the morning. That's what they were hired for after all. Let them earn their keep. Jared was not a patient man, and he had gotten as far as he did by beating others to the final punch. He treated his personal life the same. Get ahead and stay there.

A knock on his door had him striding across the room and yanking the door wide. Benny stood there with a few papers in his hand and red-rimmed eyes. Working on the computer had never been one of his strong points. But somehow, tonight he had not had too hard of a time digging up whom the man in black was. As crazy as it sounded, it was almost as if someone was directing him to the right information. He had hacked into databases that he had not even known existed, his fingers flying over the keys with a will of their own. He'd printed out what he found and now handed it over to his boss. He stood still as he watched Jared read over the information he had collected, and hoped his job was finished for the night. He was fried.

Jared nodded his head as a smile spread over his face. It was not a pretty sight, cold and hard as stone. "Good job Benny, good job. Get some sleep. I'll need you to do a job for me, soon. Just as soon as I figure out how to take care of this little "problem."

Jared shut the door in the bodyguard's face and stroked the papers. *Well, well, well,* he thought to himself. This was the first real challenge he had had in a long time. Pest control was one of the things he was really good at. Get rid of the competition. Set a goal and achieve it. At any cost, and leaving no trail that could lead back to him. Jared wanted to know why Sam Barnhart was in Vegas. The number one assassin for the U S Government did not, according to records, surface in the outside world unless something was going down, or someone. Information like this could be very valuable, he was sure. Having some big wig in his debt was always a good deal. An ace in the hole for future use. Jared intended to put his best team on this and in seventy two hours or less, he would know everything Sam was doing and why. Jared loved a challenge and this was going to be a good one.

CHAPTER 32

Leonard rubbed his hands together and laughed in glee as he floated outside the window of James' penthouse. Benny did have help. His help, and with it he had become one of the greatest hackers alive, or dead for that matter. He had worked that computer like a pro. If anyone had come upon him they would have seen his eyes roll back and with only the whites glowing as he sat mindlessly in front of the keyboard. His fingers flew and information was emerged as if by magic, time had no meaning for Benny as he worked and gathered.

When Leonard had finally released him, Benny had looked down at the pages printing and wondered fuzzily what had just happened. He read the reports and was amazed at what he had done. "How could this be?" he wondered. Since when had he been able to work a computer like this? Who was Sam Barnhart anyway, and what did it mean that he was the government's number one assassin? He did not feel capable of deciphering any of what he read.

He had gathered it all together after the printer had stopped spitting out the papers, as if it was a bulimic ridding itself of its last guilty meal, and taken them to the door of the bedroom. His hands and arms had felt heavy as he had raised them to knock, standing dumbly as he waited to be admitted. The door opened and he had given all he had to the waiting hands of James, then had the door slammed in his face for his efforts.

Bastard, he thought tiredly. He really did work for an ungrateful prick. He stumbled away from the door to find his bed and fall face down into an immediate and deep sleep.

For the moment, Leonard would let him sleep. He had worked him hard and did not want to ruin his mind just yet, as he still had need of him and his services. Leonard floated for one more minute as he surveyed his handy work. He remembered, without knowing how he knew, a saying that fit his plans perfectly, *The enemy of my enemy is my friend*. Well for now, James was his new best friend. Leonard had given him the tip of the iceberg, but had yet to reveal that it was he, James, who was the target of the Messenger. No one else.

That ought to provide some amusement for Leonard as he watched the fireworks the information would cause. James was way to into himself to take the information and run, going into hiding as most smart men would do. Not that it would do him any good. Sam was too good to let his target get away. The only way James was leaving was under a coroners, bloody sheet.

If all came to pass, as Leonard planned, there just might be two for the price of one here. He did not care if the world was rid of James, only that he got what he wanted. That was still Ashton Rider. He had every intention of giving Ashton another visit after giving her a few days to think about changing her answer and her attitude towards him and his offer.

His work was finished here for the evening. Tomorrow he would work on directing events in his direction. He spread his arms and slowly twirled in space. Life was good. Well, life was not the right word to describe his existence, but it would have to do for now. He began to rise into the night sky, then on a whim he stopped and looked down on the humans scurrying around like busy ants, believing that their meaningless lives had purpose. He began to grin, and for the fun of it he let loose bolts of lightning followed by rolling claps of thunder. He allowed a couple to hit the towers of two-man made monstrosities and watched with a child's awe the sparks that few, lighting up the night sky with colors and fire. He watched until the last ember faded away and then let himself fade into nothingness, leaving behind destruction and fear.

CHAPTER 33

Sam made it back to his room without incident, and shut his door on the outside world. He took off his clothes and hung them up, preferring a neat and orderly room. He liked to know where his things were at all times. He went to the shower and made quick work of cleaning up. The night spent watching a scum bag like James had left him feeling grimy and dirty. Wrapped in a hotel robe, he made himself a nightcap before going to his computer and settling into a comfy chair, prepared to listen in on James until he went to bed.

Strange as it was, Sam heard very little. Then he remembered James was still at the club and would probably be there for a good while yet. He went back through the tape until he found the footage before James had left for the club. Noting useful, as James sat around drinking and taking phone calls until about 11:30. He had then gotten ready to leave and the room had fallen silent. James had not worn the suit with the device on it, so Sam would have to be satisfied with his surveillance of James at the club.

Sam stretched out on the couch and relaxed until the James party returned. He drifted into a light sleep until the opening of the door in the penthouse suite brought him back to wakefulness. He got up, retrieved a pair of earphones from his room, plugged them in, and was ready to take notes of what he heard.

James barked orders to one of his goons, then slammed a door immediately afterwards. Sam didn't hear much else, except the constant clicking of computer keys and an occasional grunt. He closed his eyes and listened hard. He could hear the constant, barely audible sound of what he thought was someone pacing over the thick carpet. Something was worrying James enough to make him wear holes in the carpet.

Sam had almost given up when he heard the printer start up. Whatever was printing took a while. He heard a knock on a door, then James telling his guard "Benny" "good job" and the slamming of a door again.

After about a minute James opened the closet door and Sam could see him placing some papers in a briefcase hidden on the floor under suitcases. He stood for just a few seconds seeming to be pleased about something, and then, without closing the door, went to the bed, turned off the light, and went to sleep.

Sam knew he was going to get into that room and get a look at those papers. When James left the next time, if he did not reveal what was contained in the briefcase, Sam was going to break in and find out for himself. You could never have too much information about your target. Information was critical and Sam would leave nothing untapped while digging.

Sam left his computer on record and went to catch some zz's himself. He lay down on top of the covers and closed his eyes. He needed to sleep, but before he went all the way under, a picture of Ashton floated in. The way she looked when she smiled, the deep, rich color of her hair, and the haunting green of her eyes. He wanted to reach out his hand and touch her. He wanted to do a lot of things with, and to her. Then another picture came to his mind and he replayed the last conversation they had had. She was dead.

Sam rolled over restlessly and a frown marred his brow. Did he believe her? Was she crazy? Why would she say something that far out? Was there a grain of truth to her story? Sam put the questions on hold and buried them in the back of his mind. Even in sleep, he knew he could not afford to be distracted until he was finished with his business. But once he was done, once he was finished and home, Ashton would get his full attention, and he planned on getting to the bottom of that mystery.

Having made the decision, Sam relaxed and no longer was troubled. He fell into a deep dreamless sleep, and slept like the dead.

CHAPTER 34

Sam woke up rested and refreshed. His mind was clear and firing on all cylinders. His plans for the day were to continue monitoring the goings on of the occupants in the penthouse across the strip. This, he found, was the tedious part of his job, but necessary if he was to succeed and stay alive. He was very meticulous, never overlooking any tidbit of information, no matter how trivial. In the past, he had found that sometimes the littlest thing could make the difference between success and failure. Sam did not fail. He would not start now.

Grabbing a quick can of soda and an even quicker shower, Sam gathered the supplies he would need for the day and turned on the T V, no sound, to pass the time until sleeping beauty's beast rose for the day. Sam sat still, his eyes and ears alert, while he waited. He could hear James snoring like a buzz saw, indicating that it would be a while before anything began to happen over there.

Sam made a few notes while he waited, going over different scenarios in his head, while trying to get a feel of what would work. His notes were in code, so if they were to fall into the wrong hands nothing could be connected with the hit. It was well into the afternoon before the snoring came to a choking halt and Sam observed James rolling over, stretching, sitting up on the edge of the bed, scratching his balls and farting like a feedlot full of fat steers. Sam shook his head and wondered if he did that? Probably.

James got up, stumbled his way into the adjoining bathroom, and turned on the shower. Fog clouds of stream were rolling out of the room before James finally shut off the water. Sam could hear James humming to himself as he completed his toilette, and if he wasn't mistaken, he could pick out the words "I did it my way." Figures, coming from this egotistical pig.

James came back into the bedroom with a towel wrapped low upon his hips and strolled over to the closet. He stopped in front of the mirrored doors and looked at himself from all directions, preening like a banty rooster. Sam could only shake his head at the vanity the man was displaying. Sam hoped with all his might that he would not drop the towel right in front of his camera. No such luck, as low and behold it was whisked away with a dramatic gesture and there James was in all his glory. From where Sam sat, his glory left much to be desired. Maybe that was why James acted the way he did. Trying to make up for his *short comings*. Sam shook his head in wry amusement, who said this job did not have any humor in it?

Sam watched as James got ready for the day. He pulled out a casual polo shirt and a pair of khaki slacks. By the way he was dressing, Sam knew James had no plans to leave the penthouse for the time being. The outfit did not have the splash and price tag James usually wore in public. James took the suit with Sam's spyware on it, and for some reason hung it on the bedroom door. That was lucky for Sam, as he now had a view of the bedroom and the living room at the same time. Cool.

James sat down on the sofa, picked up the phone, and ordered enough room service to feed an army. Bacon, sausage, eggs, pancakes, waffles, toast, omelets, crepes, three different kinds of juices, coffee and milk. And of course he expected it right away. Sam looked at his half empty can of soda and shook his head. If James were going to live longer he would be running towards fat in no time at all eating like that.

Sam came back to attention when he heard James bellow out the name of his bodyguard, Benny, demanding he get his ass in here right now. Sam's lip curled at the way James treated the people who worked for him. He wondered why Benny didn't do this job for him and save the Government his fee. Was any job worth being treated like something found on the bottom of your shoe? Not in Sam's opinion. Sam let that irritant pass as Benny appeared, looking a little worse for wear from the late night before. He stopped before James' seated on the sofa.

"Yes sir?" he said with a question in his voice.

James seemed to tense up a little as he confronted his employee. "Have you found out any thing more about him?" he asked.

Benny stared at James with a question in his eyes, "No sir, nothing since last night. Was there something else you wanted me to look into?"

"Hell yes" he said, giving the man before him a look that portrayed his exact thoughts on Benny's intelligence. "I want you to get a hold of my contacts, give them everything we have, and tell them to dig deep. I expect to know the color of his underwear before the day is out."

Benny opened his mouth to remind James that the person they were researching would not have information floating around like dandelion seeds in the wind, ready to be snatched up by anyone passing by. But, with one look James silenced him and the words were not uttered. "Yes sir," he said turned and left the room.

Sam was left wondering who was so important that James wanted to know all about their life. He sat a little closer to the screen and watched James pace the room. Something was going on, he could tell.

About that time the bell on the penthouse door rang, followed by a soft knock. James looked around, expecting someone to answer the door. When no one came, he let out a disgusted snort, strode to the door, and opened it himself. On the other side of the door was the mountain of food James had ordered. Sam watched as two carts were wheeled into the room. *Christ*, he thought, *you could feed a third world country with all that food*. The two bellboys were rudely waved away by James as he started to lift lids and eat with his fingers. Both seemed to hesitate and waited for James to remember to tip them. James stopped, a strip of bacon half way to his mouth, and stared at the two young men who had made no attempt to vacate the premises. With a grunt he finally realized what they were lingering around for, reached a greasy hand inside his pocket, pulled out some money, and flung it at them. It fell well short, making one of them bend over and retrieve it from the floor. The indignation on the bellhop's face was plain, as he straightened up and mumbled a, "Thank you sir," before both exited the room.

Sam knew that these guys basically worked for tips and they worked hard, having to put up with shit like James had just dished out all the time. To make them bend over and pick up their money from the floor was humiliating and way wrong. If Sam was looking for a reason to off this guy, watching him was giving him all the reasons he needed.

Sam had assumed that the food would be for James and his guards, but he watched as James ate from every dish and made no attempt to include his men. He didn't eat half of what he ordered, but eating sloppily with his hands out of each dish kept him from, even if he wanted to, offering it to anyone else. What was left would go to waste. That thought had probably not even entered his mind.

When he was done, James sat back, pulled out a big fat cigar and lit it up. Sam made a face and let his tongue hang down his chin as he imagined the stench of the smoke now hanging around the ceiling of the room, smelling like someone had lit a bag of dog shit on fire. But James seemed to enjoy his smoke as he slowly puffed away and looked at some unseen spot of interest on the ceiling.

He was interrupted as, once again, Benny entered the room and waited to be acknowledged. James sat up and looked at him, "Well," he said, "what did you find out?" Benny once again gave him some papers, not as many as last night but apparently just as important. James read them and then seemed to read them again. Sam sat up straighter, sensing this was going to be important. He could feel it and see it in James' body language. When he was done, James tapped the papers on his chin for a few minutes, his face going from disbelief, to fear, to anger, then rage, before settling into a cold sinister smile.

He snapped his fingers at Benny and said, "Give me the phone. You know Benny," he said, as Benny walked up to his left elbow, picked up the phone from its cradle, and handed it to him, "there is an old saying. Keep your friends close but your enemies closer." With a ruthless smile on his face, James dialed the phone, sat back on the sofa with his arm draped over the back, and waited for the party he had dialed to pick up. Sam could tell when they did as James snapped up straight and said slowly into the phone, "Give me Sam Barnhart's room."

CHAPTER 35

Sam sat up, his back ramrod straight, on the edge of the sofa. He had not just heard what he thought he had heard, had he? Where had James gotten his name? What did he know about him? With questions whirling around his head, he watched as James waited to be put through to his room.

Sam looked at the ringing phone as if it were a coiled snake ready to strike. Should he answer it? He took a deep breath, gathering his wits about him, and decided he would wait and see if James left a message. Depending on what the message was, Sam would decide what his next move should be. Sam turned his attention back to his laptop and watched as James prepared to leave a message. Sam would have no need to retrieve it, as he was hearing it live.

With a smug look on his face, James stood up and paced the room, as he waited for the rings to stop on his end of the line. He listened to the beep, then began his message, "Hello, Mr. Barnhart. This is Jared James, and I am calling to invite you to the opening of a new club in town that I have an interest in. Although I'm sure you've heard of me," he said as he preened in front of a mirror hanging in the room, "you may be wondering why I am calling you, since we have not met. My staff was instructed to compile a random list of visitors in town this weekend, from which a lucky few were chosen to attend this event. Your name came up in the random drawing," he explained. "You would, of course, be my guest at the opening which is tomorrow night at eight p.m. The name of the club is the "Snake Pit" and is located in the "Top of the World Casino." Dress will be black tie. Your name will be on the guest list at the door, so all you have to do is check in and ask to be directed to my private table. I know this is sort of last minute," he apologized, "but hey, this is Las Vegas, with a winner every minute, right? I hope you will be my guest for a "memorable" evening, Mr. Barnhart. See you then."

James hung up on his end, a smile a mile wide covering his face. "Damn I'm good," he told Benny. "See how it's done? That's the way to get ahead in this world. Think fast on your feet and make sure you always have the upper hand." James puffed out his chest and strutted around the room. He stroked his ego as he went on and on to Benny about how he was the best, and how no one could put anything over on him. When he finally finished bragging, he instructed Benny to go and add Sam's name to the guest list and to make sure Sam was seated at his table.

Benny left the room to play errand boy, glad to get out of there for a while. More hot air was just let out in that room than a hot air balloon could hold, and he had forgotten his hip waders for the crap that went with it. Benny did as he was told, then decided to take a few minutes for himself to just relax and breathe. There were a few times in the last couple of days that he had just not felt like himself. He couldn't explain it, but something felt off inside. He decided to take a walk around the outside of the casino to clear his head and to get a little exercise. After wandering aimlessly for a time, Benny found himself standing at the front entrance, once again. Instead of going inside, he turned and looked up at the casino across the street. His eyes seemed to find and hold on a window partway up its tower. Was there a figure standing at the window? Benny could not tell but that window seemed to hold a fascination for him. He stared at it for a long time, before mentally shaking himself, turning away and entering the Casino at his back, returning to the blowhard he worked for.

Two steps into the bright and pulsating casino floor, Benny stopped short. An idea had just entered his head and, without knowing how he knew it, he knew his boss was to be the next target of the assassin, Sam Barnhart. What to do? He was developing a strong dislike for the gasbag who had hired him, but if he sat on this information the easy money he was making now would dry up and he would have to go looking for another gig. Benny figured he did not have a choice, so he headed to the elevator and made his way to the penthouse suite. Just before he entered he considered one more time what he should do. He felt as if the two sides of him were warring and he was being torn in two. His head ached and he was slightly nauseous. In the end he again decided to let James in on his hunch. Pulling down his jacket and squaring his shoulders, Benny walked in and headed straight to where James stood.

Looking out over the strip stretching before him, James stood with his arms crossed over his chest, rocking slightly back and forth as he thought about what to do with his day. He felt good about having invited Barnhart to the opening tomorrow night. But what should he do after he got him to his table? What should he say? How should he act? How could he make this situation work to his advantage? Hmmmm.

James became aware of someone else in the room. Turning his back on the vista, he faced Benny, and with irritation in his voice he asked, "What do you want? Did you take care of the arrangements I asked you to take care of?"

Benny shuffled his feet and cleared his throat before answering. "Yes sir. Everything is as you wanted."

"Good," James said. He started to turn his back on Benny in dismissal, but before he got all the way around Benny stopped him with a raised hand. "I have something to tell you,

Mr. James," he said. James waited with impatience etched on his face. "It's about Barnhart," he said.

With that one statement he had James full attention. "Well?" James barked as Benny hesitated. "Give it to me."

Benny looked James straight in the eye and almost decided to say nothing. James really was a jerk. Was the world any better off with James in it? Probably not. Once again Benny felt torn in two as he fought with himself. Then, his mouth opened and without really wanting to, the information began to spill out. "It's about Barnhart's next target."

Again he hesitated, and James annoyance with him grew. "Are we playing twenty questions, Benny, or are you going to tell me what you think you know? I don't pay you to make me wait," he said arms crossed, tapping his foot impatiently.

"It's you," Benny finally said. "His next target is going to be you."

"Bullshit," James screamed. "That's just bullshit!" He was waving his arms in the air, pacing the room angrily now. "How do you know this? Have you found some kind of information on that computer of yours that would make you think that? And if not there, who is your information coming from?" Questions flew at Benny and each one was fired like a dart making Benny wince as James got into his face and stood nose to nose with him.

"It's you," Benny said again not backing away from his angry employer, his voice getting stronger with his conviction. "I don't know how, I just know it. You have to trust me, let me do my job. Isn't that what you pay me for, protection? You're next," he said with conviction staring into James' disbelieving eyes.

James stood there listening to Benny and his eyes began to bulge with anger. "Do you have any proof?" he demanded.

"No," Benny shook his head, "but I know."

"You know," James sneered, "you know. Did this information come to you in a dream or did some fortune teller give it to you when she read your palm?" James mocked the bodyguard.

Benny squirmed uncomfortably but stood his ground. "As I said, you have to trust me. I'm telling you the truth."

"Get out!" James bellowed his face turning almost purple with rage. "You dumb asshole, get out of my sight," he waved his arms angrily dismissing Benny from the room.

Benny turned and made his way to the door. As he rested his hand on the doorknob he turned one last time to look at James. James was staring at him, unwilling to consider that what he had been told was true. Benny tried one last time to get it through James' fat head. "Believe me, trust me. If you don't, you're a dead man." Then, shrugging his shoulders, he gave James a look of sympathy as he said, "Knowing Barnhart's reputation, you're probably a dead man any way. You just don't know it yet."

With that, Benny walked out the door, hearing it shut behind him with a ominous click.

CHAPTER 36

James watched Benny walk out the door, wanting to kill him. How dare he try to scare him by lying to him? What did he think he would gain by making such an outrageous statement? No one would dare to try to take him out. He was Jared James. He was a rich and important man. He was somebody. People would notice if he was gone or missing. Of course gone and missing was not what Barnhart was good at. Erased was what the report had said. He erased his targets. James just could not believe, would not believe, he was the reason Barnhart was in Vegas. How outrageous was that idea?

He paced and ranted, going back and forth across the room like a duck in a shooting gallery. Suddenly, in mid stride, James stopped in front of the big glass window showing the strip he had been admiring shortly before. A voice in his head that would not be denied screamed until he felt his head would explode. "It's true, it's all true. YOU'RE NEXT! Think, what are you going to do about this? You have been given one chance to beat Barnhart to the punch and save yourself. What are you going to do?"

"I don't know," James repeated over and over. "I don't know what to do. I can't think." All of a sudden James fell to the floor, face down and flat as a pancake. *Oh my God,* he thought, *OH MY GOD. I've been walking in front of the window and I could have been shot. Just like in the movies, a bullet being fired from a long way off and coming through the window to splatter my head all over the walls.*

Deciding he had to get away from the windows, Jared crawled across the floor, hugging the walls, looking like a crab, his arms and legs pulling and pushing, with his rear poking up as if it was suspended by wire from the ceiling. He made it to the corner of the room and sat with his back pressed tightly against the wall. Sweat dripped down his shirt collar and a dark stain was beginning to grow in his pants. Fear did funny things to people, making them cower, or in some, charge into the fray, having no plan, just reacting. It seemed James was in the first group. Weeping, shaking, and being unable to think straight, he sat where he was, not moving, not thinking, until the same little voice once again intruded.

"Get up, you coward. Get moving and make a plan. Make it a good one. Use the opportunity you have tomorrow night to your advantage. Barnhart does not suspect anything and if he shows at the opening, you could have someone get to him when the music is loud and the crowd is three sheets to the wind. No one would notice a man slumped in the corner, until it was too late to figure out who had done the deed."

Yeah, yeah that sounded good. That sounded just like it might just work. Good thing he came up with it, James thought to himself. Some of his confidence and bravado returned, as he stood up on his slightly shaking legs. He looked around the room and made sure he was alone. He was good. No one had witnessed his moment of weakness. "No, not weakness," he told himself. He had not been himself for a minute, that was all. Something had come over him, something he could not explain. He'd just pretend this little incident had never happened. In fact he was now sure it never had. It had just been a waking dream.

James looked down at his clothes and cringed. He hurried into his room, stripped off the wet, stained offenders and took a hot shower. He needed it to calm his nerves and marshal his thoughts. He spent a long time under the stream of hot water, emerging only when the water had turned cold and he was totally in control again.

Emerging from the bathroom, he was no longer scared. In fact he was just the opposite, he was angry. He was past angry. No one was going to off him. No one was going to even get the chance to try. Sam Barnhart was the one going down.

James pulled out his cell phone and dialed a number. When the call connected, he did not bother with a greeting, but barked his order into the phone. "Get in here, now!" He did not wait for an answer from the party on the other end, but snapped the phone closed almost before the command was completed. A full thirty seconds later, the door was opened and both of his guards came in. He looked from one to the other before deciding which one he needed.

"You," he said pointing at Benny, "stay."

"You," he said to the other one, "go, but I'll need you later."

Benny stayed where he was until they were alone. "What do you need?" he asked.

Jared stood before him, his legs spread, arms folded over his chest, brows drawn together in a frown, a challenging look in his cold eyes. "Since you are so sure that Barnhart is going to hit me, I'm giving you the assignment of taking him out. Tomorrow night at the opening. I want it quiet," he said. "When the dancing is going strong and the drinking has almost everyone on their heels, I want him stuck and left in a booth. Make it look like he is just sleeping or passed out when you carry him to the booth," he instructed Benny.

Benny looked at James, thoughts running rampant in his brain as he absorbed what James had just instructed him to do. "He wanted him to kill a man for him. Guess who was going to take the fall if it was discovered he was the one to put the knife in Barnhart? It wouldn't be him," Benny vowed.

"At least not alone. He would sing like a bird and take James down with him."

Benny looked at James and said out loud, "Sure boss, I'll do this for you."

James had never had a doubt and nodded his head. He opened his mouth to speak but Benny interrupted him before he could begin.

"Quarter mil," he said.

"What?" James asked in disbelief.

"You heard me," Benny said. "I want a quarter of a million dollars to do what you want done or you can find yourself another boy."

James' eyes closed to a mere slit and his face took on a reddish hue. "I already pay you a sinful wage. Now you want more?"

Benny stood his ground and replied, "You want me to commit murder for you. That's going to cost you more then the paltry amount you pay me now."

James was over a barrel, and he knew Benny knew it too. It was too late to hunt up someone who would kill for hire. Like Barnhart. James knew Benny, that slimy parasite, had him by the short hairs, and there was nothing he could do about it.

"Fine," he said. "Done. Just do the job and don't tell me any of the details. I don't want to know." He turned his back and walked across the room trying to dismiss his, now, partner in crime.

But Benny wasn't done yet. He followed James, coming up close enough behind him that James could feel his hot breath on his neck. "You're in this up to your neck and don't you forget it," he said quietly. "I fry, you fry. I'll pick up the money tomorrow morning, have it ready."

With that, it was Benny's turn to walk out of the room with the last word being his.

"One more thing," James said just as Benny reached the door. "I want you to make sure, right before Barnhart takes his last breath, that he knows it was me that did this to him. You tell him, you tell him Jared James is the one sending him to hell."

CHAPTER 37

Leonard was exhausted. Directing Benny had been draining, but getting Jared James to understand he was Sam's next target, and to get him off his butt to do something about it, had been worse than walking through hell's fires. How the man had gotten as far in the business world as he had, was beyond Leonard's comprehension. The man was a coward and an idiot. Leonard had had to pull him up off the floor, where he was blubbering in fear, and plant the idea to take Sam out in his head. If it had been left up to James, he would still be laying on the floor wetting himself, an easy target for Sam Barnhart, or anyone else for that matter.

Leonard stretched his small wings and his even smaller arms. He opened his mouth and yawned so big that it caused a small back draft on the world below. He needed to rest and be ready for the night. But before he could, he had one more puzzle to work out.

When he had been *helping* Benny, he had felt some resistance in Benny. Resistance that should not have been there. Where had that come from? Was Benny stronger then he looked? Or, were there forces at work trying to crash Leonard's plans? Leonard dismissed the thought that Saul could, once again, be challenging his plan. He had taken care of that obstacle, hadn't he? It was just not possible that any other immortal would care about the situation. They had their own assignments and problems to worry about.

A trickle of apprehension lingered in Leonard's mind, as the new day began to unfold around him. He felt weary after his recent intervention with Benny and James, and decided to take some time to recoup. He would have to leave the humans to their own devices for a while. *How much trouble could they cause on their own, anyway*?

CHAPTER 38

Sam was glued to the computer screen, watching James pace his room. Back and forth, back and forth he walked, until Sam began to feel dizzy just watching him. He listened as James ordered his goon to add his name to his guest list for the opening, and bragged about being smart and staying on top of things. The bodyguard, Benny, had left the room, obviously to do his bosses bidding.

Sam waited impatiently until Benny returned, eager to see what their next conversation would hold for him. Benny confirmed Sam was on the guest list and then seemed to have something important to tell James. Sam listened intently, as Benny said it had something to do with him. Sam leaned in closer to the screen, sure that it was going to be something very important and something he was going to want to hear.

The screen went black. The lights went out in Sam's room, even the cheesy clock on the table was not blinking 12, 12, 12. The electricity had gone out. Sam flung himself back on the sofa, not believing what was happening. At a surely critical moment, he was left in the dark, literally.

Sam sat there thinking about the recent turn of events. It seemed James had discovered who he was, and now the question was, how much did he know? Sam wasn't worrying about how he found out, that would be left for later. Now the question was, did James know what he did for a living, and if he did, did he know he was next on the Messenger's list? Sam doubted his current plan had been uncovered, but decided it would be to his advantage to play it like it had. He would assume that James knew he was a man living on borrowed time. Sam got up and walked over to the window. He looked out on the strip, not really seeing the busy scene below. He could call off the hit for now, but decided that the circumstances were perfect and the timing felt right to him. This turn of events, however, changed everything. The element of surprise was no longer his. His only advantage would be that James' would not be aware that Sam knew he'd been discovered. Sam would have to be on his guard from here on out, increasing his risk a thousand fold.

Having James aware of his plan, also limited the ways the hit could be completed. Sam's employers wanted it public and messy, so a rifle from a distant window was out. Poison could be long and drawn out, causing great pain before death, but not necessarily public if James died in his penthouse bed. Not what was wanted. A car bomb would do the trick, but innocent bystanders could be taken out along with James. Not acceptable.

Sam knew that a knife, up close and personal, was the best method for his current assignment. Knives were deadly when placed in the proper spot in the body, left a gory mess, and using them in public, if done correctly, allowed the assailant plenty of time to disappear undiscovered. So a knife it would be.

The club opening would be the perfect place to take James out. Lots of people, noise, booze, and cover. The only wrinkle would be that his name would be on the guest list, and the police were going to have to interview everyone on the list once the deed was done. He would have to do the job, get rid of the knife and clean up, then be sitting calmly enjoying the party when the police arrived. Or maybe he could just do it and then walk right out the front door before anyone even realized what had happened. That sounded better to him.

He would pack his things into his car this afternoon and be ready to leave at a moments notice. He would be long gone before James was discovered and the alarm was raised.

Again, he would change little about his appearance, a man dressed in black blending in with the crowd. When questioned about his clothes, witnesses would only remember, "A man in a tux, like everyone else. What did he look like? It was dark I couldn't tell. Color of hair and eyes? Again it was dark." Yes, the opening should be a good place to hide in plain sight.

Sam walked into the bedroom and pulled out one of his small bags. He carefully opened it and removed its contents. Spread before him on the bed, were three very different knives. One big, wide and heavy. No good. It went carefully back in the bag. The next one was smaller, but still too big and did not fold up. Back in the bag. The last was what he was looking for. More like a gang bangers switch blade, hidden by the handle until a button was pushed, releasing the long, pointy, sharp as a razor, blade.

It was clean, and mirrored Sam's assessing eyes back at him. Bright blue, cold and deadly, they looked at the blade from every angle to make sure there would be no tell tale links to him. No fibers to match up. No prints to dust for, and no DNA, except for James', when it was over.

Sam took the blade apart, cleaning it down to the bare insides, then putting it back together, again cautious about leaving nothing to trace it back to him. He wrapped it in a soft cloth, placing it on top of the dresser until it was time to go to the club.

He spent the afternoon packing, then checked his computer to see if he had missed anything from the recording device. Why, he did not know, because he had no electricity for the better part of the day. Some glitch in the system, they told him when he inquired as to the cause of the outage.

Sam took his bags and other items down to the car, preparing for his exit from Sin City. He planned on driving his car to the other side of the strip, leaving it parked about a block away from James' club opening. Close enough to get to easily, but far enough away to stay off camera. Sam had thought about the cameras in the club also. A small jammer which would fit in his pants pocket would take them out, leaving his hit unrecorded. All that remained was to shower and get ready for the evening.

Realizing he still had two hours before he had to leave for the opening, he sat on the sofa and went over his plan one more time, examining it in detail to see if it had any flaws or any chance of being thwarted. He would walk confidently into the casino and take his place at James' table. Sickening as it seemed to him, he would suck up to his host, stroking his huge ego until he had James believing he was just another of his many drooling groopies looking for a step up in life. When he had gained James' confidence, he would, without any regrets, deflate that ego and enjoy watching the look in the man's eyes as he realized he had been duped. Even though he wouldn't be able to stick around and watch the bastard die, he was more then satisfied that his plan would work.

Going around his room, he wiped every surface until it shone, freeing them from any telltale prints that he may have left on them. Using a small hand held vacuum that he had brought with him, he made sure there were no hairs left behind, a sure way to trace DNA if one was left in some inconspicuous place. His room was spotless when he was done. Sam would clean the bathroom after he was finished getting ready. No hairs left in the drain there either, no prints under the toilet seat or on the wall beside it. Clean everything. Sam was the best, and with some of his jobs his skills had been pitted against the best csi's law enforcement had to offer. He always left them with no leads and no clues as to his identity. This time would be no different.

It was time for Sam to get ready. He showered, cleaned the bathroom, got dressed, put all of his things by the door, and made one final trip around his "home away from home" for the last few days. Sam nodded his head in satisfaction, deciding he was going to make someone a great wife some day.

At that thought, Ashton popped into his head, causing Sam to catch his breath with her remembered beauty. He stood still in the middle of the room, and watched as her soft hand floated up and caressed his cheek. "Take care of yourself Sam. Come back to me," she said in a soft and husky voice. Then, as suddenly as she had appeared, she faded away, leaving a tingling sensation on Sam's cheek where her cool fingers had been. He shook his head, and with an effort, once again put thoughts of Ashton away in his heart.

He felt in his pocket for his jammer and his knife. Both were there. He would be taking the card for the room with him, destroying it somewhere between here and home. Walking to the door, he picked up his remaining bags and set them outside in the hall. As he pulled the door shut behind him, he discreetly wiped both sides of the knob.

Sam felt good about tonight, confident that all would go as planned. As he turned down the hallway, Sam again thought he heard Ashton's voice, only this time it was not soft and smoky. It was dark and filled with warnings as she spoke only three words, "Watch your back!"

CHAPTER 39

Ashton had spent the week alone, seemingly anchorless. She drifted around her cabin, doing light chores, and took long walks in the mountains, taking in as much beauty as her senses could absorb. Still there seemed to be something missing, and that something was Sam.

She longed to look into those teal blue eyes and see her own reflection, as he studied her from beneath those thick dark lashes of his. She missed his crooked smile and that smoldering lust that lingered just beneath the surface as he tried to deny his attraction to her. SHE WANTED SAM. She had come to terms with that realization and planned to do everything in her power to make him feel the same about her, if he ever decided to come back.

He had left on a bad note, and Ashton longed for another chance to fix what was wrong between them. She debated about walking over to his cabin to see if he had returned, but was leery of going over there again, for fear of running into Leonard. The last conversation she had had with the little angel had left her shaken and angry. Because of him her life would be over in a little over a month, and she felt cheated and wronged. She knew there was nothing she could do to change the outcome, but that did not make her feel any more forgiving towards him.

Saul, on the other hand, had tried to help her, so she had tried everything she could think of to summon him. He was the only one who had answers to her questions, but she had not been able to reach him. Where was he? Had he done his job and now she was on her own? Somehow that did not seem like him. He had seemed warm and compassionate to her situation.

As Ashton sat at her kitchen table in the cabin, she realized that she hadn't eaten much since Sam left. She had lost her appetite for the food they had bought on their one night together. Even the knowledge that she pretty much could eat anything without the worry of having to take the extra weight off, could not compel her to eat. The food, in her mind, had been bought to share with Sam. And he was not here.

That fact was brought to mind over and over as the days dragged on for her. She wondered where he was and what he was doing. She had a nagging feeling deep down that something was going wrong with him, and she could not get to him to help. Her dreams at night were filled with him in danger, of him being hurt, and of him being lost to her forever. If she kept going the way she was, she would drive herself crazy in no time flat.

She tried to keep busy with her walks, and she even tried her hand at arranging the rocks she collected into a garden. It had turned out okay, but her heart and mind were just not in it. Ashton knew, without a doubt, that she was meant to be with Sam, making it all the harder to bide her time until he returned.

He would return, she knew it. The question was, when? Would it be in time for them to be together before her time was up? She hoped so. Letting out a deep sigh, Ashton went to sit on her back steps, trying to soak up the late morning sunshine. She closed her eyes and raised her face to the light. It was warm and gentle on her cheeks, seeping into her body and making her feel relaxed and drowsy. She leaned back against the steps, closed her eyes, and opened her mind to her surroundings.

She heard small animals scurrying in the undergrowth, she heard birds tending their young chicks, and she heard light footsteps approaching her house. She slowly opened her eyes, her breath stopping in her chest as she saw Sam standing before her.

The breeze gently lifted his hair to play around his face in soft curls, reminding Ashton of a child's locks with their shine and softness. His teal blue eyes locked with hers, and what she saw in their depths made her pulse gallop and her tongue feel thick. His lips were slightly parted as he drew deep breaths into his chest. His shirt was unbuttoned down the front, giving Ashton glimpses of his bare chest as it rose and fell with those breaths. She caught teasing peeks of the dark mat that lightly covered his hard belly, and that line of soft darkness that pointed like an arrow downward to disappear inside the waistband of his old jeans. The top button was undone and the faded material molded itself to his hips and thighs like a second skin. It covered his long legs and lay in folds on the tops of his worn boots.

He looked so good that Ashton had trouble finding the words to welcome him home, so she simply raised her open arms in an invitation for him to come to her. He moved towards her in unhurried strides, his eyes locked with hers as he came towards her. Ashton could sit still no longer and rose to meet him as he stopped before the bottom step. She raised her hands and, with care, slipped them inside the open folds of his shirt. Her hands felt the heat and smoothness of his skin, as they travelled from his shoulders around to his hard stomach. His stomach jumped and quivered at the light touch of her hands. She let her thumbs slide inside the front of the waistband of his jeans, then slowly circle around to his sides. She let them climb his sides and, again, brought them to his shoulder caps under his shirt.

The shirt became a barrier she wanted gone, so she pushed it down his arms, following its progress with her hands until she reached his fingertips. She helped the shirt slide from his body and let it fall to the dirt, forgotten in her pursuit of the treasure beneath it.

She let her eyes devour the perfection in front of her. The colors, the texture, the expanse of his naked torso filled her vision, until she could see nothing else. She moved a step closer, until the distance that separated them was barely a whisper. She let her lips rest on his flesh, and when that was not enough, she let them travel the hills and valleys of his masculine form, tasting the saltiness of his sweat, feeling the heat roll off him, breathing in the scent that was uniquely his. She knew his body, his smell, his taste, the feel of his skin as well as she knew her own.

She let her hands move to the buttons of his jeans, as her lips continued their journey of discovery. She opened each one slowly, stopping to give small feather like caresses, prolonging the anticipation of freedom. When all had been undone, she inched her hand inside to find he wore no cloth between himself and his jeans. She had the freedom of touching him and releasing him into her waiting hands. He filled them with his length and girth, hot and heavy, smooth to her exploring touch. Her attention had him jumping with reaction and growing in size.

She raised her head from his chest and, immediately, her lips were captured greedily by his. He had been waiting for her to get her fill of his body, to become familiar, to realize this was her home, but he was tired of waiting. Gently he gathered her into his arms and held her tightly against his bare chest, not as if she was breakable but with strength and with their whole bodies touching and learning.

Ashton buried her hands in his so soft hair and held his head still while she rained kisses, soft as feathers, over his face, loving the roughness of his whiskers against her sensitive lips.

She wanted more, slowly moving against him, letting him know without words what she wanted, what she needed, what her intentions were. She pleaded with her body for him to come to her, releasing them both from the restraint they had kept over themselves.

And Sam did. His hands rode up her sides, taking her shirt with them until she was bared to the sun and to his gaze. She felt no embarrassment as his eyes feasted hungrily on her nakedness. Sam placed his hands under her arms and lifted her until they were eye to eye. Lowering his head slightly, he buried his face between her breasts, breathing in so deep that Ashton was sure her scent was permanently imprinted in his senses.

His lips and hands began a journey of discovery of their own, and she arched her back and dug her nails into his shoulders with the pleasure it brought her. She wanted it all, and she wanted it now. They'd have time later to go slow and be more detailed in their lovemaking, but for now she needed him inside her.

She dropped her hands and pushed his jeans down over his lean hips. Down until they could go no farther without taking off his boots. There was no time for that, it could come later. She took his hands in hers and placed them on her hips, urging him to imitate her actions, and he did, pushing her jeans down her long silky legs. Hastily, she kicked off her shoes so she could be free of the denim that stood in the way of how she wanted Sam.

When she was free, she rose on her tiptoes and gave a jump, letting Sam catch her bottom in his hands, as she wrapped her legs around his waist. She opened herself to him, letting him lower her until she was filled with him to the point of bursting. She put her hands on his shoulders and leaned back, locking eyes with him as they found their rhythm together, relying on his strength to keep them both upright.

Ashton had never felt this connection with anyone else, and wanted to burst with the happiness she was feeling. She began to draw herself inward as both neared their peak. She felt herself tighten around him and the sun began to fragment and burst behind her eyelids as she arched her back bringing herself more flush against him. She held on while wave after wave rolled through her and finally flung her to rest on its shores, Sam beside her.

She could not move and her eyelids felt too heavy to lift. She lay where she was, in no rush to end the encounter. When her breathing began to resemble something close to normal, she opened her eyes to gaze at Sam and to tell him what she was feeling. But instead, she screamed.

She screamed long and loud, as the face before her was not Sam's, but Leonard's.

CHAPTER 40

Leonard needed to rest and regain his strength, but he had one more thing to do before he could. He wanted to see Ashton and try to convince her one more time that they should be together for all time. He wanted to see if she had changed her mind about coming with him now, instead of making him wait until her time on earth was up. He would try to make her see that they would have fun, running through the clouds playing tag, hide and seek, and anything else they wanted to. She did not need Sam. He had to make her see that.

He appeared at her house in the mountains, and found her reclining on the steps of her back porch. She seemed to be asleep but he heard a moan escape her lips and thought she might be in pain. Standing over her, he tried to read her thoughts but could not understand what she was dreaming. He knew she was with Sam in her dream, but what they were doing was beyond his knowledge. As he watched Ashton, her cheeks became rosy and her breathing grew faster. Suddenly she slumped back against the step and her body seemed to have no bones as it melted against the steps like liquid silk.

Leonard continued to stand over her until her eyes slowly opened. Instead of the greeting he hoped she'd have for him, she screamed. She screamed so loud, the echo bounced off the mountains and continued long after no more sound came from her throat. Her face had lost the sleepy look of contentment, and was now etched in shock.

"What are you doing here?" she demanded, her voice coming across sharp as a whip. "How darc you come to spy on me!" Ashton was embarrassed at the thought that Leonard may have been able to see into her mind and her dream, robbing her of her most intimate thoughts. It was her fantasy and hers alone. He had no right to sneak into her mind and share any of what was there. All she wanted to do was to bask in the sweetness of her desires and instead she woke to find this little imp in front of her. "What do you want?" she asked again.

Leonard straightened up to his full height, trying to appear threatening, and looked down at Ashton. "I have come to see if you have changed your mind and will come with me now. I have given you ample time to consider my request and become accustomed to the idea." He puffed out his chest, seeming more mature and bigger then he really was. "What say you?" he demanded.

Ashton sat with her mouth open and found it hard to answer the little booger. He did not take no for an answer, did he? Either that or he had short-term memory loss. She distinctly remembered telling him, in no uncertain terms, that she did not want anything to do with him. Yet, here he was again, intruding in her life.

Ashton stood up slowly and she, too, rose to her full height. "I will tell you this one more time," she said facing Leonard and speaking slowly and clearly as if to an ignorant child. "Because of what you have taken from me, I want nothing to do with you. Not now, not ever. Am I making myself clear?" she asked in an angry voice.

Leonard could not believe he was hearing her correctly. His eyes, as they bore into Ashton's, began to take on the reddish hue that had been present so much of late. "Do you understand what you are refusing?" he demanded. "Do you even care what I am capable of doing to Sam?" he threatened her with what he knew she held most dear.

"What will you do to him?" she cried, "take his life too? You do realize that that would not be such a bad thing for me, right? I mean if you want to kill him, go ahead. That way I won't have to be without him for a lifetime. We can be together in eternity as soon as my time here is up."

Leonard's face took on a look of surprise before he smirked at Ashton's naïveté. "What makes you think Sam will be allowed to be with you and not be sent to Hell where he belongs?" he asked.

It was Ashton's turn to be surprised, and her face lost all of its color as the realization of what Leonard said hit home. She had not considered the fact that they would not be allowed to be together after they both passed from this earth.

Leonard watched Ashton's reaction and knew he had struck home. She had not thought about that, had she? Leonard smiled rather nastily. He was sure she would now consent to his plans and he reached out his hand to her. "Take my hand and come with me. Sam will be left alone if you do."

Ashton felt confused, but thought fast on her feet. "No," she said. "No!" this time with more conviction. "You will not blackmail me with your threats towards Sam. Sam will be alright and you will not be able to do anything about it." She stomped her foot and crossed her arms over her chest as she delivered the last sentence.

Leonard knew anger beyond anything else he had felt before. "You think not?" he said, his eyes turning blood red as tears of rage and disappointment ran down his cheeks like lava. "Because of your refusal, Sam will know pain. Pain that will be worse then anything you can imagine. You have sealed his fate and no pleading on your part will save him now," he vowed.

Ashton was shaken but would not let Leonard see. "Saul will have something to say about your threats," she bluffed. "He won't let you harm Sam."

Leonard's laughter started quietly and grew until Ashton covered her ears, so great was the volume. "Saul is dead," Leonard boasted. "Dead because he tried to interfere with what I wanted. You will get no help from him. Mine was the only mercy you should have asked for. But that door is now closed to you. Sam will suffer beyond anything you can dream of. And it is now your fault."

Leonard began to rise up into the sky, but then stopped, looked down at Ashton and left her with one last barb. "Think of that as you enjoy what little time you have left on this earth, the hell of your own making."

In a blinding flash of light he was gone.

CHAPTER 41

Saul grew stronger with every second that passed. His injuries had been severe and the road to wellness had been long, but he felt the end was in sight. His pain was now almost nonexistent. At first, so much of his concentration had been used to block the rolling waves of pain, that nothing else had been able to get through to his mind. But things were changing. He was able to open his mind now to the things and beings that needed his attention and guidance. The first being Ashton.

He had had to leave her at a critical time, her questions unanswered and with no help in directing her relationship with Sam. Time had been short then, and was even shorter now. Saul concentrated on Ashton and brought her into focus. He could see her as if he were standing right beside her. He was unprepared to see who it was that she was talking to. It was Leonard. Why was he with Ashton? It was not allowed.

Saul focused harder to bring their voices in clearer, and listened as Leonard tried to persuade Ashton to come with him, giving up Sam and the time she had left on earth. He was dismayed when it became apparent that this was not the first time the two had met. What was this he was hearing? Leonard was threatening to hurt Sam if Ashton did not do as he asked? It seemed Ashton had learned a few things on her own while he had been busy, for she rightly told Leonard that he, Saul, would not allow any harm to come to Sam or Ashton.

What he heard next held him paralyzed. Leonard boasted that it had been he who had attacked an unsuspecting Saul from behind, leaving the older angel dead. This bit of information answered one of Saul's questions. Why he was still here. If a stronger, full grown immortal had attacked Saul, as Leonard had done, it would have ended Saul's existence instead of just injuring him.

Saul felt the sharp blade of betrayal as it slid into his being. He had taken the young angel under his wing, and tried to be a good role model for him. He had shown him the error of his ways with Ashton, and had felt he had gotten through to him.

Leonard had fooled him. And he had bought it. Saul believed in the good in everyone and tended to believe what was told to him as truth. He did not believe in retaliation, but this time, this time he would break his own code. Before he could help Ashton, he was going to have to take care of the root of the problem, and that was Leonard.

Saul's body began to vibrate, ever increasing in speed. When it seemed he could withstand no more, his wings burst open, sparks flew, and a light to rival the sun burst forth from his being. He hung suspended in the air, with wings outstretched and arms spread as if to embrace the world. Bringing his arms to his sides, Saul folded his wings in close to his body and hurtled towards earth, faster then the human eye could see. A fiery tail shot out from behind him as he began his search for Leonard. Leonard thought Saul was defeated, he should have known better. Saul was nowhere near defeated. In fact Saul was back. Back with a vengeance.

CHAPTER 42

Sam didn't go directly from his hotel to the opening, but drove his car, as planned, and parked it a block south of the Top of the World Casino. Locking his car, he got out and walked a few blocks in both directions, checking out the media coverage and the police presence. He walked around the outside of the casino, paying special attention to the doors leading to the street. He didn't see any extra security coverage on any of them. Feeling satisfied that exiting the casino would be no problem once his task was completed, he made his way into the Casino.

Sam kept his head down and melted with a group of well-dressed men and women, whom he assumed were also attending the opening. He was correct, as they all made their way to the Snake Pit. There was a brief wait at the entrance to the club, as each person's name was confirmed with the guest list. Sam waited his turn, occupying himself with observing and listening to the chatter exchanged by those in line. Most was just drivel, but Sam found some of it interesting, as a good many did not seem to want to be here. *So why come,* he thought. Was *it such a big deal to be seen at an event like this?* To some, appearance was everything. Look at his host for the evening, a prime example of a publicity seeker if there ever was one.

Sam was finally at the front of the line where he had a nice, unexpected surprise. One of the employees checking names and providing security for the evening, was none other than Tyrone, the bouncer who had let him into the club where he'd first scoped out James. Sam waited until Tyrone looked up from his clipboard, then he smiled and stuck out his hand.

"Hey man, nice to see you here," Sam greeted him.

Tyrone looked a little taken back that a guest would talk to him let alone offer to shake his hand. When he finally met Sam's gaze, recognition dawned in his own deep brown eyes. "Nice to see you again, sir," his bass voice rumbled. "If you need anything this evening, you come find me. I'll take care of you," he promised Sam.

Sam nodded his head and when he withdrew his hand from Tyrone's ham-sized paw, the hundred dollar bill that had been discretely hidden there was gone. Sam always hedged his bets, and he just might need Tyrone's help before this night was over.

The lighting in the club was dim, allowing for an ambience of discretion, as Sam made his way inside. He was met by a tall, good-looking, young man who asked Sam if he could show him to his seat. Sam gave him James' name, and was led to a table situated right up front and to the left of a small, raised platform. It had a podium and a mike on it, from which Sam expected his host would be speaking when the festivities began. His guide motioned to a chair at the table which would allow Sam a good view of all the activities going on inside the club. Sam tipped the young man and thanked him for his assistance.

He glanced around at the others already seated at the table, recognizing a few actors who had had some minor success in films. Unbuttoning his tux jacket, Sam took his seat. He made eye contact with his host, Jared James, mentally preparing himself for the upcoming evening. The game of cat and mouse had begun, but who was the cat and who was the mouse?.

"Mr. James," Sam said as he rose out of his seat and extended his hand to James.

James hesitated a fraction of a second before he took the hand and shook it.

Sam had to hide his distaste, as James' grip was wimpy and slightly damp. "Wus," he thought.

James played dumb as he waited for Sam to regain his seat before he asked, "And you are?"

"Sam Barnhart," Sam replied. "I received a message that I was to be your guest tonight at this opening. Some kind of lottery pick it seems, and I was one of the lucky winners. Right place, right time, I guess," Sam told James as he made eye contact with the man.

"Oh yes," James said in a friendly tone of voice that was more for the other guests at the table than Sam, "congratulations, we're glad you could join us. The two locked eyes for a few seconds then James asked, "What do you think of the Snake Pit so far?"

Sam took his time as he let his eyes roam the room. It was too loud and pretentious for his taste, exactly the kind of place he would have avoided like the plague on a normal basis. "It's great," he lied convincingly. "Really great. I was very surprised to receive an invitation to the opening tonight. Before you told me about the lottery pick, I thought it might have been because you'd heard I was looking for a new investment opportunity while I was in town," Sam told him. "Either way, I can't tell you how honored I am to finally get to meet *the* Jared James. I've read and seen a lot about you in the media. You are a very important man in this country," Sam said stoking James ego. He paused to give Jared a chance to speak. The sticky sweet tone of his own voice was beginning to gag him. He raised his glass of champagne and took a small sip trying to wash the foul taste it left from his tongue.

James looked closely at Sam. He was trying to figure out if the information Benny had given him could have been a mistake. Sam did not seem like a killer to him, and was showing no signs of being uncomfortable in his presence. In fact, he seemed to be rather in awe of the great Jared James. And rightly so, he decided sitting back in his own chair.

"Well now, Sam," James said in a boastful tone, "it's always a pleasure to meet a fan of mine. I don't know much about you, but if you are looking for some place to lay some money, this little gem right here," he said motioning his hand around the club, "would be a great place to place your bet." Having made the offer, James sat back to see where the conversation would go.

Did Sam really have money, he contemplated. The report given to him had said nothing about his financial situation. James was always looking for good investors to boost his projects and self-image.

Sam smiled and looked eagerly at James. "You know," he said in the same ass-kissing tone of voice, "that would be worth a look. To be in a business venture with you would be an honor." James preened as Sam continued to pour on the syrup, "You're bigger in real life than you appear on TV, and much younger looking also. I just can't believe I'm at your table." He shook his head as if he just couldn't believe his good fortune, then told James, "I usually do all my business behind the scenes, but this seems like a great opportunity, right here and now."

Jared's gaze became a little keener, as if he was trying to decide if there was a double meaning behind the words Sam had just delivered. Did he mean that he was going to try to kill him right here, right now, tonight at this public event? Jared continued to look at the man across the table trying to read his expression. It seemed open and a bit awestruck to him. He had always prided himself on reading people and all he was getting were good vibes from this Sam Barnhart. Was Benny wrong?

"Well, Sammy, can I call you Sammy?" Jared asked

"Sure," Sam replied thinking to himself that no one called him that and lived. "You can call me anything you want as long as it's not late for dinner." Both laughed falsely at the old joke.

At that moment James' attention was drawn away as an older man approached the table and whispered in James' ear. Nodding his head, James returned his attention to the table, focusing his attention on the other guests at the table. While he was preening for them like a peacock on parade, Sam watched him and made his own evaluations as to how much James knew. He had seen James look more closely at him when he'd dropped a hint to his intentions. Jared knew something, that was for sure. But what and how much? Sam decided it did not matter how much James suspected, the hit was a go.

For the next hour Sam and James sparred with each other, Jared trying to get information from Sam and Sam sucking up to James so much that he was sure he was going to have chapped lips the next day from all the time they spent on James' ass. Sam thought it was kind of funny that no other unknown people, besides himself, had come up to James and thanked him for an invitation to the opening. So, he surmised, the lie about the promotion was just that, a lie to get him here and watch him. Maybe James was trying to put Sam at ease as he tried to reverse the tables.

The hour reached eleven as James rose from the table and stepped up to the podium. He was met there by the same older guy as before, and, after a brief conversation, the older man stepped up to the mike and turned it on.

"Good evening ladies, gentleman, and friends," he smiled as he welcomed the audience. "We would like to welcome you to this special event tonight, the grand opening of the Snake Pit." Applause came from around the room as all turned their attention to the spot lit platform. "I will personally guarantee that this will be a night you will never forget." James eyes looked over the crowd, his eyes settling on Sam.

Amen, thought Sam, *amen*.

CHAPTER 43

Sam had applauded with the rest, and now sat calmly in his seat listening to the old guy's introductory speech. It was time to start looking for an opening to finish the job. All Sam needed was an instant in time to bury the knife deep, give it a twist, pull it out, and then walk away. He was in no hurry. You never rushed a job or things could end up going very, very wrong.

Sam listened with half an ear while the old duffer praised the club and its patrons. *Blah, blah, blah,* he thought as he droned on for another fifteen minutes before Sam's attention was caught and held.

"Again, thank you all for coming. Now I would like to introduce to you a man who had a large part in making this wonderful place a reality. A man who really needs no introduction, Mr. Jared James." He motioned toward James and stepped away from the mike.

The applause was light and seemed somewhat unenthusiastic to Sam, as James stepped up to the mike. Seeming not to notice, James held his hands in the air like he was a politician and turned from side to side begging for attention. After the smattering of applause had stopped, James ran his hands through his hair, pulled down his jacket, and bent towards the mike.

"Thank you, thank you all for coming," he said. "As my esteemed colleague mentioned, we are very glad to have all of you with us tonight to celebrate the opening of the Snake Pit. I personally have invested a huge amount of money in this place to insure it's success, and your presence here tonight is a tribute to the success of our plan."

He paused for a few seconds, before continuing, "I'd like to take a few minutes to explain what MY vision for this club is. This club will be a place for the *elite* of society to come and enjoy the best food, the best drinks, and the best entertainment any club can offer. No riff raff will be allowed into this club," he emphasized with a look of distaste on his face. "Members must meet a certain level of financial success to be allowed to enter. They will be allowed to bring guests into the club, however, the guest will also be required to meet a certain level of financial status in the community and in the business world. Like me," he said using himself as an example of the coveted clientele, "they must have obtained success in a way that makes them a household name. After all, anyone who reads a paper or watches TV knows who I am."

James stopped there to smile at the crowd and seemed totally oblivious to the fact that they had troubled looks on their faces and were murmuring behind their hands to each other. The hum sounded like a hive of angry bees, and the noise was growing.

Sam sat back with a wry smile on his face as he watched and listened to James dig himself a hole, deeper and deeper. Sam smirked to himself that if James didn't shut up soon he, Sam, would not have to do the job because the crowd was going to do it for him.

James unbuttoned his jacket and placed his fist on his hip as he strutted back and forth on the platform. "I would also like to inform you that if any of your older children or grand children for that matter, want to find out how the business world works, we will be hiring only the elite to work here.

We will not be subjecting you to the presence of people off of the street as your waiters, bartenders or cooking staff. We, as celebrities should surround ourselves with our kind. The elite. The cream of the crop. The top of the heap. Only the best and elite will be tolerated here in my club, in every capacity."

James was really on a roll, seemingly ignorant of the chaos he was creating around the room. "As you can tell from tonight, the portions of food will be kept small. I know most of you are watching your weight, as you should," James said as he winked at a table of women sitting right in front of him. Horrified expressions turned to anger and rage as he threw out insults left and right.

"As I look out on the beautiful people here tonight, I see that some of you have had work done to your faces and bodies," he said nodding his head toward a few seated around the room. "This club will be a place where you can come without being hounded by the paparazzi until all signs of your recent surgeries are gone. I know how important public image is, and so do you."

James continued to spew out crap, not realizing that everything he said into the mike was being broadcast live throughout the casino to the horror of the same riff raff he was trying to keep out. But Sam knew. He had glanced over to the entrance and saw a crowd of angry people, who had come in off the sidewalks, gathering in protest. They had been enjoying their time gambling and playing when the speech had started. Now the fun was forgotten, and security had their hands full trying to keep them out. It was their job to try to calm the angry mob, reassuring them it was not they that James was discriminating against.

Voices grew loud, as the press of people grew larger with each passing second. The few security guards, including Tyrone, and the flimsy velvet ropes were not enough to contain the mob, as they finally surged through and pushed their way right up to the stage. Men and women wearing loud, sparkly shirts, jeans and shorts, tee shirts and thong sandals mixed with the guests wearing thousand dollar dresses and designer tuxes. Oddly, there was no separation of class, as all were united in their voicing of disapproval to Jared James and his pompous attitude.

James looked out over the crowd from behind the flimsy podium, and instead of recognizing the threat he called loudly for security. He apologized for the unsavory mix of people who had gotten in and assured the *elite* things would be back to normal in just a few minutes.

Sam wondered why he could not see that the *elite* he was trying to segregate were mixed in with all the rest. Sam stood up and mixed in with the crowd. He made his way to the front, with little effort, as the mass pushed and surged in that direction. Angry men waving bottles of beer climbed the stage and surrounded James, getting nose to nose with him and demanding he step outside with them. Everyone seemed to want a piece of him, and were not going to wait that much longer to get it.

All sorts of threats were flung at James as the crowd pressed in so close that Sam felt himself swept forward until he was nose to nose with James. James' face was turning an unhealthy shade of purple, as ordinary humans evaded his space making it impossible for him to escape. His eyes swung wildly around the room looking for a friend to help him, coming, instead, face to face with Sam Barnhart.

He looked into Sam's eyes and saw his own death mirrored in their depths.

"You!" he screamed accusingly, "you caused all of this to happen. "I know who you are. You are a common murder. If you think you are here for me, think again. I out smarted you. You're nothing," he smiled evilly at Sam. "Benny!" he screamed, the veins on his neck bulging from effort.

The cold smile that covered Sam's face and the flat, dead eyes that looked into his, let James know that he had made a grave mistake in underestimating his killer. The crowd parted for just an instant and James caught the gleam of unforgiving steel held in the Messengers' hand. He tried to take a step backwards but the crowd would not budge. He was held where he was and had to face the grim reaper before him.

"Benny!" he screamed again. "Benny!"

Sam pulled his arm slightly back and moved in for the kill. Just as Sam was about to strike, he felt a burning pain deep in his right side that left him momentarily paralyzed. He looked into James' gloating face and barely heard him speak. "I told you, you were nothing. I'm better then you. I, Jared James have been the undoing of the great, legendary, feared Messenger."

Sam could not think clearly, so great was the pain. Over his shoulder he heard Benny whisper in his ear as he held the blade still in Sam's side. "Mr. James said to tell you this was from him. To make sure you knew who was sending you to hell."

At that moment Sam felt the crowd surge forward, slamming him into James. He felt the warmth and wetness spill over his hand and arm as his own knife was buried to the hilt in James' gut, right above his belly button. The slight satisfaction he felt as the shocked look came over James' face was not enough for Sam. He gathered all of his strength and pulled upwards with his arm. The knife sliced it's way up to the underside of the breastbone and then deep underneath the ribs, almost burying Sam's hand in James' guts as they spilled out and hung to the floor.

Holding the shocked James impaled on his knife, Sam's voice came out guttural and deep as he pressed his mouth close to James' ear. "The people of this country hate you. You are nothing more then a self-serving asshole whose time has come. The government of this country sends its regards. I may go to hell, but you're gonna beat me there." With that Sam gave one more twist to the blade and then pulled it free. He wiped it on the arm of James's sleeve, shrugged himself free of James death grip, and stumbled back into the crowd.

The knife that had been in his own side had dislodged with the movement of the crowd. As he made his way to the exit, Sam kept his legs under him with sheer will power, but was beginning to crumple. Thoughts of Ashton moved through his mind, and he felt deep regret at not being able to return to her. His vision started to dim and the sounds of the crowd got farther and farther away.

As he reached the edge of the crowd, his legs gave out and he started to go down. Just as Sam had given up hope and accepted his own death, he felt big, strong hands lifting him, giving him support. "I've got you," Tyrone whispered. "I've got you. Now let's go."

CHAPTER 44

It had taken Saul some time to find Leonard. Time he did not have. When he did get to him, he was too late to stop what Leonard had set in motion. He may not be able to stop it, but he could alter the outcome.

Saul now knew Leonard's intentions. Leonard planned on killing Sam Barnhart, allowing him and Ashton to be together now, instead of having to wait for Sam's natural time to come. Leonard was too angry or too inexperienced to factor into the equation that Saul would not let that happen.

Saul could see Leonard whispering into Benny's ear and guiding his hand as it aimed for Sam's back. It seemed that was Leonard's favorite striking place, the back. After all, Saul had had first hand knowledge of that.

Saul moved quicker than a heartbeat, and at the last second, deflected Benny and Leonard's aim. The knife stuck and held in Sam's right side. Saul moved the crowd aside, and the knife came free, but not before the damage had been done, and the pain settled in. It was not normal pain either. Saul could detect the excessive agony in Sam's face, and knew Leonard had intensified the pain with burning hell fire to hurt Sam all the more before he died. Saul would not let that happen, Sam would not die today.

He switched his attention to the smaller angel and felt a deep satisfaction at the disbelief on Leonard's face. That disbelief turned to white, hot rage as Leonard let Benny's mind go and faced Saul.

"You!" he screamed, "I ended you. How are you here? Why are you here? Get out. This is no longer your concern. I have control, this is my plan and you can't stop me." Saul looked on as Leonard threw a fit and all but fell on the floor and kicked his feet with the tantrum.

For all the trouble Leonard had caused to himself, Saul, and the humans, he still felt pity for him. Leonard was not going to give up easily. Pointing his hands at Saul, he let streams of power fly from his fingertips in Saul's direction. He had caught Saul off guard last time, but not now. Saul easily deflected the attack, and letting loose his own energy, wrapped Leonard in a cocoon of immobility, arms and wings folded tightly against his sides.

"Let me go. Let me go!" Leonard screamed as he tried to struggle free of his restraints. "It's almost done. I've planned for this, worked for this, and now it's happening. Can't you see this has to be? Let. Me. Go!"

No matter what Leonard tried or said, Saul held him tight. He had a choice to make. End Leonard's existence or send him back to earth to be reborn in another body. It was not a hard decision for Saul to make, as he drew Leonard in close to him before he spoke.

"Leonard, you have gone against every commandment known to man and heaven. Normally in a situation such as this, there would be no question as to the consequences," he told the young angel with a very somber look on his face. "But, because of the way you prematurely came to us, your young age, and your inexperience, I will grant you another chance." Leonard had stopped squirming and trained his eyes on the older angel's face as he weighed his fate. Saul continued, "You will be stripped of your immortality and be sent back to earth to be born and live as a mortal. You will have the chance to learn your life lessons and will be reborn again and again until you have gathered all the knowledge your soul needs to be complete. Once this is done you may be allowed to rejoin the ranks of the immortal again, providing you live a good life each time and show compassion and understanding for and to your fellow man."

As his future was revealed, Leonard yelled, "You can't do that! You have no right to make that kind of decision for me or about me. I'm telling!" Leonard said sounding again like the small child he was.

Saul again felt pity move through him and reached out a hand to cup the little ones chin in his palm. He raised Leonard's chin until their eyes met and held. "We will meet again," he told him in a gentle voice.

Saul closed his eyes and willed Leonard's wings to separate from his body. Once they did, the beautiful wings disappeared, leaving nothing but glittering particles, floating to the floor as fairy dust in the wind.

Leonard felt strange without the weight of the wings he had become accustomed to on his back. He had liked them; they kind of made him feel like a super hero or something. His lip stuck out in a pout, Leonard began to fade from Saul's sight.

It only took a second for him to disappear, but it was enough for Saul to catch a glimpse of the red tinge in the wide, angry eyes. *Trouble*, thought Saul. t*hat one is going to be trouble.*

CHAPTER 45

Saul pushed Leonard to the back of his mind and turned his attention to Sam. Without seeing him, he could feel Sam's pain as he made his way to the edge of the crowd, coming in waves of fiery desperation. He closed his eyes and looked into Sam's mind, watching as Sam began the process of losing his grip on life.

Looking around the gathering of people, Saul tried to get a sense of someone he could trust to assist him with Sam. His mind found and fixed on a big man, Tyrone was his name. Saul remembered that Tyrone knew Sam already and felt no ill will towards him. In fact he liked him. Saul guided Tyrone through the mob to Sam's side, planting the thought of help and escape in his mind.

He then turned his attention to Sam. Laying his hands on him, he gave Sam some of his strength. Although he could not heal Sam, he could keep him alive until he could get back to Ashton.

Tyrone put his arm around Sam's waist and half dragged him across the floor and out a side door. He had no idea how Sam had come to be in this condition, but he felt a sense of responsibility to the man and wanted to help him in any way he could.

"My car," Sam mumbled, "it's setting down the street. Just get me to my car."

"Which way?" Tyrone asked, practically carrying Sam as they made it to the sidewalk outside the casino.

Sam focused his eyes and looked around to get his bearings. His pain, that god awful pain, seemed to be getting a little better in the last few minutes, as he located his car on the street to the right and directed Tyrone that way.

Once there, Sam gave the keys to Tyrone and leaned against the car until it was unlocked and the door opened.

"Get in man," Tyrone instructed Sam as he handed him in gently like a piece of fragile glass. "Do you have somewhere to go?" he asked. "You can crash at my place if you need to. It's safe." Looking Sam in the eye, he repeated, "It's safe."

Sam shook his head as he settled himself into the seat, "Thanks for your help, but I think I can take it from here. If you ever need anything, call me." He handed Tyrone a plain white card with only a phone number on it. "If you need me, I'll be there for you," he promised.

Tyrone slipped the card in his front pants pocket and started to duck back out of the car, but Sam stopped him with a hand on his arm. "Take this," Sam said a little out of breath. He turned Tyrone's hand over and placed a wad of hundred dollar bills in it.

Tyrone looked down at the money that had blood smears on it, then back at Sam. "I shouldn't take this from you, but God knows I have a need for this right now. So thanks." In a voice that rang with sincerity and promise he gave Sam what he needed to hear. "Don't worry, man, I'll keep your secret."

Sam took the hand he held out and nodded his head. "Yes," he said, "I believe you will. Find me if you need me," and with that Sam pulled the door shut and started the car.

He let it idle for a moment as he took stock of his condition. He didn't feel as bad as he had. He didn't feel great, but he was beginning to feel like he would make it, at lease for a while longer. He turned on his blinker and merged with traffic. A last look in his rear view mirror showed Tyrone still on the street with his hand in the air, waving goodbye. Sam smiled slightly and lifted his hand in farewell. He doubted Tyrone could see it, but he was okay with their parting. He trusted Tyrone. No reason why, just a feeling he had.

Sam drove carefully till he hit the edge of town. He hadn't seen any flashing lights behind him and no roadblocks barred his way up ahead. It had all happened so quickly, that maybe the police had not even found James' body yet. Hell, with the size and emotion of that mob, they'd be lucky to find anything at all.

He left the neon lights behind him and drove out into the dark night. His head felt fuzzy and his eyes didn't seem to want to focus, but for some reason Sam stayed on the road. He remembered thinking that he must have an angel on his shoulder that night, keeping him alive. But he was wrong. His angel was sitting on the front seat beside him.

CHAPTER 46

Sam left Vegas at a little after midnight, and should have made the trip back to Colorado in about ten hours. But he had no sense of time, as his brain floated in and out of awareness for most of the drive. He'd needed to stop for gas, but wasn't sure he had. The whole trip seemed like a dream. He sat slouched behind the wheel of the car, his hands gripping the steering wheel as he tried to sit up and focus on his driving. He would stay that way for a short time before he, once again, would slide down in the seat. The next thing he knew he'd be passing some landmark that should have taken him hours to get to from his last conscious thought.

One thing he DID remember, was being in constant pain. The only time it left him alone, was when he was unconscious. No that could not be right. You can't drive when you are unconscious, can you? He remembered checking his side a few times to try to determine the extent of his injury. It had stopped bleeding for a while and then it would begin seeping again. Or maybe it had been seeping and then it had stopped bleeding. He wasn't too sure on the order of things at the moment. All he knew, when he was aware, was that he had his hands on the wheel and he was driving.

He kept his car pointed in the right direction and between the lines on the pavement that seemed to stretch on forever.

Sam's eyes felt dry and heavy as he attempted to concentrate on the road. His mouth was pasty and he was so thirsty he would gladly have drunk a lake dry if one had been available. His skin felt hot and stretched over his body, as if it was a size to small for him. He ached and wanted to change his position in the seat, but it seemed like too much of an effort to do anything.

He found himself wondering if he was going to make it back home, or if someone would find his body sitting behind the wheel of his car on the side of the road. Not that it would matter to him if he was dead, but he'd rather not go out that way, sitting on the side of the road with the sun beating through the windows, making his body blow up with gasses that would only come out when it popped. Everyone wanted a little dignity, and he was no different. If he had to go he wanted it to be in his mountains where the air was cool and clean.

Just the thought of the cool air made Sam almost weep. He wanted to be home. He needed to be home. He wanted Ashton. He sounded like a whinny baby, but he didn't care. There was no one around to hear his moans of pain and see his damp eyes. He wanted to have loving arms wrapped around him and a soothing voice telling him he would be alright. He wanted a cool, healing touch to take away his agony and make things all better.

These thoughts finally brought a slight smile to Sam's dry, cracked lips. It sounded like he wanted his mommy. But Ashton was nowhere near being his mommy. He wanted everything from her and with her, and was very glad she was not his mother. He remembered her sparkling emerald eyes staring into his just before his lips met hers, the feel of soft skin against his roughness, and the dream. Sam decided he must not be at death's door or these thoughts would never have had the effect they were having on his body at the moment. Thinking of Ashton made him feel very much alive.

With renewed determination, Sam flexed his fingers gripping the wheel and peered out of the windshield, looking at the stretch of road that seemed to go on forever in front of him. It seemed to dip and weave, as if he were looking at it through a heat wave. *Maybe he was*, Sam thought. It did seem awfully warm to him, so maybe the view was being distorted by the heat.

As the miles passed by the window, Sam's neck seemed unable to hold his head up as it bobbed up and down, back and forth. *I've got to make it home*, he thought. *I've got to make it home.* With that one thought playing over and over in his mind, his head sagged onto his chest, while his car continued in a straight line down the long highway.

CHAPTER 47

Saul was with Sam for every mile that passed under the spinning tires. Although he'd never driven a car before, he found himself forced to do so by using Sam's body. He'd taken control over Sam's mind, allowing him to drive while Sam slept much of the time. He guided Sam's hands, worked his feet, and kept his vigilance over Sam's wound. Even though Saul was in the passenger's seat, threads of light connected him with Sam, sharing his strength and doing what he could to keep Sam alive.

He had to get him back to Colorado. Back to Ashton. Once there, he was sure he could guide her hand to make Sam well. Ashton had already lost much of her life to interference, and Saul wouldn't let the same thing happen to Sam. Life must take its course and be played out as planned.

Saul had been an immortal since the beginning of his existence, so he didn't have mortal experiences to rely on. He had always used his wings to get where he needed to be, or just appeared or disappeared in places. This time he'd been forced to tap into Sam's knowledge of driving and take over the wheel right after they had left Vegas. He had to admit that even though the situation was grave and demanded all his concentration to control it, he was having a great time driving.

It hadn't taken him long to learn that Sam's car could get up and move if it had to. Saul would have loved to press his foot to the gas pedal and feel the car respond to his demands, but he also knew that if he was pulled over there would be no way to get Sam out of the trouble it would cause him. Imagine Sam not only trying to explain his speeding, but the wound in his side and the events that had led up to it. The cop might even have been smart enough to connect the dots, and put Sam at the scene they had just left behind in Vegas. Saul would be forced to use his influence on the cop's mind, which was something he tried not to do unless absolutely necessary.

So, even though it meant getting Sam home a little sooner and scratching a new itch that Saul hadn't known he possessed until this moment, Saul resisted the urge and kept the car at a reasonable speed. Instead he rolled the windows down, feeling the wind rush through his hair, and listening to the sound of the tires whapping their way over the uneven pavement. Smiling to himself, and realizing there was no one around to hear him, Saul threw back his head and let his voice sail into the universe, "Whoopeeeeeeeeeeeee!"

CHAPTER 48

It was just past noon when Ashton walked into her kitchen. She wasn't hungry, but decided it was time she made herself take in some nourishment, as her clothes were beginning to sag on her already lean frame, and she didn't need to lose any more weight. The fresh fruits and vegetables had long since been thrown away, having taken on the look of old shrunken heads seen on a late night horror show. So that left her with a choice of something frozen or canned in the cupboard. She looked in the freezer without interest and then shut it with a snap. Nope, nothing of interest there. The cupboards held little more interest, but she finally settled on a can of chicken noodle soup that was tucked in the corner of one of the shelves.

She heated it up and dipped a modest amount into her bowl before sitting down at the kitchen table. She swirled the noodles around and around in the steaming broth with out taking one bite. The steam rising from the bowl smelled good, finally tempting her to sample a small spoonful. Her eyebrows rose in pleasant surprise as she realized that it tasted good. In fact, with her second spoonful her appetite came roaring back. She attacked the bowl as if it was going to be her last meal, gulping down the soup, not minding that it burned her tongue, and not coming up for air until it was empty. She got up and brought the pot to the table, pouring the rest of the soup into her empty dish. She bent over the steaming dish and, again, devoured the contents. Only when nothing remained in the bowl, did she sit back in her chair and relax. She realized that this was the best she'd felt, since finding out Sam had left.

With the thought of Sam, her stomach clenched and almost rebelled. Ashton placed her hands, palms down, on the table and took a few deep breaths, bringing her belly and her emotions under control. *Get a grip*, she thought. *He's gone and not coming back*. He'd never even bothered to call, and she must face the fact that he was done with her before anything could get started. It would be very easy to let herself be depressed and give up, but, with a squaring of her shoulders, Ashton shook off the feelings that had dragged her down of late. She still had time to live and there were things she wanted to do and to see. If she had to do them by herself, then she would.

Ashton got up from the table and washed her dishes clean, setting them in the drainer to dry. She wiped her hands on her pants and decided the next order of business would be to take a bath, since it had been a few days since she had taken one. Not that she had done anything to get dirty or smelly; it was just that she suddenly felt a need to stand under the hot water and cleanse her body, and maybe even her mind. She would send all her negative thoughts swirling down the drain and have a fresh outlook on the life she had left.

She took the stairs two at a time and rushed to get into the shower, dropping clothes wherever they landed. She stepped into the shower and enjoyed a long, hot, renewing soak. The hot water worked it's magic, seeming to bring her back to life, and she got out feeling like a new woman.

She was not sure why she had all this energy all of a sudden, but it felt good to be moving and doing things. She dressed in fresh jeans and a light sweater, then picked up her dirty clothes from where she had haphazardly discarded them on the floor, raced down the stairs, and placed them in the washer with a pile of other laundry that had accumulated in the hamper.

Again she took the stairs two at a time, as she made her way back to her bedroom and stripped the sheets from the bed. She replaced them with crisp, clean ones, made from Egyptian cotton. She held them to her face for a moment, feeling the cool softness of their fiber and breathing in their fresh, mountain air goodness. *Yum,* she thought. *Was there anything better then fresh smelling sheets*? She fluffed the pillows into their cases and took the comforter out to hang on the old line in the back yard. By the time she was ready for bed this evening, it would have absorbed the freshness and pine smell of the woods. She was going to sleep well tonight, she decided. She needed it.

She spent the afternoon dusting and rearranging her cabin. She threw open the windows and watched as the curtains danced in the fresh air that moved in and took up residence. She turned on the TV, which she and Sam had had connected during their trip to town, for noise, and to give her company. She had never gotten into soap operas, and there was nothing else on, so she left it low and paid no attention to what was being said. It was just background static to fill the otherwise quiet walls. Ashton kept herself busy all afternoon making her home clean and cozy. She should have done this a long time ago, she thought, but she was doing it now and that was okay with her.

As the sun began to set, she went outside and retrieved her bedding from the line, took it upstairs and spread it over her clean sheets. The whole room filled with the scent of outdoors, and Ashton smiled. She placed a vase of wildflowers, that she had spotted growing in her yard, on the nightstand beside the bed and turned the lamp on low. It looked so inviting, she was tempted to succumb to the urge to curl up and take a nap.

The rumbling in her stomach changed her mind, and she made her way to the kitchen to make herself some supper. Her attitude and appetite was much improved from the last time she had eaten. She realized, with a smile, that she was ravenous after her afternoon of cleaning, and began looking through the cupboards for the makings of a hearty meal. Her search revealed a jar of Prego spaghetti sauce, her favorite, a can of Green Giant niblets corn, and some sliced, canned peaches in thick sauce for desert. There was a bag of angel hair pasta in one of the drawers that she set to boiling on top of the stove. After turning on the flame under the sauce and vegetables, she went in search of bread to finish off her menu. She found a loaf that was slightly stale, but not moldy, sliced off two thick pieces, slathered them with butter and garlic salt, and placed them in the oven to heat. She opened a bottle of white wine she and Sam had splurged on while shopping, and poured herself a glass. She placed the bottle on the table, then took dishes from the cupboard and silverware from the drawer, and set the table, lighting a candle in the middle for ambience. Standing back, she clapped her hands at the inviting site, then turned her attention back to the preparation of her meal.

The noodles were tender and the sauce bubbling in the pot, so she drained the spaghetti and poured the two together into a large bowl, stirring until the noodles were wet with the thick, zesty sauce. She added butter to the corn and pulled the toasted bread from the oven. It was not five-star but it looked good and smelled even better. The aroma in the kitchen was enough to make her mouth water as she settled into her chair with the feast in front of her.

Once again she ate everything she'd prepared, noticing each particular flavor and texture as the food touched her tongue, was swirled around in her mouth, and found its way into her stomach. Ashton pushed back from the table and patted her full stomach with satisfaction when she was done. Maybe she should lean back, belch, loosen her belt and smack her lips, like she'd seen people do on TV after a particularly satisfying meal. She had never done anything so gross, and even though she was by herself and could do anything she wanted, she decided it was not her style.

Instead she got up, ran some hot, soapy water in the sink, and washed her dishes. She placed them into the drainer to dry and be put away tomorrow, before pouring the remainder of the wine into her glass, and making her way into the living room.

She set her wine on the end table beside the couch, and squatted before the dark fireplace, deciding a small cheery blaze might be just the ticket to warm the cabin which had become chilly with the setting of the sun. She would sit and watch the flames before going up to bed.

She laid the logs, tucked some kindling into them, and struck a match, watching as the small flame turned into a dancing fire within minutes. She had a knack for making fire come to life, a true mountain girl if there ever was one. Wrapping a light blanket around herself, she tucked her feet up underneath her bottom and settled on the small sofa, which she had moved before the fireplace today. She slowly sipped her wine and lost herself in the dancing of the flames.

Mesmerized by the magic of the dancing flames and warmed by the clear liquid in her glass, Ashton's muscles unwound and her dark green eyes no longer fought to stay open. She relaxed into the cushions, settling into the corner with her blanket wrapped tightly around her. Warm and safe in her little nest, she gave in to the urge to close her eyes and drifted into a contented sleep.

CHAPTER 49

Ashton woke with a start, feeling slightly disoriented, heart pounding like she had just finished running a marathon. The fire had died down to glowing embers, and the room seemed to have taken on an unnatural chill. A shiver ran up Ashton's back and made the hairs on her neck stand up. She tried to remember what she had been dreaming that had caused her to jolt upright. She couldn't remember anything, no matter how hard she tried. Maybe it was just a feeling. Whatever it was, it was giving her the creeps.

She looked at the clock and saw that it was almost 11:30 p.m. The time was important, she knew it. Why? What was going on? Ashton pulled the blanket a little tighter around her shoulders and huddled deeper into the corner of the couch. She knew she should get up and poke the embers and add a log to the dying fire, but for some reason could not seem to move from the couch.

One moment she didn't want to move and the next she couldn't. The right side of her back was on fire! She had never felt such an all-consuming pain. It felt like she had been stabbed by a blade that was red hot and coated with malice. Where had that thought come from? Where ever, she knew it was a true and correct description of something that had happened. But to who, and why was she aware of it?

She sat on the couch a while longer feeling the pain leave her body until it was only a memory. When she was able to breathe again, she rose dragging the blanket with her. She walked through the house, stumbling over its trailing edges, looking in every nook and cranny, trying to find a clue as to what was going on. Finding nothing, she retuned to the couch and sat down on the edge, gnawing on her fingernails and frowning as she tried to get a handle on what was making her so jumpy.

She went to the kitchen, made herself a cup of hot tea, and sipped it as she paced the wooden floor around the table. She set down her cup, extending her arms, rolling her shoulders and arching her back, trying to determine whether the pain she'd felt had been hers or something imagined. So far so good she figured, finding no body part that was causing her any pain.

She picked up her tea and continued pacing the length of the house over and over, trying to keep her mind open in case something else wanted to come to her. But nothing did.

Dawn was just breaking when she finally gave in to exhaustion, and settled onto the couch, once again, hoping to catch a nap for a few hours. Her eyes had just begun to feel heavy when something on the T V caught her attention.

The newscaster for the world news was saying something about a murder. Intrigued, and once again wide-awake, Ashton reached for the remote and turned the volume up.

"It was reported that last night, at about 11:30 pm, oil magnet Jared James was fatally wounded in a night club in Las Vegas. The club, the Snake Pit, was hosting its grand opening and James was one of the major investors in the property," the handsome reporter with his charcoal grey suit and red tie told the die-hard viewers still unlucky enough to be awake at this hour. "Eyewitnesses are saying that the large crowd had gotten out of control, rushing the podium where James had been giving a speech. When security and the police arrived on the scene, the crowd's mood had been ugly. It had taken law enforcement half an hour to disperse the crowd, and empty the club." He paused for effect, a brief frown crossing his handsome face before continuing, "When they reached the podium, police found James on the floor, originally thinking he had been trampled by the crush of people. Further investigations revealed that James had been stabbed and disemboweled, presumably some time during the "riot". His face grew pale as he revealed this detail, then regained it's impartiality as he continued to read the story from the prompter, "A spokesperson for the Police refused to comment on whether any suspects have been detained in relation to the apparent slaying. According to an employee of the club, there was a malfunction in the surveillance system, thus hampering the investigation and providing no visual evidence of the incident. Many of the clubs occupants had left the scene before the crime was discovered, so police are trying to get the names of the people on the guest list for the evening. If anyone has information that could aid in this investigation, they are urged to contact the Las Vegas Police Department," the reporter finished and turned to the next story on the prompter.

There had been a picture of Jared James covering the full TV screen at the beginning of the news report, and then in the upper left hand corner, as the reporter gave the details of the apparent murder. Ashton did not know why this story seemed so important to her, but it was. She did not know Jared James personally, but she knew who he was. She listened to the report in its entirety, before lowering the volume on the set once again. It dawned on her that the time of her back pain and the time of the alleged murder, were one in the same. Was there a connection? Why should there be? She was in Colorado and he had been in Vegas. Not even close. But something was going on here and Ashton felt like she had just come in during the middle of a show and was trying to catch up.

Once again she was off the couch, the blanket dragging around her feet as she paced the chilly wood floor. She walked and considered the happenings of the evening for another hour, before she finally gave up, crawled up the stairs, and fell into the soft comfort of the bed that she had been anticipating all evening. The sun was well up and the day had started but Ashton was exhausted and needed to shut down for a while. She closed her eyes and fell into an uneasy sleep.

CHAPTER 50

Ashton dreamt that she was at the club. She could see what had happened as if she had been among the crowd in the room. She could feel the heat of the angry crowd as they pressed their bodies around James like a heavy smog. She could see the look of shock on his face, and then the glassy emptiness in them as he disappeared under the feet of the mob. There had been someone standing in front of James, but he or she, appeared out of focus, and no matter how hard Ashton tried, she could not see their face.

Ashton tossed and turned for the better part of the three hours she spent in sleep. When she finally swam slowly up from the depths of her slumber, the once tucked sheets were tangled around her perspiring body, and she felt as tired as if she had not slept at all. The dream and the events of the night still circled around her head like angry bees and would not leave her alone.

Rubbing her hands over her face and dragging them through her tangled hair, Ashton swung her legs over the edge of the bed, and stood up, unfolding one creaking muscle at a time. She walked on wooden legs to the bathroom where she splashed cold water on her face, brushed her teeth, and ran a comb through her tousled hair. She had fallen asleep in her clothes, and decided they would do until she decided to take a shower.

She made her way down the stairs into the kitchen, where she decided to make herself an omelet. She broke two eggs into a bowl, added some shredded cheddar cheese, a little salt and pepper, and poured the mixture into a sizzling pan of hot butter. She turned the heat down under the skillet and watched as the orange cheese began melt into the plump yellow puddle. She flipped it over once, added a bit more cheese and folded it onto her plate. She toasted a couple pieces of the bread she'd found the night before, and spread them with grape jelly she'd found in the refrigerator. She poured herself a cup of the hot coffee she had perked while preparing the rest of her breakfast, and settled herself at the table. Ashton ate the food, paying only half attention to what she put in her mouth, the dream and her connection to the events of the night before still occupying much of her mind.

She was not sure what she wanted to do with her day but felt she should stick close to home. She cleaned up her breakfast dishes, then went in search of a book to read. Choosing one from the bookcase along the wall in the living room, she settled on the couch in front of the fireplace and tried to get lost in the pages of the book. Her attention span was that of a gnat, so she scratched that idea. She tossed it on the coffee table beside her, and once again found herself pacing the wooden floor. Boy, she had been doing that a lot lately. If she wasn't careful she would wear a path in the boards, but moving felt better than sitting still.

She had finally convinced herself that the events of the previous evening had been just a coincidence, when the low growl of a powerful engine brought her back from her concentration. She waited, expecting it to pass by on the road, but instead it slowed and came into her yard. She wrinkled up her nose and frowned, not feeling like unexpected company. Besides, who knew she was here? Just Sam.

Her feet were frozen to the floor as if someone had nailed them down tight. Should she go to the door? Should she wait until there was a knock to go to the door? Why wasn't she moving? She heard a car door open and close and the creaking of her back steps before her paralysis lifted and she started moving. She waited expectantly for the one deep male voice she longed to hear call her name, but instead all she heard was silence.

She slowed her headlong flight to the back door and approached it with caution. Before she got there, she grabbed the heavy pan she had fixed her breakfast in from the drainer, having every intention of using it if trouble decided to show up. She kept the pan hidden behind her back as she opened the door and prepared to confront the intruder on the other side.

Instead of a stranger she was met by Saul looking the same as he had the first time she'd seen him, dressed in white, floating slightly above the ground, wings half spread, but looking like he was on a mission. Before she could open her mouth to ask questions, Saul moved aside and Ashton dropped the pan with a loud bang. Behind Saul stood Sam.

Both Sam and Ashton took a step towards each other, but before they could meet Sam reached out a hand to her, palm up and covered in blood. He said two words that Ashton had to strain to hear, so low were they spoken before he pitched forward into her extended arms. "Help me."

CHAPTER 51

Ashton caught Sam as he fell into her stunned, outstretched arms. She stumbled backwards under his weight, and would have fell down with Sam on top of her if Saul had not stepped in. Using his powers, he levitated Sam until he was chest high. Sam's body was suspended in mid-air, as if by invisible wires, his arms hanging towards the ground, head lolling back, and drops of blood splashing onto the old wood of Ashton's porch, sounding, to Ashton's ears, like a bass drum as they hit.

Ashton saw it all as if it were in slow motion, the slight breeze stirring Sam's hair, the barely visible rising and falling of Sam's chest as he struggled to take each breath, the pallor of his face, and the nightmarish soaking of blood on his clothes. She looked down at herself and saw the blood that had transferred onto her arms and clothes where Sam's body had touched hers. Her hands started to shake and her stomach to roll. She had been desperately wanting to see Sam again, but never in her deepest, darkest dreams had she imagined it would be like this. *Not like this*, she thought as she shook her head from side to side. *Not like this*.

Ashton turned her questioning eyes to Saul for answers. "What happened?" she asked with a shaky voice. Saul stared back at her with regret and apology in his eyes, giving Ashton reason to believe he had something to do with Sam's current situation. But before he could reply, she gathered her wits about her and took control of the situation. "Get him inside and put him in my bed," she ordered the angel. Turning to lead the way, she stopped and turned back, squarely facing the immortal on her steps. "Don't even think about disappearing until you explain this whole mess to me and until Sam gets better. You owe me and I'm collecting."

Saul merely nodded his head as Ashton turned to hold the door open so he and his precious cargo could pass through. Stepping past them, Ashton led the way up the stairs to her bedroom and flipped back the cover so Saul could lower Sam to the waiting mattress. The fresh sheets she had slept on just a short time ago, now supported and folded around Ashton's new charge. Fresh blood slowly stained them, leaving Ashton to believe that the blood flow was not gushing but rather seeping from Sam's wound. She'd seen enough episodes of Grey's Anatomy and House on TV to know that this was a good sign.

Rolling up her sleeves, she looked at Saul as he stood off to the side of the bed and began to fire orders at him. "We need to get him out of his clothes, clean the wound, and apply pressure to it to get the bleeding stopped. Stay here with him while I go get hot water and the other things we'll need." She gave him a warning glance to do as she expected and rushed out of the room.

She flew into the kitchen first and filled a large pot with hot water, then put it on the burner to heat. While she waited for the water to boil, she went into the washroom and gathered old, frayed wash rags, towels, and sheets to be torn into makeshift bandages. She found a bottle of alcohol in the bathroom cabinet for disinfecting the wound. Ashton paused for just a second, realizing that she did not even know what the wound looked like, what caused it, or how bad it was. No matter, she told herself, she was going to fix it and make Sam better, or die trying. No, there would be dying today, hers or

Sam's, she promised herself. Sam would get better, even if she had to make a deal with the devil for him to do so.

Throwing the rags over her shoulder, she picked up the pot of hot water, carried it up to the bedroom, and set it gently on the bedside table. In her absence, Saul had removed Sam's clothes, and he now lay with the sheets riding around his waist. Ashton had been waiting to see Sam naked, but she barely took the time now to admire the lean muscles and light furring on the chest that lay bare to her. Time for that later.

"I'll need you to roll him over onto his uninjured side and hold him there while I see what we are dealing with," she barked at Saul.

Saul did not move, but Sam began to slowly rotate until his injury was exposed to the sunlight. It was a cut, about two inches in length. The depth was unknown to her, but she was going to assume the worst and figure it was deep. Sam had been stabbed.

She moved to the other side of the bed facing Sam, and spread towels on the bed underneath him to catch the water as she washed the wound. Looking at Saul again she said, "Roll him on to his stomach and let him lay there while I clean him up. I assume you can keep him asleep while I work, so he will not feel the pain?"

Saul took his eyes off Sam long enough to meet her gaze and again nodded his head. "I will spare him the pain and let him sleep to heal, while you clean the wound and stitch it closed."

The white threads that connected Sam and Saul had been visible this whole time, but now glowed brighter as Saul fed more energy into Sam, putting him farther into unconsciousness. He did not tell Ashton that the pain he would be sparing Sam, would be felt by him. He would take on this burden as long as he stayed connected to Sam. As Ashton began to gently wash the wound and the areas around it, Saul stood steady, not a sound coming from his lips.

Ashton took a deep breath, knowing she needed to clean the wound and disinfect the whole area before closing it. She had never done anything like this, but her hands were steady and sure as she soaked and cleaned the area over and over until the skin was pink from her efforts. The water, on the other hand, was dark red and smelled of copper with the blood she had cleaned from Sam. She soaked one of the rags with alcohol and went over the same area twice before she was satisfied that he was clean, and that she had done what she could to prevent infection.

She rose from the floor where she had been kneeling and arched her back saying, "I need to go find a needle and thread. I'll be only a moment." With this said she turned to leave the room, but her eyes were held by the sight of Saul.

While she worked over Sam she had not glanced at the angel, but now she was stopped in her tracks by his appearance. His immortal beauty had not been dimmed by the pain he absorbed, but had intensified. A glow seemed to radiate from his body and his face was a mask of serenity. He took Ashton's breath away as she continued to stare at him. Saul looked at her and when he smiled it almost blinded her, so bright and breath taking was the sight.

Ashton knew she had no time to dwell over Saul but she needed to know. "What's happened to you? I don't understand," she questioned.

Saul let his gaze rest on the pretty human, then with a low voice he shared with her the information very few other mortals knew. "I have taken on Sam's pain and suffering. When an angel does this, gives of himself to help another, his powers are enhanced. The burdens we carry for others make us stronger and enable us to give more. Greater strength is the reward for our sacrifices." The angel paused for a minute and his gaze turned to Sam on the bed. "Sam's pain was great but he felt nothing. When he awakes, he will remember nothing of what happened while you cared for him."

Ashton's face paled as she realized the pain the angel had gone through for Sam. "Are you hurt now? What do you need?" she asked Saul with concern.

"I need nothing," Saul reassured her. "This is my purpose, to help my charges. I will continue to give healing forces to Sam as long as he needs them," he promised her. "But you, Ashton, are not finished with him." He waved her from the room saying, "Go get the needle and thread and finish the job. As great as my powers are, I cannot make him well alone. You have to help. Go now. Time is of the essence," he urged her toward the door.

Ashton ran down the stairs into the kitchen looking in the top drawer nearest the phone jack for a needle and thread. Everyone had a junk drawer in the kitchen filled with duct tape, pens and pencils, and yes, even a needle and thread she discovered, as she rummaged through its contents. As she made her way back upstairs, Ashton wondered to herself, "Was what Saul doing for Sam considered a miracle?"

Entering the bedroom, she paused at Saul's side and turned her face to his. Their eyes met and, although no words were spoken, in them he could read her thanks and gratitude.

Ashton moved to Sam's bedside, where she soaked the needle and thread in the alcohol before reaching out with one hand, pulled the sides of the wound together, and slowly began slipping the needle in and out. She pulled each stitch tight before going on to the next. She had never been very handy at sewing, but a half hour later she looked at the closed wound and felt a sense of satisfaction. Thirty neatly placed stitches now took the place of the ugly hole that had marred Sam's side. No doubt there would be a scar, but it should heal nicely and be something he could show his grandchildren when he was old, telling them some tall tale of how he had come by it.

Ashton placed a bandage, made from the torn up sheets, over the wound. Then, as if reading her mind, Saul lifted Sam off the bed just enough that Ashton could anchor the bandage in place with strips of cloth, which she wrapped around his torso. She removed the wet towels from beneath Sam, then looked to Saul to finish the job. Sam was lowered, as gentle as a baby, to rest again on the bed. Ashton pulled the sheets up to Sam's shoulders, making sure he was as comfortable as he could be.

Looking down on his sleeping face, she raised her hand and gently stroked the hair from his brow. She lowered her lips to his cheek and kissed him. His skin carried a stubble of whiskers, but Ashton didn't mind as she lay her cheek next to his for a few seconds. When she came away, her own cheeks were wet with tears.

"Don't let him go, Saul," she sobbed brokenly. "Don't let him go."

CHAPTER 52

Ashton stayed by Sam's side for a few minutes, holding his hand and stroking his face. She needed to touch him and reassure herself that he was still breathing. Slowly getting off of the bed, Ashton cleaned up the mess that had accumulated on the floor. Blood stained rags, damp towels and thread littered the floor, lying where she had dropped them while tending to Sam. Looking down at the bundle she held, she decided she was not going to wash or save any of it. No reminders were needed to remember what she had seen and done.

Holding the bundle close in her arms, she turned to Saul. "I'll be right back. Don't leave him." She started for the door but stopped and turned back. Raising her eyes to meet the angels she said, "Please? And thank you for bringing him back to me." She was rewarded with a gentle smile from the angel. He's going to make it isn't he, Saul?" she pleaded with a warble in her voice.

Saul could feel her desperate need for confirmation and gave it to her. "I believe so. You have done everything you could, my child, and I will continue to help as much as I can." The soothing tone of his voice and the truth Ashton could see in his eyes, were all she could ask for.

She turned without another word and went to the kitchen trash, dumping everything she held inside, then closed the lid.

She stood very still for a few seconds, her closed eyes downcast, then she began to shake. Reality had set in.

She had not allowed herself time to think while Sam needed her, but now she found herself seeing it as it really was. There had been so much blood, more blood then she had ever seen in her life. She had never seen an injury like this one, dealing with minor cuts and burns throughout her childhood, but never a stab wound of this magnitude. She was not sure how she knew it was a stab wound, but she did. Why would anyone want to stab Sam, and how was Saul involved in all of it? The questions whirled around in Ashton's mind.

Ashton allowed herself a few more precious moments to fall apart and then clamped down on her emotions, set her resolve back in place, and stiffened her spine. She needed to clean herself up and return to the bedroom so she could be near Sam if he needed anything. She turned on the hot water and lathered her hands, scrubbing the dried blood and antiseptic smell from her fingers, watching the pink bubbles spinning down the drain. She washed until the water was clear and her skin was pink.

She made her way up the stairs, weary from the many trips up and down, and the events of the day. Going back into the bedroom, Ashton gathered clean clothes for herself and went to take a quick shower. Washing in the sink may have taken care of her hands, but wasn't going to rid her of the blood that had gotten everywhere else on her body. As she undressed she looked at her image in the mirror. There was a blood smear on her brow and cheek, probably where she had pushed the hair from her eyes while tending to Sam. Her eyes looked shell-shocked, like someone who had just weathered a tragedy and lived to tell about it. Boy was that an ironic thought considering her supposed car crash and death.

Throwing her clothes in the trash, she hurried through her shower. In less than twenty minutes she had showered, dressed in a pair of ratty old sweats, and was back at Sam's side.

He had not moved since she had last seen him. She watched as his chest rose and fell with each shallow breath. She bent to lay her lips on his brow, but before she was even close to him, she could feel the heat coming off him in waves. He felt like a furnace someone had left on high.

Ashton whipped her head around and looked at Saul in alarm. "He's burning up, we have to do something!" she said.

Saul could see her pupils constrict down to the size of pinpoints, her panic beginning to take control. Not meaning to be cruel but needing to snap Ashton back, Saul put strength in his voice as he answered her. "Stop!" he commanded. "You will be no help to me or Sam if you go off the deep end now. Take a deep breath he told her," placing his hands on her shoulders and looking into her eyes. "Now!" he demanded, leaving her with no thought of disobeying.

Ashton did as Saul ordered, drawing air deep into her lungs several times. She began to feel the panic receding. "Saul was right," she told herself, "now was not the time to panic."

Remembering back to the times she had been sick and a fever had been present, she recalled her mother wiping her forehead and face with a cool damp cloth over and over. She remembered how it had felt so good. Not only the coolness, but also the love in her mother's touches. The ache of that loss tried to surface, but Ashton squelched it and focused on Sam. "We need cool water, wash clothes and towels again. I'll be right back."

She again rushed out of the room and down the stairs. Saul was satisfied that she was back on track. In no time she returned with an armload of towels and a big pan of cold water. She set it down on the bedside table, and once again laid towels around Sam before she wet a cloth and began washing his face. She dampened the cloth many times as it only took a couple of passes for it to become warm from the heat of Sam's fever. Over and over she repeated the process. She placed a cool cloth on Sam's forehead, then turned her attention to his neck and chest, lowering the sheet and pooled it around his hips. She bathed his torso with cool water, all the while talking to him, telling him to fight and to come back to her.

She poured out her love to him, hoping some of what she said would get through to him and make him wake up. But the hours wore on and the sun began to lower in the western sky before she felt a little less heat coming from Sam's body. A small flicker of hope, that maybe the worst was past, took root in her heart. She worked with renewed purpose, taking turns with Saul checking the bandage over Sam's wound, making sure it was clean and dry.

She herself was bone tired, and the strain of the day and its events were beginning to show on her face. Tired, dark smudges lay under her emerald green eyes. Her voice was dry and crackling as she spoke to Sam, giving him encouragement and declarations of love. The muscles in her arms quivered as she dipped the cloth in the cool water and wrung it out over and over. Her back began to ache, as she bent and stretched, keeping Sam's fever at bay. But she never faltered.

Saul remained quiet in his vigil, watching as Ashton worked and cared for her destiny. Because that was what Sam was, her destiny. They had been meant to meet, fall in love, and make a life together. That life now had only a few short weeks left.

Saul had come to like and care for Ashton and Sam. He sighed as he thought about the loss these two were about to face. He touched Ashton's shoulder, drawing her attention.

Weariness was in the eyes she turned on Saul. "What is it?" she questioned "Is something wrong with Sam? Is he in more pain? What can I do?"

Saul smiled at her and shook his head. It is not Sam, but my own thoughts that make me restless. He looked at Ashton and saw the relief in her face. "I believe it is time for you to eat something," he told her, fatherly concern lacing his words.

"I'm not hungry," her reply was immediate and stubborn.

"That may be, but you will need your strength and rest if you are to help me heal Sam. I will be here to watch over him, and will alert you should the need arise," Saul promised motioning her toward the door.

Ashton opened her mouth to protest, but Saul cut her off with just the raising of one beautiful eyebrow. "Go now," he said. "Return when you have eaten. I will be here when you have finished."

Ashton placed the cloth in the pan and rose stiffly to her feet. Looking from Sam to Saul she rose to her feet and headed for the door. "I'll just fix something and bring it up here to eat."

"No," Saul said, "you need a break and some fresh air. Eat your food out on the porch, if you feel the need to combine the actions to save time, but do not return until you are refreshed."

Ashton wanted to protest, and tell him he had no right to boss her around, but she knew he was right. She needed a moment to breath. Still, she wanted to be with Sam so, again, she opened her mouth to protest. This time the eyebrow of the angel did not raise, but lowered and looked ominous. She snapped her mouth shut and sighed in defeat.

"Fine, but I will be back shortly," she conceded.

Saul watched her leave and marveled at the strength mortals were capable of. They were such fragile beings, easily swayed and guided. But when the situation called for it, they could be fierce and loyal, guarding and protecting what was theirs.

But Saul had things to do. He had business with Sam, and he needed Ashton to be out of the way for him to concentrate. He was going to have to wait until Ashton went to sleep tonight. Then his true work with Sam would begin. Saul crossed his arms over his chest and prepared to wait, but not for long.

CHAPTER 53

Ashton made her way down the stairs and into the kitchen to rustle up something to eat. She wanted something quick, so she could get back upstairs to Sam. Rummaging through the freezer, she located a TV dinner that looked like it had been in the freezer since Christ was a corporal, but it fit the bill of fast and easy, and if the truth be known, nuking food was Ashton's only real talent in the kitchen. So she pulled it out, dusted the crystals of ice from the box, opened it, and placed the tray in the microwave for the allotted five minutes.

While she waited for the timer to sound that her food was done, Ashton pulled out a chair by the table and eased her weary body into it. She laid her head on her arm, thinking she would rest her eyes for a few minutes. However, rest evaded her, as thoughts and images of the day started replaying behind her closed eyelids.

Not yet wanting to relieve the experiences of the day, she opened her eyes, got up from her chair, and busied herself around the kitchen. She thought that if she kept her hands busy the time would go faster, as she moved the placemats on the table a fraction of an inch one way and then moved them back the other way, pushed on each cupboard door to make sure it was secured, and rearranged the silverware drawer. "Why did five minutes on a microwave always seem to take thirty," she wondered to herself, impatient to eat and get back upstairs.

The microwave finally beeped, signaling her meal was ready. Ashton gathered her utensils, grabbed a potholder, and removed the cardboard looking burrito from the microwave. She decided a little fresh air would do her good, so she carried her tray to the small table on the porch, and settled into one of the chairs.

Instead of digging right into her food, Ashton took a moment to look out over the mountains and the sun that was beginning to set. The beauty of the outdoors never failed to amaze and inspire her. She had been here about a month, and had never seen two sunsets exactly alike, their colors and cloud patterns were ever changing.

Ashton tried to look at each day as if it were her last, because it might be. She wanted to take everything in, drink in the sights, and absorb the wildness of the mountains. Saul had been right, she'd needed the fresh air and a little time to unwind.

Thinking of Saul brought Sam back to mind, prompting Ashton to lift her fork and begin eating, so she could return to his side. She took a bite and thought, *Hummmm, looked like cardboard, tasted like cardboard, must be cardboard.* The thought brought a slight smile to her lips. It was nice to still be able to find humor in life, despite the recent chain of events that would send anyone into an emotional downward spiral.

Ashton ate about half of her meal then turned up her nose and pushed it away from in front of her, considering herself a saint for forcing that much in. *Maybe I should have checked the expiration date before I ate it,* she thought. Finding the humor in that she smiled and reminded herself, *What's the worst that could happen, I could get sal and die?* Not likely, considering she was already dead.

Ashton carried her tray and silver into the kitchen, disposing of the tray in the garbage and tossed her silver into the sink. She grabbed a soda out of the fridge, popping the top as she made her way back out to the porch. She leaned against the railing, once again studying the colors of the sky. She tried not to think of the future but sometimes, like now, it snuck up on her. She wanted to be spending this time with Sam, having his arms wrapped around her as together they watched the sunset, anticipating a quiet evening together. She didn't know if you could take memories with you when you died, but she was going to make sure she had plenty of wonderful ones with Sam stored up.

She set her can down on the porch railing, reached her arms over her head, and arched her back, stretching each muscle and joint in turn until they creaked and popped.

Shaking her arms loose at her sides, Ashton took one more deep breath of mountain air, drank the last of her soda, and then went back inside the cabin. She looked at the clock ticking above the sink, and found she had spent a relaxing forty-five minutes outside, something she'd sorely needed. She threw her empty can in the trash, washed her hands and face, and headed back up the stairs, ready for another bedside vigil beside the man she loved.

When she entered the room, she noticed that Saul had moved Sam into the middle of the bed, where he appeared to be resting comfortably. His skin, when she touched it, was not as warm as before, and his breathing was deep and steady.

"We did good, didn't we Saul?" she asked, pride and accomplishment in her voice as she gazed up at the angel she now considered her friend.

Saul had been standing by the door, watching the way Ashton fussed over Sam, touching him here and there as she rearranged the sheets and checked his condition.

"Yes, Ashton," he replied, "we did very good. Between the two of us, we have saved a life."

Ashton's eyes grew wider and more desperate as she looked into Saul's eyes with her own that were huge and damp. "Can't we save mine, Saul?" she quietly implored.

Pain, worse than that he'd transferred from Sam, rushed through the angel. He wanted, with all of his being, to be able to say yes to Ashton's simple request. He wanted to grant her a reprieve from death so she could know the happiness of life with Sam, bear his children, and be old and satisfied with her life's work when death finally came for her. But he could not. He wanted to shriek with his frustration.

"Come here, Ashton," he said quietly holding out a hand for her to take.

Ashton came to stand before him and grasped the hand held out to her. As they stood there holding hands, Saul's body took on that same glow Ashton had noticed when he took Sam's pain from him. She began to feel an inner warmth fill her chest, and a sense of well-being came over her. Saul had done the only thing he could for her, and that was to take the sadness from her heart and replace it with anticipation of her time to come with Sam. Ashton's sadness was now his, and he wanted to weep with the emotions that now filled his being.

Saul held Ashton's hand tight trying to reassure her all would be well. "You will be happy, Ashton," he said looking deep into her eyes. "What has happened to you is not fair, nor was it right, but it cannot be undone. Make the most of the time you have left. Feel everything and do everything with all the strength and wonder you can."

Ashton felt the warmth travelling up her arm, infusing her whole body. She knew Saul was helping her, and she gave herself over to his powers. They held hands for a moment longer, then she gripped the angel's hand tighter as if to say thanks. Gently removing her hand from his, she turned her attention back to Sam's motionless figure on the bed.

She sat on the bed beside Sam, resting her hand on his chest that was gently rising and falling with each breath. She could feel his heart beating strong as she fixed her eyes on his face and studied him. With her other hand she traced the features of his handsome face, the dark brows that covered beautiful blue eyes, the slope of his nose, the full mouth that she longed to kiss, his cheekbones and chin now covered in a soft dusting of whiskers. She ran her fingers through his silky black hair, pushing it gently from his brow. She memorized every detail with her eyes and hand, storing it all up for the time when she would no longer be able to see or touch him.

As the time ticked by and Sam continued to rest beneath her bedside vigil, Ashton began to feel sleepy, and was finding it more and more difficult to keep her eyes open. She would find her eyes drifting shut and her head bobbing onto her chest, before she would snap them back open, blinking rapidly to chase away the fatigue that threatened to take over. Finally, giving in to her fatigue, Ashton lay down carefully, snuggling in beside Sam, and pulling the sheet and blanket up under her chin.

"It's only for a minute, Saul," she said without opening her eyes.

Saul watched as she entwined her fingers with Sam's, gave a final sigh, a gentle smile on her lips, and fell into a much-needed sleep. He watched her a few more minutes, making sure she was truly asleep, and then he too closed his eyes.

But he was not going to rest. He had work to do, and it was time he got started.

CHAPTER 54

Sam floated in the darkness. It was warm, comforting, and all encompassing. There was no pain, no discomfort, only a feeling of being wrapped in a cocoon of dark velvet. It felt good to him. He liked it. *Maybe*, he thought, *I'll just stay here forever*.

"You won't, you know. You can't," said a voice as deep and dark as the blackness around him.

"Why not?" he asked. "And who are you?" he looked deep into the blackness surrounding him.

A dim light began to glow in front of Sam, growing in size and intensity until he could make out a figure in its middle. It appeared to be a man, but Sam could not make out the details of his face, as the intensity of the light coming from behind him, kept his face in the shadows.

"What are you doing here?" Sam asked the shadow. "This is my place, you can't stay here."

"Neither can you, Sam," the voice said.

"Why can't I? Did someone die and make you God? Who are you, anyway?" Sam asked again.

The figure floated towards Sam. *That can't be right*, Sam thought, *people did not float*. But as he continued to watch, that's just what happened. Floating slowly towards him, the figure came close enough that Sam could make out a face. A handsome face, framed with long dark hair. He saw the man was clothed in a snow-white robe that seemed to move with an unfelt breeze.

Sam wanted to rub the aberration from his eyes, but his arms remained at his sides, powerless to move at his command.

"My name is Saul, the figure said, "and for lack of a better explanation, I am an angel."

Yeah right, Sam thought to himself. *There are no such things as angels.*

Really," the voice said, amusement rich in its tone.

He had Sam's attention now, seeming to be able to read his thoughts before they escaped his lips.

"Who is to say what is real and what is not? Does this place feel real to you?" Saul asked.

Sam opened his mouth to say, "of course," but then shut it, as it dawned on him he didn't really know where he was. "What was this place that was so dark and comforting?"

"Okay," Sam said, "let's say for the time being that you are what you say you are. What do you want with me? Considering my past, I never really expected to see one of you guys"

Saul nodded his head and moved a little closer, "I am here to help you, you and Ashton."

Immediately grabbing Sam's attention at the mention of Ashton's name, Sam asked in a demanding voice, "Where is she? What have you done with her?"

"Nothing, she is safe," Saul replied.

A memory of Ashton telling him that she was dead, and that she'd been brought back to earth to live for two months to find her destiny and purpose, suddenly filled Sam's mind. Maybe he was dead too.

"Am I dead?" Sam asked. "Am I dead like Ashton claims to be?"

"No," Saul said, "you are suspended in a state of unconsciousness." He watched Sam's look of puzzlement as he struggled to understand what was happening to him. "Do you remember what happened to you?" the angel asked. "Tell me what the last thing is that you remember." He crossed his arms and waited as Sam filtered through his last conscious thoughts.

Sam squeezed his eyes tight, trying to wrap his thoughts around whatever it was that was tickling the back of his mind.

He remembered meeting Ashton, beautiful Ashton, a woman so perfect it hurt a man to look at her. He remembered the way she had gotten under his skin faster than any other woman ever had, how they'd seemed to be meant for each other. Then he remembered her telling him a wild tale of untimely death, and being granted a two-month extension because it had all been a huge heavenly screwup . He remembered the disbelief and the disappointment of having her turn out to be a whack job.

He remembered running away from her unbelievable story, leaving his mountainside, and travelling to Vegas to take out Jared James. As this memory came back, the rest rushed in like a tidal wave. The riot, the hit, being stabbed. After that things became fuzzy and unclear.

"Are you sure I'm not dead?" Sam asked again. "I remember being stabbed in the side, and then nothing. Why can't I remember what happened after that?"

"I picked you up and guided you back to Colorado, to Ashton," Saul said filling in some of the blanks for Sam. "We, Ashton and I, have cared for you, and you are healing from your injuries."

I'm on drugs, aren't I? Sam thought. *That's it, this is all a hallucination. It's not real.* He looked at Saul with a sneer on his mouth. "You're not real. Jared's people must have captured me and want information from me. So they drugged me."

Clever of them to plant images in his head to make him feel comfortable and trusting Sam thought. "I'm on to you pal," he said to Saul. "It isn't going to work."

He prepared to ignore the image in front of him until it disappeared, but Saul was running out of patience and time. With a bolt of lightening, that lit up the darkness surrounding him like the 4th of July, and a clap of thunder that rocked Sam's world, Saul grew in height and unfurled his immortal wings.

"Do not doubt who or what I am, mortal," Saul's voice thundered in the darkness surrounding Sam, "for time is short and I have much to tell you." Seeming to have captured Sam's attention, he continued, "I have come to you to let you know that what Ashton told you was true. All of it. She was taken before her time, and because her death was premature, she was granted two months time in which to learn her destiny and live her life to the fullest. She has one month left, and if she is to do what she needs to, you have to be made aware of the facts."

"And what would the facts be?" Sam asked, listening but still skeptical. Even the sight of the winged angel in front of him did not completely convince him.

"Fact one," Saul began, "is that the Messenger is no more. The James' job was your final job in that profession."

"Who is the Messenger?" Sam asked, bluffing in an innocent voice.

Again a flash of lightening and a clap of thunder boomed in the darkness.

"Do NOT play me for a fool!" Saul ordered in a threatening voice. "I have told you and shown you who and what I am. I know everything about you and your life. I am here to give you guidance and direction. If you are as smart as you think, mortal, you will listen to my words and learn from them. The last job you did almost cost you your life, and would have if I had not intervened. If you value your life, you will retire and not go down that path again."

"All right," Sam said. "I had decided this would be my last job anyway, so I will agree to your request."

Saul looked sternly at Sam, "That was not a request, it was a command."

Sam hated to be forced into doing something that he did not want to do, but in light of the current situation, and the fact that he really had decided to quit the business, he figured he would go along with what was happening, for now.

Saul could read Sam's mind like an open book, so he knew he had won the point.

"Fact two," Saul continued, "Ashton was telling you the complete truth. She risked everything when she trusted you with a story that most, including yourself, would think she was nuts for saying out loud. You handled that badly," he scolded Sam, "and I caution you once and only once, do not hurt her again. Her time is short and she should not have to finish it in anguish because of you."

"Sounds like a threat somewhere in there," Sam said.

"No," Saul said, "I never threaten." He smiled at Sam and Sam felt it all the way to his bones. This being would not threaten, but would make good on everything he said.

Sam nodded his head once in understanding and Saul continued. "If time was not of the essence there would be no need to direct the course of events."

"You mean interfere, don't you?" Sam butted in.

Saul wanted to take control of Sam's mind and just make him believe, to sidestep all the wise cracks and the attitude and get on with business, but he didn't. He wanted Sam and Ashton to come together because of the attraction and love that was meant to be. If Saul had been standing on the ground he might have started tapping his foot in frustration.

"You and Ashton's destinies are intertwined. You were meant to be together, to share love and life as one. I tell you this only so you will look into your heart and know the truth of my words. Although your time will be short together on earth, I can promise you that your time after this world will be eternal."

Sam's mind whirled with the knowledge he had just been given. Was that why he had felt such a strong attraction to Ashton at his first glimpse of her? Why he had dreams of her? Why all he could think of when he had been stabbed was not being able to see her again?

Sam looked into the eyes of the angel in front of him and what he saw was truth. Sam tried on the idea, wiggled it around a little, and found that it fit like his own skin. It was right, it was good, and Ashton was his. He smiled to himself, and then because he could not help it, shared the smile with Saul. Sam could almost feel the happiness radiating from every pore in his body. Sam stood a little straighter, looking around in the darkness. Turning back towards Saul, Sam made his own demands known.

"So, how do I get out of here? What are you waiting for? Don't just float there, get me home!"

CHAPTER 55

Ashton's eyes opened slowly as she crawled up from the warm cocoon of sleep. She had been so tired last night from the stress of having Sam delivered to her doorstep wounded and bleeding, tending to his wound, and fighting his fever, that she had slept like the dead. Speaking of Sam, she suddenly became aware of his body spooned up against her back. She had forgotten that she had crawled into bed with him last night, wanting to be close by in case he should wake and need her.

His arm lay heavily across her waist and a large, warm hand had crept up under her loose sweatshirt, resting just under her breasts on the warm skin of her ribs. It rose and fell with Ashton's breathing, which had become slightly faster at this discovery.

Ashton moved her own hand under the covers, pushing up her sweatshirt in order to twine her fingers with Sam's while he slept. She knew she should get up and check to make sure he was okay, but she wanted just a few more moments of him holding her close, his hand on her bare skin.

Ashton had never spent the whole night with a man, so she had no experiences to compare this with, but it felt so good and so right that she wanted to stay in bed, like this, forever. A smile spread across her lovely mouth as she wondered if she was taking unfair advantage of the handicapped. Giggling softly, she wiggled her butt more firmly against Sam and pulled his arm a little tighter around her. The heat coming off of Sam's body did not seem to be excessive to Ashton, and she was relieved that she would not have to repeat the care that had been so taxing yesterday. She felt like Goldie Locks, not to hot, not to cold, just right.

Wanting to get as close as possible, she inched her shoulders back until she could feel Sam's bare chest through her shirt. His breath tickled her neck and stirred her hair, as the two dark heads shared one pillow. Ashton lay relaxed and totally content. *Five more minutes*, she thought. *Just five more minutes, and then I will get up and start the day.*

She lay with her eyes closed, and had almost drifted back into slumber, when a low clearing of a throat brought her back to wakefulness, fast. She had forgotten about Saul. Her eyes scanned the room until they zeroed in on the angel standing in the far corner.

"Good morning, Ashton," he said with smug humor in his voice. "Did you sleep well?"

Roses bloomed on Ashton's cheeks, as she struggled to get out of bed. During the night, Sam had moved in close behind her and lain on her hair. Ashton now found herself brought up short, as she attempted to get out of the bed and face Saul with some semblance of dignity. Instead, she was forced to kneel beside the bed, pulling hands full of hair out from under Sam, until she was free.

Well, this is embarrassing, she thought, finally standing up straight. She turned with a look that challenged him to say something. It was all Saul could do not to burst out laughing, which immortals rarely did. Her hair, from its recent rough treatment, now looked like a birds nest had exploded on her head. Ashton, unaware of her appearance, smoothed down her baggy sweats and tried to look composed and casual. Placing her hands on her hips she adopted an unconcerned air and returned Saul's greeting.

"Good morning to you too, Saul. Did you sleep well? Uh, you do sleep, don't you?" she asked, unsure if angels needed sleep or not.

Saul smiled as he answered her question. "No, we do not need sleep the way mortals do, but thank you for asking." He found himself enjoying watching her fidget as she tried to make light of her situation.

Ashton stood in front of Saul shifting her weight from one foot to the other. She knew she was a grown woman, but she felt like she'd just gotten caught by her parents making out with a boyfriend in her room while they were not home. "Oh don't be ridiculous," she chided herself.

Pointing her finger at the closet door, Ashton inched her way sideways as she told Saul, "I'll just grab some clothes and go get dressed. It'll just take me a minute." She moved at lightning speed, away from the angels knowing smile.

Saul said nothing as he watched her grab clothes willy-nilly from their hangars, then rush into the bathroom, slamming the door behind her.

Ashton nearly fainted as she got a look at herself in the mirror. A mixer held to her head would have given her the same effect, as the bed head she now saw reflected back at her. It was a good thing Sam had not woken up and gotten a look at her. The sight of her probably would have scared him right back into unconsciousness.

Jumping into the shower, Ashton lathered her hair and body, then stood under the hot water only long enough for the bubbles to find their way into the drain. Not bothering with lotions or perfume, she pulled on her clothes, combed her hair, and applied a little mascara, before taking one last look in the mirror and deciding she was as good as she was going to get.

Ashton went back out into the bedroom, feeling better then she had in a long time. Sam was on the mend, he was here with her, and she was in love. In love. She liked the sound of that. She sat on the edge of the bed and gave Sam the once over. His brow was cool to the touch, telling her his fever was gone. The sheets binding his wound remained white, which told her that the wound was no longer bleeding. Satisfied that all was well with her patient, Ashton looked at Sam in a different light, admitting to herself that he looked good enough to eat, all warm and tousled from his night of sleep. She wondered when he would wake up, as she ran her fingertips over his face and stroked the arm that had been wrapped around her only a short time before.

Looking at Saul over her shoulder she was about to ask his opinion on the matter, when he obviously read her mind and answered, "It won't be long now. He is well on the road to recovery."

A tingle of anticipation ran through her as she heard those words. Turning back to Sam she bent down until her mouth was so close to his ear that she could feel the soft fuzz that covered his lobes, as she whispered, "Wake up, Sam. You're home now. Everything is going to be fine." When he didn't respond she increased the pressure on his arm and spoke a little louder into his ear, "You need to wake up and look at me, Sam."

Still he slept. The temptation of his ear so close to her lips was too much for Ashton. She finally gave in, placing tiny, nibbling kisses on the outside of her fascination. Slipping the tip of her tongue out from between her lips, she lightly, teasingly traced the shape, then gently used her teeth to pull the lobe into her mouth. She used her tongue and lips to grasp and taste it, and when she let it go, she could feel the dampness of it as she nuzzled it with her nose.

"Wake up, Sam," she pleaded with the still form on the bed. "I've waited forever for you and I need you to be with me now."

She continued to whisper tender words into his ear, branching out her kisses to include his neck and bare shoulder. "Please Sam, my love, open your eyes and look at me." Ashton tried for a few more minutes before sitting up and letting out a sigh of resignation.

"Soon," Saul said, waiting until Ashton had pulled back from Sam. He did not want to interrupt her, as he could feel her love for this man consume her attention.

When she turned her eyes up to his, Saul was amazed at the emotion he saw in their depths. The emerald green was arresting at any time, but now they shone as bright as a beacon on a stormy night, lighting the way for Sam to find his way back. Back to the land of the living and to his life with her.

Saul could almost feel envy for the two mortals before him and the journey they would be taking together very soon. Immortals did not have mates or the intimate connections these beings did. They were forced to tap into human feelings and experience these joys through them. The emotions in this room were some of the strongest Saul had ever felt. Love was amazing, he had discovered. It could make honest men do things that they would never dream of doing, or could bring the strongest of men to their knees. He never tired of watching love take hold and bloom, as two people discovered their destinies lay within the other.

"I believe Sam does not need my help in his recovery any longer," Saul informed Ashton.

"What do you mean?" she asked, rising from the bed to go to the angel.

"The connection I have been maintaining with him, to help him heal and to keep him alive, is no longer needed. He is strong enough and well enough to finish the job on his own," he explained, looking into her anxious eyes. Saul looked from

Sam to Ashton, then, taking her hand in his, gave her one more piece of advice as he prepared to sever his ties with Sam. "He may not be in danger of dying anymore, Ashton, but he will need your care for a while longer. Take care of him and watch over his recovery. Do not let him do harm to himself by attempting to do too much too soon when he awakes."

At Saul's pointed look, Ashton's face again became rosy. "Was he talking about sex?" she wondered. "I can control myself," she replied back, rather stiffly. "I'm not that selfish that I can't control myself and let him get better before . . . ." she let the sentence trail off and looked away from Saul, her cheeks still flushed a pretty shade of pink.

Saul let out a little sigh. Ashton had misinterpreted his advice and he needed to put her mind to rest. "Ashton," he said, "look at me." When she raised her eyes he looked at her with amusement. "It is not you I am worried about. I know Sam has a strong will and won't like admitting that he needs to be careful for a while. It is you who will have to be the strong one. Just take care of each other and nurture the love you have been given to share, even if only for a short time."

At Ashton's nod, Saul let go of her hand and turned to Sam. He closed his eyes and his lovely wings began to lift away from his body. The white ropy ties connecting Sam to him began to lose their glow and fade. When they had completely disappeared, Saul opened his eyes and watched as Sam drew in a deep breath.

The dark head on the pillow began to stir and the eyelids to flutter. Ashton went to the bed and knelt beside it so her face would be on the level of Sam's.

"Sam," she said in a low soft voice. "Can you hear me?"

Sam's eyes opened slowly as teal blue met emerald green. His, a little out of focus and confused. Hers loving and concerned.

"Ashton?" Sam's voice croaked through dry lips. "What happened? Where am I?" he asked his eyes roaming her face and the surrounding room. Just then, his eyes caught a movement over her shoulder. Years of training had him tensing, ready to attack or defend as the situation warranted.

Gentle hands pushed against his shoulders as he attempted to come to a sitting position. "Lay still, Sam," the deep, dark voice of his dream commanded. "You are in no danger here."

Sam lay back, reassured, as he cocked an eyebrow at the angel. "Hey, Saul," he said as his eyes began to close again, "nice to see you again."

CHAPTER 56

Sam slipped back into a light sleep while Ashton sat on his bedside looking from him to Saul. Questions clouded her emerald eyes, and a light frown rode between her brows. "What was he talking about, Saul?" she asked in puzzlement. Recalling the circumstances that had brought Saul into her life, Ashton's voice took on a note of panic as she asked, "How could you two possibly know each other? What business could have brought the two of you together? Is he dead, too?" She threw questions left and right at the angel.

Saul didn't even attempt to answer until she had run down and sat silently looking at him, waiting for answers. Saul weighed his responses carefully. He had given his word to Sam and would not break it. It would be his choice to tell Ashton about their encounter if he chose to.

"No, Sam is not dead. I simply went to Sam in his dreams, while he was unconscious," he finally admitted. "It was part of the healing process."

"What did you talk about?" Ashton asked, not satisfied with the puny answer Saul had given her?

"It is not my place to share that with you," Saul said. "You must wait for your answers until Sam is ready to tell you."

With that, Saul turned away from his two charges and went to the far end of the bedroom. He stood with his back to the wall looking at Ashton. "It is time for me to go, Ashton, I am no longer needed here." At her look of concern, Saul reassured her, "I will check in on occasion and listen if you call, but I feel that I am leaving Sam in very capable hands. You will be just fine together." He paused for a moment then went on, "Remember, Ashton, your time here is running short. Treasure every moment, and be happy. Until we meet again." And with that he was gone.

Ashton stared at the spot where the angel had been a few seconds before. She didn't think she would ever get used to it, him being there one minute and gone the next. Shaking her head slightly, Ashton went back to the bed and sat down beside Sam. She quietly watched him, reaching out often to touch him, stroking his face and body, learning the feel of him.

The quiet of the room was interrupted by a deep, long rumbling sound. Ashton actually jumped at the sound of her stomach letting her know that it had its appetite back and was impatient to be fed. She hated to leave Sam for even a moment, but knew she'd need her strength when he woke up. As she walked softly out of the room, it occurred to her that Sam was going to need something to eat when he woke up, too. Her cupboards didn't have much for either of them, so she was going to have to leave him for a while and go into town for food. Although she didn't have a car, she remembered that Sam and Saul had arrived at her doorstep in one. So, she would just barrow it, run into town for some supplies, and be back, hopefully before Sam woke up.

She quickly put on shoes and socks, ran a comb through her hair, pulling it back in its usual tail, not bothering with the few soft tendrils that escaped and lay on her cheeks. Heading down the stairs and reaching the door, Ashton stopped short and chewed on her lip. She had no money. *Well,* she thought, *Sam wouldn't mind if she used some of his, if he had any.*

Ashton ran back up the stairs and into the bedroom. Sam's clothes lay in a pile in the corner where Saul had dropped them the day before. She picked them up with two fingers, holding them out at arms length, making a mental note to burn them as soon as she could. It was funny, she had been covered with Sam's blood when she was tending him, but picking up his pants that were stiff with the same dried blood, made her stomach roll. She quickly went through the pockets, finding three one hundred dollar bills. These too had been soaked with Sam's blood. Dropping the pants back into a stiff heap on the floor, Ashton took the bills into the bathroom and began washing the money with warm soapy water. She smiles as a thought danced through her head, "Is this what they meant by money laundering?" Probably not, she decided. She rinsed the bills until the water from them no longer ran red. Satisfied that the bills would not raise suspicion when she presented them for payment, she pressed them between towels, then pulled out her blow dryer to hurry the drying time along. Looking none the worse for wear, she stuffed the bills into her front jeans pocket, snuck a peak at Sam to make sure he was still sleeping, and left the house.

She ran down the wooden porch steps and across the yard to the Sam's car. She put her hands to the glass and looked through the smoked windows, happy to see a set of keys dangling from the ignition. She opened the car door and prepared to get in but was stopped cold at the sight that confronted her. Once again it seemed that Sam's blood was everywhere but in his body. It had soaked into the seat, ran onto the floormats, and was smeared on the console. Bloody fingerprints covered the steering wheel, dash, and door handle.

"Oh shit!" Ashton said, as her eyes grew big and her stomach turned over at the sight. It looked like a massacre had taken place inside the car. *Well,* she thought, *there was no help for it, she was going to have to clean it up before she could get into the vehicle.*" She raced back inside and filled a bucket with hot soapy water, gathered some rags and headed back to the car. She opened the door and decided she was going to clean everything but the seat, where a large stain had worked it's way into the fabric. She would be able to cover that for now with a blanket, and then get one of those seat covers for a more permanent fix.

She rolled up her sleeves and went to work. It took her the better part of an hour and two buckets of clean water to make the car presentable. Spilling the last bucket of dirty water into the gravel on the driveway and stowing it back in the pantry cupboard, Ashton went back up to the bedroom to see if Sam was still asleep. Satisfied that he was resting deeply and comfortably, she tiptoed out of the bedroom and grabbed a plaid fleece blanket from the linen closet.

She tucked the blanket onto the driver's seat, covering the bloody stain. Ashton felt pleased that the vehicle was once again presentable and road ready for her trip to the store. Driving with the windows down and the fresh air coming in, it took Ashton little time to reach the town of Nora Falls.

Ashton parked on main street in front of a discount clothing store. *Perfect*, she thought to herself, *Sam would need something to wear when he was up and around.* She walked through the door to the store and was welcomed by the jingle of a bell and a kindly old woman. She searched through the racks, coming up with a pair of jeans, two flannel shirts, socks, underwear, boxers because he looked like the boxer type, and a pair of sneakers. She was pleased that her purchases had only set her back $50.00, leaving the rest for the groceries. Ashton thanked the lady and loaded her treasures into the car.

She locked the door of the car and made her way up the street to the grocery store. Guiding her basket up and down the isles, she filled her cart with soups, puddings, whole wheat bread, slivered ham, cheddar cheese, a variety of fresh fruit and vegetables, milk, soda, and juices. She splurged on some cookies from the bakery section, before making her way to the isle with aspirin, toothpaste, a toothbrush for Sam, and some large gauze bandages for his wound. After making two trips around the store, she was finally satisfied that she had a good variety of necessities and comfort food, and that she hadn't forgotten anything they might need.

Heading to the checkout counter she stood in line waiting her turn. She was slowly making her way to the front of the line when she felt a hand on her arm. Turning she was greeted by the smiling face of Laura May, the owner of the café where she and Sam had shared their "first date."

"Hello, Laura May," she said with a genuine smile, "it's nice to see you again."

Laura May grabbed Ashton and folded her in an engulfing bear hug. "I was wondering when one or both of you was going to surface," Laura said. "No one has seen hide nor hair of you since that night you came to my place to eat." Wagging her eyebrows up and down Laura leaned in close to as if to share a confidence with Ashton.

"Sam must be keeping you real busy, huh?" she whispered with a twinkle in her eyes. "How is he?" she asked keeping her eyebrows moving like the waves on the ocean.

Oh Lord, Ashton thought, she assumed, and probably the whole town too, that they had been holed up having wild monkey sex since the last time they had been seen together. *I wish*, Ashton thought to herself.

"Sam's fine," she replied, looking over her shoulder, willing the cashier to stop tickling the baby in the woman's cart, and get the line moving.

Laura May snooped in Ashton's basket as they waited. "My goodness, girl. It looks like you're trying to feed an army. Run low on food, huh?" again her question was accompanied by wiggling of her eyebrows.

Ashton was saved from answering as she made it to the front of the line and began placing her groceries on the moving belt. "Just picking up a few necessities," she told Laura May as the checker finished ringing up her purchases and placed them in bags. She deposited the proper amount of money on the counter, then turned to Laura May. "I'll tell Sam you were asking about him," she said. Snatching her receipt from the surprised cashier's hand, she grabbed her cart full of bags, and all but ran out of the store.

As she opened the trunk she thought to herself, please *don't let there be a body in it.* She let out a sigh of relief at the empty space that greeted her. Feeling slightly silly, she set the bags in, shut the door, climbed into the driver's seat, and headed the car toward home. *Aren't small towns grand?* she thought with a smile. *Everyone knows what you did before you even did it so, you might as well do it. I'm all for that.* Ashton laughed out loud at the thought that was chasing through her mind.

Ashton enjoyed the short trip to the cabin, rolling up the windows as she climbed higher up the mountain. It was still pretty cool in the mountains for late June, as the heat from down below grew to just a memory. When she pulled into the yard the sun was still high in the west. Ashton made three trips into the house, carrying bags until the car was empty. Her arms were tired when she was finished. She set about putting away the groceries, making herself a ham and cheese sandwich to munch on while she worked. She set some chicken noodle soup on the stove for Sam. Within a half hour everything was put away, and the soup was sending tendrils of steam toward the ceiling. She poured it into a deep soup mug, tucked the bags under her arms and carried it all up the stairs and into the bedroom, being as quiet as she could so as not to disturb Sam.

She did not have to worry on that count. As she came through the bedroom doorway, juggling her cargo, she saw Sam sitting up in bed, bare-chested and watching the door intently. When he saw it was her that was coming into the room, he leaned back against the pillows, let out the breath he'd been holding, and opened his arms to her.

CHAPTER 57

Ashton hesitated only a second as she decided what to do with everything in her arms. She dropped the clothes where she stood, then walked to the bedside and carefully set the soup on the nightstand. Slowly she lowered herself onto the edge of the bed, so as not to hurt Sam. But Sam would have none of that. He grabbed her and all but dragged her across his lap.

Their eyes met and held for a moment, each knowing what they wanted but unsure if the feeling was mutual. In the depths of the blue and green, love's flame was flickering as it came to life. Desire was there also, wanting to be let out, unleashed and satisfied. Sam eyes roamed hungrily over Ashton, learning and memorizing each lovely feature of her. She had the same bright glow that he had seen down by the lake that first day, but now it was different. He couldn't put his finger on why, but it seemed more intense. Or maybe it was just the fact that he wanted her more than he had ever wanted anything or anyone else.

He remembered being stabbed and thinking he would never see her again. But here he was, and she was in his arms, warm and soft. Her eyes were like a mirror reflecting a hunger that matched his. Sam raised his hands and framed her lovely face, tracing his thumbs under her eyes as his fingers tunneled into the soft hair at her temples. He could feel the incredible softness of her skin, the warmth of life in her body as she rested it more fully against him, and he wanted to pull her into his heart, keeping her safe and with him forever.

With his hands still cupping her face, Sam inched forward, at the same time pulling Ashton gently toward him, until their lips barely touched, teasing them both with the slight pressure and the promise of more to come. Time lay down and became still as the two stayed locked together by the mere meeting of lips. Ashton raised her hand and placed it on Sam's chest trying to steady her tilting world, but that simple act seemed to be the catalyst that broke the restraint Sam was holding over himself, as he let go of her face, wrapped his arms around her, and held her so tight that a breath of air could not have wormed its way between the two.

All of the feelings that each had held in check were transmitted from body to body, as the kiss became more demanding and the heat between the two became a raging fire, all consuming and hungry. Ashton wanted to be with Sam, right now, no more waiting or wanting, but Saul's warning came rudely to mind and would not go away. She was the one that was going to have to be strong and give Sam time to regain his strength, before they could satisfy the urge to be one. Ashton drew back, but only far enough to lay her head in the crook of Sam's neck, her arms wrapped around his waist and her chest resting on his. She brought her legs up onto the bed, curling them and enclosing Sam in a circle of protection. She could feel his heart thunder under her cheek and knew his desires were as strong as her own.

Sam kept one arm around her, and brought the other to rest on the back of her dark head, tucking it more securely under his chin. Satisfied that she was where he wanted her, he closed his eyes and rested his cheek on the silkiness of her hair.

"I thought I would never see you again," he said, his voice gruff with emotion. "You were all I could think of, the one thing that kept me going. I had to get back to you."

Ashton snuggled closer to him, then without looking at his face she asked, "What happened Sam? I know our last conversation did not go very well. Then I went over to your house the next day to try and make it right, and you were gone. I didn't know where you went or if you were coming back."

She did not put any accusations in her voice, but Sam felt the sting of his behavior anyway. What to tell her? He was not sure she could handle the truth of what he did, or would want to stay with him if he did tell her. If what Saul had revealed to him was true, then there really was no choice to be made. He would have to tell her all of it. There was no time to ease her into it, or to not be honest with her.

Sam held Ashton a little tighter to him and drew in a deep breath, then let it out as he began his story. He talked for a long time, sometimes the tail coming out fast and easy, sometimes halting and painful with truth.

Ashton listened quietly, not interrupting, letting Sam get it all out, not judging but still shocked at the profession he was in. If she was understanding things correctly, Sam was an assassin. True he worked for the government, but he still killed for a living. She never would have guessed his secret if he had not told her. Her attention was brought back to the present, as Sam's story came around to why he had left this last time.

"Even before I left, I had decided this would be my last job. I don't need the money, and it just felt like it was time to retire. It was an easy assignment, and it should have gone off with out a hitch, but something went wrong. I got stabbed before I finished the hit," he said. "I still don't know what happened. A friend helped me get out of the Casino, put me in my car, and I headed home. I had to get home, to you, Ashton." Sam paused as if thinking before he continued, his voice slightly puzzled. "I don't remember the trip home. I was in so much pain when I was aware, but those times never lasted very long, and before I knew it I was on your doorstep. Then I woke up, and you and Saul were standing over me, here."

Sam shifted a little and Ashton would have moved out of his arms but he held tight and continued his narrative. "I will admit to you that when you told me you had died and then been brought back for two months to finish you life, I thought you were crazy."

"But now?" Ashton asked when Sam did not continue.

"Now, I have to tell you that I believe you." He cleared his throat and said a little stiffly, "Saul kind of visited me when I was unconscious. He told me you were telling the truth and that we were meant to be together. He made me believe. I need to apologize to you for the way I took off, making you think it was your fault. Leaving you to wonder what was going to happen next. I need you to forgive me, Ashton." Sam said with a break in his voice. "I need you by my side for as long as I can have you. Forever would not be long enough for me. Can you forgive me, Ashton?"

Ashton could feel his body next to hers tense and prepare for the worst. Did he really think she would reject him? "Sam," she said, "there is something I have to tell you, and then it will be me asking for your forgiveness at the end. First, yes I do forgive you, though I do not feel there is anything to forgive. I would have thought my story was crazy if I were you, too. What you do or did for a living is your own business. It's not my place to pass judgment on you for that. That was your past, and I believe, with all my heart that I am your future, and you are mine."

Sam's body relaxed at her words, and he would have turned her face up once again for his kisses, but she stopped him with a hand on his wrist.

"I believe that you were hurt because of me," Ashton said, as she began her story of how she came to lose her life because of the Leonard's treachery. She told him that she believed she was the reason he'd been injured in the first place, because of Leonard's jealousy. "So you see Sam," she finished, "I believe I am the one in need of your understanding and forgiveness. If not for me, you would not be laying here in my bed trying to heal from a knife wound."

It was Ashton's turn to be tense as she waited for Sam to speak. "No," Sam said with conviction, "I don't believe either one of us needs forgiveness from the other. It would seem that our lives have become a playground for these angels. I never believed in them before, but now I have no choice."

Again Sam pulled Ashton more tightly to him before he asked in a quiet voice filled with pain and uncertainty, "Where do we go from here, Ashton?"

With eyes filling with tears for Sam's new burden, the burden of truth, she said in a small voice, "We're going to live, Sam. We're going to live, love, and be together for as long as we can."

"And how long will that be?" he asked. "How long do we have to squeeze a lifetime into?"

She raised her head finally and looked into eyes, that like hers were damp and haunted. "One month, Sam," she whispered, dealing another blow. "One month."

CHAPTER 58

Sam felt panic build in his chest as her words. One month? One month was not enough time. He wanted more, had to have more. Maybe there was a way to bargain with Saul. He would gladly give up his life so Ashton could live. He would find a way, he had to. He pulled Ashton to him for one more lingering kiss before pushing her gently away from him. "I think you came in with some food, and as unromantic as it sounds, I am starved."

Ashton was glad he'd changed the subject and lightened the mood. She put a smile on her face and nodded her head, "I went to the store and got us some food while you slept." Standing by the bed she shuffled her feet and cleared her throat before she made her confession to Sam. "I, um, didn't have any money, so I sort of barrowed some from you." She looked down at her feet then back at his face. "And since I didn't have a way to get to town, I sort of used your car, too. I hope you don't mind."

Sam was surprised that she should seem nervous telling him this. "You can borrow anything I have sweetheart. I fact you can have everything I have. Don't ever doubt that."

A smile bloomed on Ashton's face, brighter then any sun Sam had ever seen. Bending over she lifted the soup and turned towards the door. "I'll go warm this up and be right back."

She made it all the way to the door before she stopped, came back, set the bowl on the stand again, and, leaning over, gave Sam a kiss on the lips that almost started his hair on fire. Ashton pulled back a mere inch and waited for Sam to open his eyes. When he did she had to smile, as the teal blue eyes were glazed with desire so thick, it took him two blinks of his lush black lashes to come back to her. He swallowed so hard that Ashton heard it, and her beautiful, deep green eyes turned darker as smoke swirled and promises were given with just one look.

"Just thought I'd let you know that I'm hungry too," she said in a whisper that Sam had to strain to hear. Her breath caressed his lips and his blood boiled with desire.

He had never wanted anyone like he did Ashton, never needed anyone like he needed her, and all thoughts of food and injuries flew out of his head as he brought his hands up, meaning to grab her and never let her go. She stepped just out of reach and once again picked up the soup.

"I'll be right back," she said again. Tossing a saucy wink over her shoulder she left the room.

Sam sat for a second, mouth agape at her teasing, then shaking his head and smiling, he threw the covers off of his legs. He swung them over the edge of the bed and deciding to test the waters, slowly rose to his feet. His muscles felt weak, as if he had been in bed much longer then just one day. But he was not dizzy, so he figured he was doing pretty good. He had seen the clothes drop from Ashton's arms earlier and now went to dig through them for something to put on. The clothes were not expensive, but would fit him to a tee, and were just what he wore when he was in his mountains. Still he did not put on everything, just the boxers, which made him smile as he pictured Ashton holding them up and deciding what to buy.

Slipping them on, he made his way into the bathroom to take care of business. He used her comb to get the knots out of his dark hair and used her toothbrush to get the bad taste out of his mouth. He just might have to apologize again to Ashton, this time for having breath that would drop a rhino at twenty paces. He washed his face, then turned to check his back in the mirror. He unwound the strips of cloth holding the bandages in place and surveyed the damage in the mirror. He was surprised to see the cut was stitched up and appeared to be healing well. The edges showed no signs of redness or infection, but the pull when he tried to raise his right arm left him no doubts that he was far from normal. Between Saul and Ashton he was sure that he owed them his life. Something he was not going to forget. He always repaid his debts.

Sam turned off the light and made his way back to the bed. He really did not want to get back in, as that would mean he had to admit he was still sick. *Then again*, he thought, *that was exactly where he wanted to get Ashton*. Not for a quick fling but to make long, slow love to her. He wanted to know her from the top of her dark head to the bottom of her feet. He wanted to imprint her in his mind and on his body. He wanted her to know him just as intimately. He wanted to get under the covers with her and never come out. He wanted.

Sam turned on the small bedside lamp and crawled back into the bed. The light it emitted was soft and low, lending an aura of privacy and intimacy to the room. The sun had gone down behind the western peaks, leaving only the small pool of light to see by. It was quiet, with only the sounds from the night coming in the open window of the bedroom. Sam didn't want to share Ashton's attention with anyone or anything, and he usually got what he wanted. He fluffed the pillows behind his back and smoothed the blankets over his legs. He looked at the door expectantly, willing Ashton to come back to him.

He was not disappointed as he heard her soft tread on the stairs. She walked into the bedroom carrying a tray with the soup on it, plus what looked like a sandwich, chips, and a small bundle of grapes. Two cans of soda were there also and

Sam thought, *bless you,* as he realized he was as thirsty as he was hungry.

Soda was the last thing on Ashton's mind, as she stopped in the doorway to look at Sam. The soft light from the lamp fell on the man in her bed, leaving the rest of the room in shadows. He looked dark and dangerous, as he waited for her to come to him. There was nothing else in the world for her, except the man in that pool of light. Nothing outside the circle that she was interested in. *Damn, Saul,* she thought again. *This was going to be hard to resist.* Her teeth almost itched with wanting to taste the flesh spotlighted for her.

Gripping the handles of the tray a little harder, Ashton moved into the room and placed it over Sam's lap.

Uh-oh, Sam thought, as he looked at the tray. If he was not careful he would be tipping it over and making a mess.

"I thought I would join you," Ashton said as she sat at Sam's knees. She curled her legs to the side and reached for the sandwich on the tray. It was thick with slivered ham, lettuce, cheese and a hint of mayo. She took a bite and looked at Sam who had not made a move towards his dinner. Her mouth was full and she had to finish chewing before she could tip her head to the side and ask, "Is something wrong, Sam? Don't you like the chicken soup? I've got others to choose from if you want something else."

Sam looked from the soup to Ashton's sandwich, and pointing at it he said, "Can I have some of that?"

"Are you sure you can handle eating something like this right now?" she asked. "I mean wouldn't something easy on the stomach be better for you?"

Sam flashed her a killer smile and held out his hand for half. At her hesitation, he simply said "please?" and she folded. She tore the sandwich in half and handed it to Sam. He took a huge bite and closed his eyes in pure enjoyment. "This is wonderful," he said as he chewed. He reached for the chips and happily munched his way through a handful, as Ashton watched with amusement at the pure pleasure on his face. His eyes sparkled and he smiled at her between mouthfuls. When he was finished he licked his fingers off and lay back against the pillows. He sighed contentedly, as he lay there enjoying the moment, then sat back up and attacked his can of soda. He tipped it up and drank like a man fresh out of the desert, not stopping until the last drop had disappeared down his throat. Returning the can to the tray Sam belched loudly and rubbed his belly. He was a happy man. His belly was full, he had a beautiful woman by his side, he was alive, and he was in love.

Ashton swallowed her last bite, then dusting her hands off she looked at Sam and asked innocently, "Can I get you anything else?"

Sam captured her eyes with his, licked his upper lip slowly, and in a husky voice answered, "Dessert."

CHAPTER 59

"Oh look," Ashton chirped, "grapes." She held up the fat, juicy bundle, and managed to look everywhere but at Sam. *If I look at him,* she thought, *I'm going to fling the tray across the room, followed by my clothes, and have to claim amnesia if Saul finds out I took advantage of a wounded man.*

Sam on the other hand watched Ashton as she held up the grapes, avoiding his eyes. He noticed the slight trembling of her hand as she held the unwanted fruit. He wanted something juicy and ripe but it was most definitely not the grapes. Sam sat up straighter in the bed, pushing the tray aside. Dumping the bundle of grapes back down on the tray, Ashton took it from his hands and stood by the bed.

"I'll just go put this in the kitchen, and then I'll be up to tuck you in," she said nervously. Her face became flushed as she heard what she was saying, and watched humor run rampant on Sam's face. *Oh god,* she thought in frustration, *it sounded okay in my head before it came out.*

Sam chuckled low as he watched Ashton escape from the room with the tray full of dishes. He knew without a doubt that Ashton was thinking the same thing he was. Both of them wanted to put an end to the frustration and give in to their desires.

Sam had every intention of making love to Ashton tonight, and the only way she was going to get to tuck him in was from under the covers. He leaned back against the pillows and waited for her to reappear. When she didn't come back, he became restless, twisting and turning until the covers were a tangle around his body. Finally he settled and once again set his eyes on the unopened door. As the minutes ticked by, his eyes began to droop. The lids, covering half of his teal blue orbs, were so heavy that they refused to open all the way, no matter what he tried.

Ok, Sam thought, maybe *I'll just rest for a few minutes until Ash gets back*. He told himself that he could and would wake up when he heard her come into the room, so a little rest wouldn't hurt. Gently he closed his eyes and slipped into a light slumber.

Ashton took the tray downstairs into the kitchen, putting the dirty dishes in the sink and the grapes back into the fridge. She didn't trust herself to go back up just yet, so she filled the sink with hot soapy water and washed the few dishes from their meal. She wiped down the cupboards, the table, the stove, and every surface she could reach, stalling for time. Finally, when the whole kitchen was spotless and she could find no other excuse to delay, she made her way back up the stairs.

Slowly she climbed, telling herself the whole way, that she would not climb into bed with Sam, no matter what he said or how good he looked. Squaring her shoulders and pasting a smile on her face, she entered the room. The vision that greeted her stopped her where she stood. From across the room, she looked at Sam, and her heart melted. He lay in the bed, the covers bunched around him like a nest, fast asleep. His head was turned to the side and his hands lay open and relaxed on his lap.

As Ashton watched he moved, snuggling down into the bed and pulling the covers up under his chin. He looked so warm and innocent, this dark, handsome dangerous man that she had fallen hopelessly in love with.

Unable to resist any longer, she crossed the room and sat on the side of the bed. Sam did not stir, as she bent to remove her shoes. Looking down at the clothes she still had on, she rationalized that she could not sleep in what she was wearing. Crossing the room she rummaged through the dresser drawers until she found a small, stretchy pair of shorts with the words, *oh baby* written across the butt, and a spaghetti strapped tank top. These would have to do, she told herself.

She went into the bathroom, stripped off her jeans and shirt, and put on the pajamas. She washed her face, brushed her teeth, combed her hair until it shone with dark, rich highlights, and, as a final touch, she placed a dab of her favorite perfume behind each earlobe. Looking at herself in the mirror, Ashton decided that a quick swipe of the mascara wand was needed. Satisfied, she turned off the lights and walked on bare feet to the bed.

It didn't even enter her mind to sleep in another bedroom. She was sleeping with Sam. She had done so the night before and it had all worked out. Besides, if she was in another room she wouldn't be able to hear him if he needed her in the middle of the night. Feeling quite justified, she lifted the sheets and eased herself in beside him.

He was lying on his side, facing away from her, so Ashton mimicked his position from the night before and spooned up against his back. Her hair streamed out behind her covering her pillow, her head sharing Sam's. She buried her nose in his silky softness and breathed deep of the warm, male scent that was his alone. She draped an arm across his waist, and pulled her legs up to fit as best as they would behind Sam's, as she was almost a foot shorter than he. She could feel the short dark hair on the backs of his legs tickling her smooth thighs.

Her skin became acutely sensitive, the spots where their bodies touched burning with the contact. She wanted to run her hands, and lips, up and down Sam's body, learning the textures of his skin, the contours of his muscles. *No*, she thought to herself, *Sam needed to rest for a little while longer.* She could wait.

Reaching behind her, she turned off the lamp leaving the room dark except for the moonlight spilling in through the curtains, then snuggled up once more to Sam's back. Slowly relaxing, Ashton enjoyed the closeness of him. Her arm that had been firmly around Sam's waist, loosened as she slipped towards sleep.

Maybe tomorrow, she thought, *maybe tomorrow she and Sam could be closer*. Her last thought before she totally succumbed to sleep was that she was finally home, finally complete, finally whole.

Saul watched from the corner of the room, not having revealed his presence to Ashton or Sam. He smiled gently as Ashton gave in to sleep, marveling at the restraint she had displayed. He knew they both wanted and needed each other, and he knew those feelings were beyond strong. But Ashton had resisted because of her love for the man beside her, and her need for him to be well and healed. He had cautioned Ashton about rushing into bed with Sam to give them both a chance to see if they really felt strongly about each other. From what he could see and feel, they both were ready for the commitment of love.

Soft white, ropey tendrils once again extended from Saul to Sam, as Saul began the process of speeding Sam's healing. He poured energy into the body he was attached to and remained that way throughout the night. At morning's first light, he removed the connection and was satisfied that Sam was almost completely well.

He spared the couple, so closely entwined, one more glance before he began to fade from sight. He would keep and eye on them, but he felt sure he was no longer needed. *Thirty days Ashton*, he thought, *I'll see you in thirty days.*

CHAPTER 60

Sam woke first as the early morning light was just making its presence known. It peeked sleepily through the curtains in the bedroom, its light chasing the shadows from the corners, sending them to rest until the evening came again. He lay there breathing deeply of the fresh mountain air, not thinking of anything in particular, just enjoying being alive.

With that thought, he raised his arms high above his head and stretched like a cat just waking up from a nap. A slight twinge in the side of his back made him realize that he was lying on his injured side. He was surprised that this caused him very little pain. He puzzled over it for a moment and then he gave a small nod and a ghost of a smile before he whispered, "Thanks, Saul. I know it was you man. I owe you. I owe you big time." He looked around the room, seeing no one, but feeling a presence. "I know you can read my thoughts, Saul, I get that, but if you could just not do that for a little while I would appreciate it. I've got something to say to you and I haven't quite worked it all out yet."

Sam lay still and waited for a sign that Saul had heard him and he was not disappointed. As a gentle peace settled around him, he knew, he felt it, his message had been received, and his request would be granted.

Satisfied, he put his hands to his cheeks and scrubbed his face, hearing the whiskers rasp against his fingers, the sandpapery sound seeming loud in the early morning stillness. Sam stopped rubbing his cheeks and looked thoughtfully right, then left as his puzzlement grew. He held his hands up in front of his face. Yup, one, two, both there. He gingerly raised the covers and looked down his body at the third hand. The one resting innocently on his groin.

Sam's mind had been fogged with sleep since waking, but now all of his senses came alive as if he had been touched by a live electrical wire. He could now feel the warmth of a body resting against his back, feel the soft, slow breaths whispering through the hair on the back of his neck, hear the almost nonexistent sounds of sleep, and smell the unique scent of woman all around him. But not just any woman, his woman.

Her smell was imprinted on his brain. Sam was sure he would be able to find her in a pitch-black room using nothing but his nose. He almost felt cheated as he realized Ashton had spent the night in his bed, and he had slept right through it.

Innocent as it may be, just having her touch him was having an effect on him. His body began to react, rising and thickening with each tick of the clock. He lay for just a moment, relishing her touch, her warmth and the feelings they inspired. He wanted to glue himself to her for all time and never let her go. The thought of the shortness of their time together crept in and like a worm in an apple, threatened to sour the moment. But Sam grimly pushed it away and vowed to cherish each moment with her. Starting with this one.

Sam gently lifted the sleeping hand and turned over to face her. He studied the sleeping face before him, memorizing each delicate curve and contour. Her hair streamed out behind her leaving her face uncovered and bare to his searching gaze. She looked so beautiful. So soft and inviting. Sam accepted the invitation and raised his hand to trace her face with strokes as soft and light as a gentle breeze. He traced the arch of her eyebrows, felt the soft, thickness of the dark half moons that were her lashes and let one finger travel the length of her nose. He touched her cheeks, each so soft, so warm and he marveled in the fates that had made such a woman just for him. He lifted his hand and rested it on the dark cap of hair that streamed out to fall in thick, rich waves across the pillow, disappearing over the edge of the bed.

He inched closer to his sleeping beauty, until their noses almost touched. He let his eyes roam once more over the face so close to his, before he gave in to the temptation to taste. His lips met hers with the merest of touches. Small nibbling kisses were his gift to her, urging her to wake and join him.

Her lashes fluttered and she drew in a deep breath as she straightened her legs and stretched. Sam anticipated her waking, but she snuggled down again and drifted back into a light doze. He smiled a smile that was edged with humor and devilry. *Oh no, my sweet*," he thought, *it's time to wake and join me.*

Becoming more determined, he again pressed his lips to hers, but with more pressure than before. His tongue came out to lightly trace the seam that was closed to him. He wanted in, he wanted her lips to open to his questing and welcome him. He knew when she woke because the lips that had been so warm and still beneath his, had come alive. They gave back each light touch and soon grew hungry in their seeking. The hand that Sam still had buried in her thick hair added pressure to bring her lips more fully against his There was no resistance as the kiss deepened, her free arm wrapping around his shoulder and her leg raising to hook him by the hips. Sam could feel her down the length of his body and in the corners of his soul.

He wanted to be slow and gentle with her this first time, but wasn't sure he could hold back. He wanted her, needed her, and had to have her. Sam lowered his hand from the back of her head and let it find the hem of her shirt. His fingers glided underneath it, touching the silky skin of her stomach, feeling the warmth and heat she gave off. His hand moved upwards taking the shirt with it, until it was bunched under her chin.

"Raise your arms, Ash," he said, his voice coming out deep and thick with desire. Her arms lifted as she rolled to her back. Sam rose above her, using both hands now to remove the thin barrier and expose her to his hungry gaze, and even hungrier touch.

He remembered his dream, the dream of them making love in the open. This was better, so much better, the feelings were richer, the smells were added, and her warmth almost burned him wherever his hands touched. And they touched everywhere. He let his hands move from her shoulders down her torso, up the sides, over and over, cupping her breasts and laving them with attention from his hands and mouth.

Ashton arched her back and dug her heels into the bed as he worked his magic. Her world spun. Feeling she needed an anchor to tie herself to this world, she brought her hands up to Sam's shoulders and, without meaning to, dug in. But that only satisfied for a short time as the need to return Sam's touches grew.

She let her hands roam where they wanted, finding hard muscles, smooth skin, a soft matting of hair, and a hard thickness still covered by cloth. Slipping only her fingertips inside the elastic of his boxers, she drew them down, slowly, teasing him by denying him and herself the final touch that they both craved. When she could reach no farther she relaxed back and let him finish the task of removing them, leaving nothing to stand between them except the brief, stretchy shorts she had put on the night before. *Oh baby indeed.*

She wanted Sam to remove them now and take her, but instead he teased her, slowly stroking her through the cloth, making her press harder against his hand as he used the heel and fingers to drive her to the edge of madness with desire.

Ashton's breathing was coming out in little gasps followed by soft moans when Sam finally eased his fingers under the elastic of her shorts and drew them down, following their path with his lips. He kissed and licked his way down one long leg and back up the other, all the while avoiding the juncture where they met, where she wanted him the most. Making his way back up her body, Sam came to rest over her.

"Look at me Ash," he urged, "open your eyes and look at me."

Ashton had left her eyes closed while she and Sam had begun the journey of discovery. She had not needed the sense of sight to feel Sam, to know him, to cloud the intensity of her feelings. Not being able to see had allowed her to concentrate on her hands, on his hands, and the path each had taken. The sensations had been deeper and truer without her vision. But Sam wanted to see her eyes before and as he joined with her.

As she opened her eyes, Sam could see the deep green swirl and smoke with her emotions and her desires. Locking eyes with her, Sam positioned himself at the entrance of her body and waited for her to let him know she was ready. Ashton sent her message by gliding her hands down his sides, gently skimming over his wound, then stopping low on his hips, pulling him towards her.

Sam entered her slowly, but steadily, until he was buried in her warmth and wetness. She fit him perfectly, and he her, as they found the rhythm of love unique only to their union. Sam held back until he was shaking with the effort of restraint. He watched Ashton as she moved with him. He felt her reach the edge, watching as her eyes met his in stunned surprise, then went blind with her release. He followed a heartbeat later, feeling himself splinter into a million shining shards, then coming to rest with his love, leaving them both banked embers on the hearth of love.

CHAPTER 61

Sam and Ashton lay naked entwined on the bed, the covers having been sent to the bottom forgotten. A light film of sweat covered their bodies, fusing them together in the physical world. Without opening her eyes, Ashton reached out and found Sam's hand. Linking their fingers, she brought it to her lips to place small kisses over the knuckles and to rub it along her jaw line.

"I love you, Sam," she said with no preamble, no hesitation, and no regret in her voice.

Time stood still for Sam as the words she spoke echoed in the chambers of his heart. They filled it to bursting, and he was awash with the love he felt for her. It sang through his veins until he could feel every part of him respond to her love. For the first time in his life, he wanted to return the words and mean them. He had said them before, but had meant them only in the sense of friendship. This feeling in no way resembled what had come before. He felt stronger because of her. Hell, he felt ten feet tall because of her, and he was complete. He was whole, realizing he had everything he would ever want or need laying right here beside him.

He became aware of Ashton trying to pull her hand away from his, and he could feel her stiffness as she lay rigid beside him. He realized he had hesitated answering her declaration of love and had unintentionally caused her pain and embarrassment.

"No my sweet," he said, pulling her hand back into his and her body closer to him, "Don't leave me. I was lost in thought, but it was all about you." He tipped her chin up and looked deep into her emerald eyes. "You and I, and how much I love you. How your love makes me feel whole and good and complete. How I am more because of you. How I will never let you go."

Ashton met Sam's blue gaze. The light within those orbs spoke of truth and honesty, and reached out to assure her of his love. A love that was as strong and sure as hers, that belonged to her alone. Ashton's emerald green eyes held Sam's and words were not needed, as each could see for themselves the feelings the other had.

"I want to remember this moment," Ashton said, allowing herself to fall into the teal blue eyes so close to hers. "Making love with you was wonderful and I have never felt that way before, but the feelings I have now, the way I feel now is what I will remember. The closeness, the oneness, the contentment, the completeness, the love. I wish I could explain it better, to help you understand."

Sam gathered her to him and held on tight, as he saw the sadness lurking at the edges of her eyes. "Oh my god," he cried inside, "you can't take her from me. We've just found each other and I can't lose her. Not now, not ever. Please Saul?" he begged, "don't let me be without her."

On the outside, Sam held her and whispered softly into her ear, "I do understand, Ash. I understand completely. My love for you goes deeper then the physical aspect of us. But come to think of it," he said, with a devilish spark igniting his eyes and needing to lighten the mood before he fell apart completely, "that part was pretty damn good too. Maybe we'll have to have a repeat performance just to make sure. No wait, many repeats. In fact, we may never have to leave this bed again. You realize that bathing is very over rated, as is eating and other boring daily routines." He wanted her to be happy, to smile and have only good memories with him, for she was not the only one that would have to store them up.

Ashton giggled her amusement as she rose to his antics and lightly poked him in his side. "As good as all that sounds, I do have to get up now." She sat up and swung her shapely legs over the bed.

Before she could make it all the way up, Sam wrapped his arms around her nakedness and pulled her flush against him, resting her back against his chest, her hips surrounded by his thighs. He nuzzled her neck and cupped her breasts from behind. "Where do you think you are you going?" he asked, his mouth getting busy tasting and kissing all of her that was within reach.

Ashton's brain began to fuzz, but before she lost her intentions completely she pulled away and stood up. "Um," she said, her tongue feeling thick in her mouth, "I have to pee."

Sam was totally engrossed with the sight in front of him. Ashton naked, her hair in wild disarray, and her body rosy from their love making. What she said did not register for a moment, so taken was he with her beauty. The glow around her was brighter then ever, almost too much for him to take in. He was bordering on overload, but knew he'd gladly blow a gasket for her. Just as long as he had the chance to look at her, to be with her, to love her. God damn it, everything led back to the fact she was leaving him soon.

With that thought, his eyes darkened and the face of the Messenger could be seen. Dark, cold and focused. He was going to beat this thing or die trying.

"Sam?" Ashton questioned, "Is everything okay?" She had seen the change come over him and had no clue what was wrong. She was so happy right now that her insides felt like warm butter, all melted and gooey. But Sam looked like a stranger to her all of a sudden, angry and cold.

Sam blinked back to the present noticing Ashton standing uncertainly in the middle of the room. He wiped the look from his face, rose from the bed, went to her, and wrapped his arms around her. Their bodies came together, from the two dark heads, hers on his chest, his lowered to bring his cheek to the top of hers, all the way down to the legs that touched, Sam's spread slightly giving her room to move in-between, letting him surround her, protect her.

"I love you, Ash," he said into her hair, "I love you."

Planting a kiss on her head and giving her cute butt a light tap, Sam stepped back. "Go pee," he said and let his arms fall to his sides, as she turned to walk to the bathroom.

Sam wondered if she walked like that normally or if she was teasing him as she strutted her way to the bathroom, then closed the door firmly in his leering face. Sam took a step towards the door, intending to share a shower with his love and maybe a little more before they were done, but stopped in mid stride as he felt a familiar warmth at his back.

"Hello, Saul," he said without turning around. "We have to talk."

CHAPTER 62

Sam turned to face the angel that he owed his life to, but at the moment he was not thinking about that. He was thinking about Ashton and her situation.

Saul let his eyes roam up and down the naked human before they settled and locked with Sam's. The angel's warm and brown, Sam's cool with a bit of frost in their depths.

"I felt your need to talk to me," Saul began. "If now is not a good time, then I will return later."

Sam shrugged his shoulders, not really caring that he did not have a stitch of clothing on. "Now is good," he said glancing at the closed door that hid Ashton from their view.

"She will not be aware that we are talking," Saul assured Sam as he glided without a sound farther into the room. Saul knew this was not going to go well, so he dispensed with the pleasantries. "Speak," he said.

Sam moved closer to Saul, not stopping until a mere arms length separated the beings. One immortal, with the power over life and death, one mortal with the power over life and death. Different but the same.

"I've been thinking about Ashton's situation," Sam began. "In particular the two months time limit she has been given. I find this unacceptable," he said matter-of-factly. "For her to have to pay for a mistake that was not of her making, is wrong.

She was innocent in the whole affair, but yet she is the one who stands to lose the most. Not to mention what I will be losing, a future with the woman I love.

"Ah," said Saul a knowing look in his eyes. "You are thinking of yourself as well as Ashton. Correct?"

Sam's gaze became a little frostier. "The proposition I have for you is not for me alone, but yes, I would benefit as well."

Saul crossed his arms over his chest and waited for Sam to continue. At Sam's continued silence Saul again said, "Speak."

Sam looked Saul straight in the eye, so Saul would be sure to see his sincerity, as he said, "I would like to give half of the years I have left in this lifetime to Ashton. We would have more time together, to love and to die together. I don't see why this wouldn't work," he pleaded. "What could it hurt if you granted us this one wish."

Saul knew what Sam was going to ask of him even before Sam had verbalized it. Looking down at the floor, Saul took a moment to find the best way to explain things to Sam. When he finally raised his head his eyes were full of compassion for the man before him.

"I know the pain you are in, I can feel it," he said softly. "What you've suggested is a good idea, but I have no power to grant your request. The pages of destiny have been written, and must play out as such. Beings such as myself are here to watch over their charges, and to give guidance and assistance when needed. We do not change destinies, we do not make bargains. If we had that power, the world would be in chaos. We feel your pain, your wants and your wishes. We would grant all that was asked of us if we could, and in doing so, create chaos. So even though your idea is a good one and sounds feasible, it is beyond my power to help you."

"That's bullshit," Sam ground out. "One of you has already meddled with destiny, that's why we are in the mess we are in now."

"Exactly," Saul stated calmly. "Look at the mess, as you put it, that trying to rearrange destiny has caused. Each action causes ripples that affect others as well. I can not break the rules for you or Ashton, as much as I would like to." Saul held his hands palm up in front of him as he said this and Sam could see the small tremor that shook them.

"Fine," Sam said, clenching his fists at his sides, "then take me instead of her. I'm good with that also. She is young and has her life in front of her. Give her mine. I want you to."

Saul again shook his head and said, "The same rules will apply for any situation you may come up with Sam. I can't do this for you."

Saul could feel the frustration rolling in waves off of Sam. He wanted to keep the woman he loved with him for as long as possible and to take on her troubles as his own. He wanted to fix them and was grasping at straws to do so.

"I can't just sit by and let this happen," Sam said to Saul, beseeching him with his eyes. "Don't you see, I can't just let this happen? There must be something I can do, some trade I can make to help her."

"Making trades and deals is only in fairy tales," Saul said. "It doesn't work that way, it never has."

"What do you want from me?" Sam asked. "I'll do anything you say, if only you'll help us."

Saul knew the pain Sam was feeling, the need to protect and care for what was his. But there was no help to be given.

"The only way I can help you is to advise you to live each day as if it were her last. Think of the things you would do and the memories you would be making if you had all the time in the world. What would be the special moments you would share? Figure out what you would do to make those moments special, then do them. Only do them now. Do not wait for the time to be right, make it right. Make her last weeks ones she will treasure for all time."

"I can't think," Sam said running his hands through his hair until it stood straight up from his heard. "I wanted this to work so badly that I did not plan for anything else."

"That's not like you," Saul scolded, trying to make Sam pull himself together. "This is not for you Sam it's for her. Do not be selfish with your time or yourself. Do you understand me?" the angel demanded.

Sam did. But he was struggling to keep his emotions in check. He wanted to scream in anger, he wanted to beg and plead and grovel for more time. He wanted to strike out at the angel for not giving them help. But most of all he wanted to hold on to the love he had finally found.

"Don't take her Saul, please don't take her." Sam felt as if his heart was breaking as he watched Saul, willed him to give in.

"It has already been decided," Saul said quietly. "I can do nothing. You will be together in time, for all time, but for now both of your destinies have been written."

Saul began to fade from sight, but before he was completely gone he gave Sam one more piece of advice, "Make your plans Sam, start them today, make them unique and special. Hold nothing back, treasure each second with her. Consider yourself blessed with this gift of love you have found and do not dwell on the future or the past. Live in and for the moment."

With that Saul was gone leaving Sam alone in the bedroom. Sound slowly seeped into Sam's consciousness and he heard the shower start and Ashton begin to hum. Sam clenched his fists together and drew in a deep breath. He needed to be in control before he went in to Ashton. He wanted to give her and himself memories worthy of a lifetime, and he was going to start today, now, in the shower.

Sam crossed the room and quietly opened the door. Steam rolled out around his ankles before he closed the door and went to join his love. He hoped the water heater had a big tank because this was going to take a long while. He pulled the shower door open and entered, shutting them in together, close, hot, wet and wanting. Sam gathered her into his arms, her body slick and steaming. He vowed to himself not to let her go until she could not stand up on her own. And he didn't.

CHAPTER 63

The days slipped by, turning into weeks as Sam and Ashton filled each one with love and beauty. They took long walks in the woods, picked armloads of wild flowers, made love under the bright light of day and the cool softness of the starlit summer nights. They had picnics in green meadows and romantic candlelight dinners in front of crackling fires. They stayed close to each other and reached out to touch, kiss and fondle often. Never seeming to get enough of each other.

On a perfect day towards the end of July, Sam sent Ashton out to gather an armload of pinecones and what ever else caught her fancy. Anything to keep her busy for a few hours. He had a plan and he worked like a mad man to finish before she returned.

The daylight was waning before Ashton returned, arms loaded and looking like a wood nymph, a circlet of dandelions woven in her hair. Sam met her at the door. Taking her treasures from her, he put them aside and gathered her into his always-waiting arms. His kiss was long and deep, taking her breath away, leaving her drugged with love when he allowed her to come up for air.

Taking her by both hands, Sam began leading her into the house, but stopped before they'd gone too far. "Close your eyes," he breathed against her lips as he could not resist kissing her moist lips again and again.

"Close my eyes?" she asked not comprehending as her brain was fuzzy from his attentions.

"Please?" he asked. "I have a surprise for you."

Ashton complied as he led her into the living room and brought them to a halt just inside the door. Sam moved to stand behind her and wrapped his arms around her waist, nuzzled her neck and crooned, "Okay, you can open them now."

Ashton kept her eyes closed for a second longer, enjoying the feel of Sam close to her, around her. She drew in a long deep breath recognizing his scent and was content with her life. She had everything she could have wanted or wished for. At a little squeeze from her love, she opened her eyes to stand still in shock and surprise.

There before them was a beautiful pine tree decorated for Christmas. It had lights that twinkled, bulbs that glowed, tinsel that gathered in all the colors around it, and cotton around the trunk that looked like the mounds of snow that would cover the mountains on Christmas Day.

"Merry Christmas in July, my love," Sam whispered in her ear.

"Oh, Sam," Ashton breathed out, tears springing to her eyes. "It's so beautiful. I love it." She turned in his arms, wrapping hers around his neck, pulling his lips down to hers. "I love you," she said as her lips met his in a molten kiss, branding him as hers.

Pulling back, her green eyes deepening and dancing with laughter and mischief, she spun away and dove under the tree looking at the presents that had her name on them.

"I didn't know, Sam. I didn't get you . . ." she suddenly cut herself off in mid sentence, and with a graceful movement rose to her feet and backed out of the room. "I'll be right back, don't move," she admonished as with a swirl of rich locks she fled up the stairs.

Sam looked after her with a wry smile on his face and waited where he was until she returned, a gift-wrapped package in her hands. She laid it under the tree and looking up at Sam she said so softly that Sam had to bend down to hear her, "Merry Christmas Sam, I'll always love you."

Sam joined her on his knees and motioned to take her into his arms, but Ash would have none if it.

"Oh no," she said laughing, "presents always come first on Christmas morning."

Sam let her have her way and handed her the presents he had been hiding. One was a locally carved statue of a young girl standing beside a fawn. One was a lightweight sweater, the color reminding Sam of her eyes after they had made love. One was a bottle of her favorite perfume, and the last was a small box meant to hold treasures fashioned out of tiger-eye stone.

As Ashton opened each one she oohed and ahhed with the craftsmanship and the rightness of Sam's choices. She loved them all. Before she gave in and kissed Sam she reached under the tree and handed him the one gift meant for him.

"Here, my love," she said softly, "for you."

Sam took the gift and held it for a moment. He had not expected any gifts from her, as he had not told her what he was planning. The surprise of the gift was felt deep in his heart. He didn't want to open it. He just wanted to hold it and know that it was from her. But at Ashton's fidgeting he finally, carefully, slowly unwrapped his present. When it was unveiled, he held in his hands a photo of her taken sitting under a tree, looking up into the camera with all the love she felt for him shining out at him.

His hand shook as he traced the face he knew so well, and he raised eyes that were damp with tears to look into hers so close and so dear.

"When was this taken?" he asked, his voice husky with feeling.

"I took it myself, Sam. I wanted you to have something to remember me by. I wanted you to be able to see me anytime you wanted."

Sam laid aside the picture and gathered Ashton close in his arms slowly rocking her, not saying a word, not having to voice his feelings as they poured out of his body for her to feel and see. They remained that way for a long while, until the grumbling in Ashton's tummy brought Sam back to earth laughing.

"I even have supper made for you," he told her. "You sit here and I'll go get it. That is if you don't mind eating around the tree?" he asked.

Ashton wiggled her butt into a more comfortable position, and smiling at Sam she said, "I think this is the perfect place to have a romantic dinner with the man I love. Can I help?"

Shaking his head, Sam left the room holding up one finger to let her know he would be back in one minute. When he returned he carried two heaping plates filled with turkey and all the trimmings. Potatoes, gravy, sweet potatoes, buttered corn, dressing and big fluffy rolls with butter melting over them.

Ashton clapped her hands, and taking one of the plates from Sam nabbed a piece of turkey to sample. "How did you prepare a turkey dinner without me knowing?" she asked.

Sam sat cross-legged beside her and began to pour wine into glasses he had hidden behind the tree. "I didn't," he said, "Laura Mae made it for me and delivered it right before you came home. I hope you like it."

Ashton could wait no longer, and dug into the delicious meal, closing her eyes in ecstasy with every bite she took. "This is wonderful!" she admitted between bites. "I love Christmas in July."

Sam ate his meal, all the while watching Ashton and the pleasure she got out of every thing she tasted. By the time the food was gone and their bellies were full, the sun had gone down and the shadows began their nightly appearance. Sam crawled over to the fireplace and started a small crackling blaze to go along with the mood. Ashton waited until he returned and then leaned her back against his chest.

Watching the fire and sipping her wine, she was content and happy with the day and more in love with Sam than ever. That he had thought to give them a Christmas memory together was amazing to her. He knew her better then she knew herself. She would have loved to have thought of this for them, but was happy with the outcome anyway. They really were two halves of a whole. Each anticipating the others wants, sometimes even before they had thought of them themselves.

Sam and Ashton sat that way, looking into the fire and enjoying each other's nearness, for the better part of an hour, sharing kisses and touches, never wanting the night to end. As the fire died low, casting soft shadows across the room, Sam turned Ashton in his arms and rested his hand along her soft lovely cheek.

"I love you, sweetheart," he whispered, his eyes delving deep into hers. "For now and forever. You will always be with me and me with you."

He kissed her so sweetly, that when Ashton opened her eyes they swam with tears and glowed with the love she had for him. Kissing her once more, softly, gently, Sam drew back until he rested his forehead against hers, swallowed once and asked from the very depths of his heart, "Will you marry me?"

CHAPTER 64

Ashton's eyes opened in stunned surprise. She knew that if she and Sam had had time on their side, they would have married. But, with the knowledge of what was to soon happen, the idea had been buried in the back of her mind only to be brought out and cherished as a wish never to be.

"How, Sam?" she asked in a choked whisper. "How can we get married?"

"I can't give you a traditional wedding," Sam said, grasping her hands with his. "But I can say the words with you and mean them with all of my heart. Tomorrow there will be a full moon and I thought, if you agree that is, that we could meet at a little secluded glade I know of and under the full moon and all the stars we could exchange our own vows together. Will you join me?" Sam asked, "Will you marry me and be my wife?"

Ashton's heart melted as she listened to Sam's plans. He was trying so hard to make everything perfect for her and she found it hard to speak around the lump in her throat. She gazed deep into his eyes, leaving him no doubt that all the stars he had mentioned were now in her eyes and he knew her answer. He could see it, but he wanted to hear the words.

Feeling his need, Ashton's smile was dazzling as she said "Yes, Sam, yes I will marry you."

Two souls came together, as lips met and hearts entwined in the rightness of their love. Little sleep was gotten that night as plans were made, details worked out and two bodies came together to make long, sweet, slow love. Each knew that words would make the commitment no stronger, but each also wanted the normalcy of the act.

Ashton was so excited that at dawn's first light she was up digging through her closet, as she tried to find something just right to wear. After all, this was her wedding day and she wanted to be beautiful for her husband. Just the thought of Sam becoming her husband made her giddy with joy. Trying not to wake Sam, she quietly went through her closet pulling clothes out one at a time only to reject them and put them back. She had no idea what she wanted, but was sure she would know when she found it. She dug her way to the very back and out again before she finally stopped, convinced and disappointed that what she wanted was not there.

Blowing hair out of her face Ashton turned to face the bed and saw Sam raised up on one elbow grinning at her efforts. Her face was flushed from being buried in her closet, some of her hair was still caught up on clothes she had looked at and rejected, and a slight frown marred her smooth brow in frustration. But her eyes took on a glow when they met Sam's. She hurried to the bed jumping in the middle and landing on top of the covers, reminding Sam of a new puppy with buckets of energy to spare.

"Happy wedding day, my darling," she said before she planted a kiss on his lips that had his mind turning to more immediate needs. Ashton giggled and pulled away from his seeking hands, as she sat back on her heels at arms length. "You have to wait for tonight, Sam."

At his slight frown, she laughed and bounced off of the bed. "I have to find something to wear today, and I would like time to think of just the right words for my vows. So, you're on your own for a little while."

In the face of her enthusiasm, Sam gave in graciously, deciding he had his own list of things to take care of before tonight, anyway. "You're right," he said, also getting up from the bed. "I'll grab a quick shower and then run some errands before lunch." He moved towards the bathroom asking over his shoulder if she needed anything from town. Assuring him she didn't, he jumped in the shower and made quick work of cleaning himself up. He dressed and gave Ashton a lingering kiss before getting into his car and disappearing down the driveway.

When he was gone Ashton went into her parent's bedroom and opened the closet they had shared. She had never cleaned out the clothes, pretty much leaving everything the way it was, as if they were going to show up at any minute. Memories washed over her as she ran her hands over familiar objects she had played with as a child. She missed them still, and would have loved for them to be here today to share the joy of her marriage to Sam. *Soon, Mom and Dad*, she thought, *I'll see you soon.*

She began to go through her mother's things one at a time, and was sure she could still detect the faint scent of her favorite perfume. Pulling a handful of fabric towards her, she buried her nose in their folds, and there it was, she was right, the scent was still there. Brushing the clothes back into place, Ashton began her search in earnest, flipping garments aside until she came upon a flowing, deep emerald green gown.

It shimmered as she moved it and felt as if it was made of rich, dark satin. Ashton pulled it from the closet and went to stand in front of the full-length mirror on the door. She held it up under her chin, turning first one way and then the other. She loved the way the gown moved as she twirled with it, and she knew this was going to be the dress she would wear. It made her skin look creamy and white and her eyes darkened with the color. It was not the white of tradition but it was what she wanted. She took it off of the hanger and shook it out to see if it needed to be pressed, or cleaned, or even repaired, but it was perfect. Almost reverently, she laid it on the bed to await her later in the day.

Closing the door behind her, Ashton left the room and went into the kitchen, where she packed a small basket with a bottle of wine, two glasses, and a clean white tablecloth to sit on. She added a few grapes and pieces of other fruit in case they became hungry. This would be for toasting her marriage to Sam in the glade following their vows. Setting the basket aside, she glanced out the window and noticed Sam just pulling into the yard. Her heart did a little flip flop at the sight of him and she hurried to the door. She met him on the back porch and shared a kiss filled with longing, as if they had not seen each other in weeks.

"Umm," she said, "you must have missed me."

"Always," he said holding her close. Grabbing her hand he started to lead her away from the house.

"Where are we going?" she asked skipping to keep up.

"I want to show you the way to the glade before it gets dark. I'll be going a little bit early to do some things, so I want you to know how to get there."

Ashton paid close attention, and found the distance not far and the way easy to follow. When they stepped out into the small clearing, Ashton knew Sam had chosen the perfect spot. Open to the sky but surrounded on all sides by bushes and trees, the ground was covered with wild mountain flowers, and the air fragrant with nature. It had an air of privacy and intimacy about it that promised secrets would be kept and memories would be long-lived and relished.

"Thank you, Sam," was all Ashton could say. "It's perfect."

Squeezing her hand, Sam led the way back to the cabin, and they spent the afternoon hours eating a light lunch and trying to hide the impatience each was feeling. When darkness fell they parted, each to get ready for the upcoming event.

Sam showered and shaved, then dressed in a dark suit with a crisp white shirt and teal blue tie. He gathered the things from the car he had picked up in town and made his way to the clearing. He set up a small stone table and covered it with candles and flowers. He placed a small stereo on the ground and put in a CD of romantic instrumental tunes, and waited for his love to join him.

Ashton took her time showering. She dried her hair and fixed it in a rich, dark fall that hung down her back. She slipped on the dress, relishing the way the fabric clung to her curves as it slid down her body. She added light makeup and a dab of the perfume Sam had given her yesterday. Stepping back, she looked at herself in the bathroom mirror and was amazed at the woman staring back at her. The love on her face gave it a radiant glow, and she almost didn't recognize herself.

Ashton noticed a small patch of fog clinging to the corner of mirror, and on impulse she took her index finger and penned Ashton Barnhart through the middle. She smiled to herself and left it there as she walked out of the room, turning the light off as she went. She went to the kitchen, but noticed the basket was gone, so she knew that Sam had taken it on ahead. There was nothing for her to do but go to the clearing. With a nervous little breath, she stepped out the back door into the moon lit night. She stood for only a moment staring at the moon that would bear witness to their vows this night. "Thank you for Sam," she said to no one, nothing, everything. She walked down the steps and, as beautiful as a dream, disappeared into the forest.

CHAPTER 65

Sam lit the candles, placed the glass globes over them so the breeze could not disturb their flame, and waited for Ashton to join him. He heard the soft rustle of her footsteps shortly before he saw her enter the clearing. She was a vision of beauty as she glided across the small space toward him. Again, Sam noticed the glow that seemed to surround her, as she moved to strand straight and tall by his side. He handed her a single white rose to hold for her wedding bouquet as they turned to face each other in the quiet of the forest.

The music he had selected was only a mere whisper of sound and did not detract from the night sounds of nature. The brilliant moon, the blanket of stars, the droning insects, and the small animals would be their witnesses as they exchanged their vows of love on this night.

Sam raised Ashton's hands to his lips and kissed them reverently one by one before he began to speak. "My love," he started, his voice low and vibrating with the emotions he felt. "Never in my life did I think I would find the one person who was meant for me, made for me, my other half. But fate and destiny have brought you to me and I will thank the gods every day for the rest of my life that it was you. You are kind and sweet. Your laughter is music to my ears. Your smile fills my heart and warms me every time I see it upon your face. Your touch lights a fire inside me that will only and forever burn for you. You have made me more then I could ever hope to be and I owe you my life. You have changed my life by showing me the goodness and love that can be found with one's soul mate. And you are my soul mate. I have no doubt that we were and are meant to be now and forever."

Sam paused as he reached into his pocket and withdrew a wide gold band. Raising Ashton's left hand he slid the ring on to her third finger before once again, looking deep into her eyes, letting her see all that he was, all that he felt for her, he continued. "I love you, Ashton Rider, and I want more then anything in this world for you to be my wife. To join me in this life and in the next as my one true love. I will give you anything, do anything, you have only to ask it of me. I would give my life for you. I promise to love you all the days of my life and to do what is right and what is good so you will never be disappointed in me. I enter into marriage with you with no regrets and with only love for you. Thank you, thank you for being my love, my life, my wife."

When he was finished, Ashton wiped a tear from first her cheek and then his, before she kissed his trembling lips with all the love she held inside for him. Then, taking one small step back from Sam, and smiling into his face, she began to speak.

"My one love. I can think of no greater pleasure or honor then to be your wife. All that you are, all that you have shown me, makes me love you more each day, until I feel as if I will burst with the emotions you stir inside me. You came into my life and have made me whole and complete, until there is nothing more I could ever ask for. Only your love. That you love me and that you have accepted my love in return is the greatest gift I have or will ever have. Each morning I wake up and greet the day knowing you are by my side and in my heart. Each night I close my eyes and cross into sleep knowing that you are by my side and in my heart. That is where you will always be, by my side and in my heart, as I will be with you."

Ashton lay down her flower, and removing a ring she had placed on her right thumb, she lifted Sam's left hand and placed a gold band on his third finger. "This ring that I place on your finger, is a symbol of the love I feel for you now and will feel for you forever. I only want your love and your happiness. That you have asked me to share this life with you, is a precious gift to me, and I will hold it inside me and guard it for all time. My one true treasure in this world is the love that I have found with you. I am rich because of it, and will be thankful all of my days that I have you. From this moment forward I will know you as my love, my life, my happiness, my husband."

Ashton held both of Sam's hands in hers and brought them to rest over her heart. She drew him to her and placed a kiss of promise and hope on his lips and shared the kiss each bride receives from her husband.

"I love you, Ashton, Sam said as he gathered her to him.

"I love you, Sam," Ashton returned with love and joy beaming from every pore of her body. "Did you bring the basket I had in the kitchen, Sam?" Ashton asked her head snuggled under Sam's chin.

"Uh huh," he said not wanting to move.

"Let's pour the wine," she said.

Sam let her go only long enough to retrieve the basket and open the wine. Ashton spread the cloth and poured two glasses before lowering herself to sit. Sam joined her and raised his glass to touch it to hers.

"To my wife," he said, "to Mrs. Sam Barnhart."

Ashton smiled into his eyes and touched her glass to his saying, "To my husband and to our love."

Sips of wine were mingled with kisses and murmured declarations of love. Soon the glasses were forgotten and the warm summer night became their blanket, as they made love for the first time as man and wife. The moon dimmed and the stars paled before the light that their love cast towards the heavens.

At the Window to the World, Saul closed his eyes and the window became dark as the angel bowed his head and said, "Destiny has been fulfilled."

CHAPTER 66

On the first morning after they had shared their vows, Sam asked Ashton to remove her ring and read the engraving he had had placed inside. She pulled the ring from her finger and read the inscription, "Forever in my heart, S." Ashton kissed him sweetly, and with damp eyes had once again confessed her love to this man. She told him that there was a story attached to his ring as well, and asked him to take off his ring also. Before he could read it though, she had covered his hand, and looking into his eyes explained her decision.

"This ring, the one I chose for you, was my fathers. I have kept it, along with my mothers, since they were taken from me four years ago. I kept both sets here at the house, because it was the place I remember all of us being together and happy. After you asked me to marry you I took it out, knowing that they would have approved of you and our love. I wanted you to have something special, which is why I gave it to you."

She removed her hand and let Sam see the inside of the circle of gold. Sam noticed two inscriptions inside the ring. The first read "Soul mates M & P", and the second one said "For all time S & A."

"The M is for my father Matthew and P was for my mother, Piper," Ashton explained. "They were very much in love from the first day until their last, and I wanted us to be that way also."

Sam slipped the ring back onto his finger and made a fist of his fingers as if he was afraid the ring would come off if not held tight. "Thank you, baby," he said as he kissed her to let her know he approved of her decision. "I'll cherish it, always."

The rest of the day, they decided, would be spent doing whatever they wanted. "After all," Sam said, "we ARE on our honeymoon."

Ashton had clapped her hands in delight, and packing a lunch had led them on a walk that took them all over the mountain, not bringing them home until the sun had dipped low in the western sky. They had chased each other through the trees, skinny-dipped in their lake, picked flowers, collected rocks, made love, and gotten drunk on the joy of being one. Their happiness knew no bounds, and they lived as if there would be no tomorrow. Though neither one would put voice to the thought, it was in the back of their minds, squirming to get out, threatening to make their time desperate.

When the sun finally set, Sam brought out candles, and they laughed as children over pizza and sodas, though both agreed the romantic setting made the food that much better. There was no mention of bedtime, but by mutual consent the journey was made, hand in hand, to their room taking time as many stops were needed to touch and taste along the way.

The night sped by as the two wallowed in the joy of each other until the glut of their acts saw them falling into dreamless sleep, wrapped in a cocoon of entwined arms and legs.

Sam woke first the next day, enjoying the quiet of the early morning and the feel of his wife beside him. He thought about his life and the drastic change that had taken place within the last two months. His time as a hired gun for the government was over and his new life as friend, lover, and husband had just begun. He had never been as content and relaxed as he was now, looking forward to each new dawn with Ashton.

He felt her stir in his arms and gave her his attention, neither saying a word but communicating with sighs, gasps and willing bodies.

Ashton rose from the bed and moved into the bathroom, soon to be joined by Sam. Steam billowed and fogged the mirror before two very clean people turned the water off and grabbed two fluffy towels to dry off.

Sam immediately noticed the spot where Ashton had drawn her name on the mirror the night they were married. He smiled, and before she could wipe it off, he grabbed her hand, kissed it and said, "Leave it. I like it there." Smiling a little sheepishly at being caught doing something so young and foolish, Ashton dropped her hand.

They both dressed for the day, then made their way down the stairs, arm in arm. Ashton made Sam a breakfast of french toast and bacon, filling his belly with food as she filled his soul with warmth.

"Sam," Ashton said after the dishes were placed in the rack to dry, "I saw something in the woods yesterday that I would like to get, so I need you to give me about an hour by myself." At Sam's questioning look Ashton went into his arms and stood on tiptoes to kiss him. "It's a surprise. I won't be long."

Sam relaxed and kissed her back. "Alright," he said, "I think I can amuse myself while you are gone. Are you sure you don't need me to come with you?" missing her before she had even left.

"It's a surprise," she said again, laughing as she stepped away. She grabbed a bag and headed to the door. "Be back soon, love you," she said as she let the screen door thump behind her and jogged across the yard to disappear into the trees.

It was Ashton's intent to pick some wild flowers and place them in a hollowed out log she had seen in the long grass beside a path they had taken the day before. Humming to herself she made her way into the trees. It took her about fifteen minutes to locate the log she wanted. Its weathered look and perfect bowl shape would look wonderful on the porch, and she wanted to give it to Sam. She liked finding him treasures from their mountain and watching his face as she presented each one to him. Her gifts had ranged from delicate flowers to rocks filled with crystals and pieces of petrified wood. Sam probably thought she was crazy but she loved the treasures Mother Nature had provided for them. They meant more to her then expensive things that could be purchased.

As she was bent over trying to pry the log from the ground, Ashton felt a warmth creep into her body and her hands stilled at their task. She wiped her hands on her thighs and rose to face the angel, Saul.

"Hello, Saul," she said a tremor in her voice. No more would come out of her mouth so she stood silent, dread gripping her. She knew why he was here, but wanted to deny it with all of her being.

"Yes, Ashton, it is time," he said, pity and compassion in his voice while grim determination was etched on his face.

"Are you sure?" she asked. "Is there nothing I can say or do to change this, to have more time?" She had to ask even though she knew the answer, could see it in his bearing.

"No, Ashton, I am truly sorry. This has to be."

"Can I have time to say good bye to Sam?" she asked.

"There is no need to say good bye, Ashton," he said, "you will see him again. Time will pass swiftly and your parting will feel like only a moment in time."

Ashton let the tears fall freely as she took the steps towards Saul. Saul raised his hand to her, palm up. "It's time, time for you to join me and mine."

Ashton took the offered hand and felt herself floating and falling at the same time. Her body began to fade and she found it hard to focus on the physical world as her journey with Saul began. The log by the path remained untouched and the sounds of nature that had stilled before the angel's presence, resumed there humming as life moved on.

CHAPTER 67

Sam puttered around the house, putting away the washed dishes and looking in the fridge for something he could throw together for lunch. Ashton had been gone for almost an hour, and he wanted to surprise her with something delicious to eat when she walked in the door. He thought he knew what she had gone into the woods to get. He had seen her eyeing a fallen log yesterday, and had suppressed a laugh as he knew their house would be its new home before long.

He found the makings of a chef salad, one of his specialties, so he spent the time slicing and dicing until he had all the fixings ready to put together. He looked at the clock and noticed that another half hour had passed. He imagined that before too long Ashton would be back asking for his help as the log probably still had roots embedded in the ground.

He wandered into the living room and turned on the T V for noise and to maybe catch up on the world happenings. He found a national news channel and went to grab himself a soda before settling down to watch. He had just opened the fridge door when the male announcer came on saying, "We have breaking news. The body of missing heiress Ashton Rider was discovered a few hours ago, still in the wreckage of her four-wheel drive vehicle in a ravine outside Boulder Colorado. The twenty-eight year old woman has been missing since late

May when she left her home in New York, saying in a note that she needed some time alone. Friends became worried when she could not be reached and filed a missing persons report with police after a week of no word from her. Miss Rider's parents, Matthew and Piper Rider, died almost four years ago, leaving their fortune to their only child, Ashton. A passing hiker found the wreckage and notified Boulder police, who say the investigation as to what happened is still ongoing. Stay turned for more details as they become available."

Sam had left the refrigerator door standing open as he made his way into the living room to stare at the TV. He saw a picture of Ashton splashed across the screen, but could not, would not believe what was being said. *It couldn't be true*, he thought. *She's here with me. She's here with me.*

Sam made his legs move, slowly at first and then with speed as he hit the door and ran into the woods. "Ashton!" he called, loudly, panic rampant in each word. "Ashton!" He ran until he found the spot where Ashton had been only an hour before, finding her gone, the bag she had taken, lying empty and forgotten on the ground. Sam clenched his fists and felt the bite of the ring on his left hand as it cut deep with the pressure. He cradled the hand that held his wedding ring, so new to him, against his chest, felt his legs turn to water, fell to his knees, and wept as his heart broke.

The deepening shadows finally brought Sam back, as slowly getting to his feet, he made his way back to the house. All was as he had left it hours before, TV on, refrigerator door open, and the forgotten salad ingredients setting on the cupboard. He shut off the TV and cleaned the kitchen, removing all signs of anyone being there.

He made his way up to the bedroom where he and Ashton had found love, made love, and slept wrapped in each other's arms. He gathered the few things of his that had found their way into the house, and stuffed them into a bag. Looking around the room he felt the emptiness, as if the life had gone from it. He put the bottle of perfume he had given Ashton into his pocket, wrapped the picture she had taken of herself for him as a gift in the bag of clothes.

He walked down the stairs and out the back door, setting his load on the steps and turning to lock the door before making his way back to his home. But then he stopped and reentered the house. Taking only five minutes, he came back out, pulled the door shut behind him, and locked it.

As he left he took nothing with him except the bag of clothes with their precious cargo enclosed, and the bathroom mirror.

He didn't look back.

CHAPTER 68

Ashton stood with Saul, wisps of clouds swirling at her feet. One second she had been standing in the woods with the angel and the next, well she was here, wherever here was.

"Where are we, Saul?" she asked, curious.

"This is where we live, for lack of a better explanation," he told her.

"Am I a part of "we" now?" she asked, looking around at the vast expanse of sky and clouds.

"If you choose to be," the angel replied.

"There is a choice?" she asked, puzzled.

Saul faced her, standing with his hands behind his back, his folded wings creating a backdrop of fluffy whiteness to rival the clouds. "You have earned a place here with us if you so choose. You will be given the gift of immortality, the powers, responsibilities, and all the abilities that come with it."

"What would be my other choice?" Ashton wanted to know what her options were before making any kind of commitment.

"You could choose to go back to earth, to be reborn to live as a mortal again."

Saul read Ashton's interest correctly and shook his head from side to side.

"No, Ashton, you would not go back as yourself, nor would you remember Sam or the life you just left. You would be born as an infant and live the life destiny has written for it."

Not liking that choice at all, Ashton had little to think about before she told Saul, "I choose to stay here."

Saul nodded his head, and would have walked on to begin Ashton's training, but noticed she had not followed him.

"Saul," she quietly asked, "where is Sam? Can I see him? Will I be allowed to watch over him, to see the rest of his life? Not really to keep tabs on him but, well, to just make sure he is happy and well?"

"I am Sam's guardian," Saul said, "but there is a way for you to look in on him."

He led her to the clearing in the clouds and introduced her to the "Window to the World."

"With this portal you will be able to see anyone you wish. But," he said, "you must be careful that you do not wish for him to join you now or in the future, not until it is his time to do so, or you will cause the same chaos that Leonard did. Before this window you may watch and keep track of his activities and his life, but no more. Do you understand?"

Ashton nodded her head. She would not wish the same fate on her love that had befallen her. "I understand, Saul," she said.

"But?" Saul asked, hearing the hesitation in her voice.

"I still love him. I have the same feelings inside me that I had before," Ashton answered his question.

"Yes you do," Saul admitted to her. "You bring all the love and goodness that you had and felt in life with you when you die. You will always remember all the good times you shared, the special moments he created for you, and will be able to share them with him again, in time."

"How long, Saul?" she asked quietly, "how long until we are together again?"

"That I can not reveal to you. Each guardian is entrusted with the knowledge of his charges life span and may not reveal it or change it. Again, to do so would have painful consequences," he explained.

"Okay, Saul," she said "but I miss him so much."

At her words her tears began to fall. They rained down her face, and with a wave of his hand Saul brought the Window to life. It showed Sam standing in his back yard looking out over the mountains, as a warm, light rain began to fall from the sky.

He looked up and seemed to see Ashton, as her tears turned into the gentle rain that fell about him. He could almost feel her beside him, and he ached with her loss.

"I love you, Ashton," he said out loud, his words carrying to her as if he were standing right next to her. "Please don't cry, my love," he soothed, "I have to believe we will be together again soon. I can feel you with me and I want you to know I am counting the days until we are reunited, for all time."

As he spoke Ashton saw that he caressed the ring he still wore on his left hand. The symbol of their love and commitment to each other. He closed his eyes letting the rain wash over him and felt her love surround him, sustain him. He knew she was with him and, he thought, "I can do this. I can live for a while with her watching over me. I may not like it but I'll do it, just so I can see her again some day. I miss you," he said out loud, "I miss you, my love," and let his tears mix with hers.

CHAPTER 69

The moments turned into days, the days into years. All the while, Ashton watched as Sam spent each day living his life, laughing with him over his joys and sharing his loneliness every night. She watched as he became involved with the town of Nora Falls, no longer keeping to himself, not having to look over his shoulder every second to see if someone had come for him, but making friends and being a friend. She watched as he became loved and respected by his neighbors, and was proud when he opened his doors to those in need.

He had many friends but never another love in his life. He missed her every day, as she did him. Sometimes, in the dead of the night, when the pain of his loss became more then he could bear, Ashton, with Saul's help and permission, would send him a sign of her love. Sometimes it would be a dream of their time together, or maybe just a soft caress on his cheek, or a stroke on his hand by unseen fingers. She sent him thoughts that soon, soon they would be as one again. She sat before the Window whenever she could to share Sam's life with him and watch over him.

One day, as the sun was beginning to set, Ashton was looking down on Sam, finding him on his porch rocking in his chair.

"Hello, Ashton," a voice said behind her. She turned with a smile for Saul, although he noticed that there was still the lingering trace of sadness at its edges.

"Hello, Saul," she said. He looked the same today as he had those many years ago when they had first met, awe inspiring and a gaze filled with compassion.

"It's time, Ashton," he said quietly, a beautiful smile spreading over his face, "Go get Sam."

EPILOGUE

Thirty-Five Years Later

As the sky grew dusky, Sam sat rocking on the porch of the rustic log cabin that he had called home for the last forty years. Taking a sip of steaming coffee, he looked around him and noticed that his home was beginning to show its age, not unlike him, but realized that he liked it that way. The bark on the logs had weathered and peeled away, while the steps bore imprints of the many feet that had climbed them to be welcomed within it's walls. There was no fancy green lawn leading up to the cabin, only scruffy clumps of hearty mountain grass and the natural outcropping of rocks poking up from his mountain.

His Mountain. He liked the sound of that and always had. Looking out across the mountaintops at the setting sun, Sam let his mind wander. The first thirty five years of his life had been spent working hard, playing, becoming the best at his trade, and making enough money to last him two life times. He had needed a safe place to live and the Rocky Mountains had given him all he needed and more. Eventually becoming a place where he grew old peacefully, a place where a he could step outside his front door each morning and smell fresh air, hear birds singing, and know he had nothing but time to do as he wished. The rugged quietness of the Rocky Mountains of Colorado had welcomed him, and so he had put down roots and been happy here ever since.

He'd been content to spend his days hiking and fishing, watching the sun rise and fall over the mountains, and letting the peace of the land fill his days, until that day thirty five years ago when *she* had walked into his life. He remembered that day like it was yesterday. He'd set out for his favorite fishing spot, a lake buried in a little glen not far from his cabin, where the deer and other animals came to water, and the trout were fat and tasty. She'd been standing on the side of the lake with her face raised to the sun, with that glow that always seemed to surround her. After thirty-five years, he could still feel the way she had filled his heart to bursting with the love that he had felt for her.

Ashton Rider. They had had two wonderful months of happiness and love before she was taken from his life. Just as suddenly as she had come into his life, she was gone. He replayed over and over in his mind her words promising that even if their time together was short, she would always be with him, and one day come back for him. Every day he had gone back to the spot where she had walked into his life, always hoping she would be there waiting for him, but she never came. Every day he walked home alone, arms empty and heart aching. Still, every morning when he woke up, his hope was fresh and strong that today would be the day that she would come back and make his world right again.

Today he had made his trip to the lake where he had found her those many years ago, and today he had returned to the cabin alone, once again. So here he sat on his porch, watching the colors of the sunset painting the tops of the mountains, and drinking his coffee. His hand shook slightly as he raised the heavy mug to his weathered lips. Old age, it seemed, was finally coming to call. Wrinkles on his face, dark spots on his hands, snowy white hair on his head, and the sagging and bagging of his skin were pretty clear signs that not only was old age calling, it had brought all of its baggage and was moving in for the duration.

Sam closed his eyes, leaned his head back, and slowly began rocking in his chair. He was especially tired tonight. Tired in his mind, his body, and his soul. He let his mind go, the creak of the rocking chair on the boards of the porch providing a soothing lullaby to his tired body, as he rested. Behind his eyelids the light seemed to get brighter and the air around him warmed, until it seemed to fold around him and seep into his bones.

Sam thought he was slipping into a dream, as he had never had such a wonderful feeling. "Open your eyes Sam", came a soft familiar voice. The rocker came to a sudden stop and Sam's heart began to beat so hard and fast that he expected it to jump out of his chest right then and there.

"It can't be" he whispered to himself. Sam opened his eyes slowly and there in front of him stood Ashton, looking the same as she had all those years ago. Same long rich brown hair, beautiful green eyes, creamy skin that held that special glow, and same lush body that he had held close and made love to not nearly long enough to suit him.

"Hello Sam," the vision said.

Disbelieving, Sam whispered to the image, "Is it you or am I just dreaming?"

"It's me Sam", Ashton replied with a smile in her eyes.

Sam came slowly out of his chair and raised his hand, reaching out to touch her cheek, letting his fingers trace down her neck and coming to rest on her collarbone. Feeling her heart beat strong and sure, tears filled his eyes and slowly ran down his cheeks, as he opened his arms and invited his love to come into them. Ashton stepped into his embrace, wrapping her arms around his waist, and laid her head on his shoulder. She felt real, solid, and warm. Her special scent filled his head, as he turned his face and buried it into the curve of her neck.

"I missed you" they whispered to each other.

"Don't let me wake up if this a dream. Please don't let me wake up," Sam pleaded to God and whoever else was listening.

Ashton gently pushed the hair from his forehead and kissed his closed eyelids as she whispered, "It's not a dream, Sam. I am here. I've come to get you. We get to be together now. We *finally* get to be together."

Sam squeezed her hard against him, afraid to let loose even for a second for fear she would disappear again.

"Look at me Sam, Please look at me," Ashton gently pleaded.

Sam didn't want to open his eyes. He didn't trust that what was happening was real. He wanted to stay locked in this moment forever, but then slowly he opened his eyes. Sam met Ashton's gaze and had a feeling that he was falling and floating at the same time.

"It's time my Love," her voice washed over him, and she slowly backed away from him, holding out her hand for him to take.

Sam grasped her hand tightly, afraid he was holding on too tight, but afraid to let go. His eyes lowered to their two hands, and what he saw made him draw in a deep breath. His hand was no longer spotted with age. It was as if someone had turned back time, and allowed him to, once again, be the man that she had fallen in love with. His skin and muscles were once again tight and glowed with the health of youth.

"What's happening?" he asked as he gazed at their hands joined together.

Bringing his hand to her lips, Ash slowly kissed it and smiled. "Remember Sam, this is how we were when we were together, and this is how we will be again. Together, young and strong forever. Don't be afraid, my darling. Trust me, trust us. I've come to take you where we can be together always. It's time, Sam. It's time for you to join me." Ash slowly backed down the weathered steps, all the while holding on to Sam, smiling into his eyes, showing him all the love she had for him, and reassuring him that all was well and as it should be. Sam willingly followed her, and as they reached the bottom step he turned to look back. What he saw puzzled him at first. He saw his aged body sitting in the chair, eyes closed, and a peaceful smile on his lips. Understanding came to him then, and a small trickle of fear washed through him.

"It's okay, Sam, we are done here now. Come with me, it's our time to be together," Ashton reassured him as she led him away from the cabin.

A lone tear tracked down his cheek as he understood, life as he knew it was now over. But he had no regrets. He had led a good life. The realization that all the loneliness was now coming to an end, filled him with a new kind of peace and joy. Sam nodded his head and, hand in hand with his beloved Ash, walked towards the trees.

If any one had been there, they would have seen a slight shimmering in the air and then nothing. The birds that had hushed their sounds for a moment, once again began to sing, and time moved on.